Annie's Trust

Serenity Inn Series

Annie's Trust

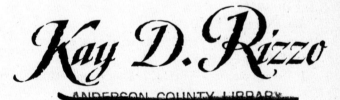

Kay D. Rizzo

BROADMAN
& HOLMAN
PUBLISHERS

Nashville, Tennessee

0-8054-2132-7

Published by Broadman & Holman Publishers, Nashville, Tennessee

Dewey Decimal Classification: 813
Subject Heading: FICTION
Library of Congress Card Catalog Number: 00-069673

Library of Congress Cataloging-in-Publication Data
Rizzo, Kay D., 1943–
    Annie's trust / Kay D. Rizzo.
      p. cm. — (The Serenity Inn series ; bk. 6)
    ISBN 0-8054-2132-7
    1. Women pioneers—Fiction. 2. Saint Joseph (Mo.)—Fiction.
I. Title. ᴍꜱ
    PS3568.I836 A82   2001
    813'.54—dc21   ᴍꜱ

                                                       00-069673
                                                          CIP

1 2 3 4 5 6 7 8 9 10   05 04 03 02 01

~ *Dedication* ~

To my "grand" niece,
Jessica.

May you always be a woman
of courage and a
woman of God.

Books in the Serenity Inn series:

Contents

~ 1 ~

Terrified by the Past, Frightened of the Future

 IN THE EYES OF THE TRAVELERS SEARCHING for the land of promise, Independence, Missouri, was little more than a pause, a comma, a place to catch their breath. But to Annie Hawkins, former slave, the town teetering on the edge of America's vast wilderness had become the home she'd never known.

Purchased from a brutal southern plantation owner, Annie had loved her rescuer, Charity Pownell, like a mother. When the wealthy New York state assemblyman's wife died in a carriage accident, the young woman grieved almost as much as did Charity's own daughter and Annie's closest friend, Serenity.

After Charity Pownell's death and later the fire that destroyed the Pownells' western New York estate, the freed slave had been bounced from place to place, never feeling completely at home. The fiery tragedy left disfiguring scars on Annie's heart as well as her hands.

Annie felt enervated by fear, fear while living in Albany, New York, with Josephine, the second Mrs. Pownell; fear while sailing on the ship to New Orleans; and fear when she was abducted and held captive by Josephine's evil stepson. With each crisis, her terror grew until she became a shadow of the bright and effervescent young woman she'd once been.

From the first moment she laid eyes on the prairie surrounding Independence, Annie knew she'd come home. Independence. The lovely name symbolized her new life. For the first time in a long time, she felt safe in the wide, untamed land.

Day or night, the prairie was magical to the poetic young woman. She loved the way the moonlight turned the prairie into a ghostly fairyland; the tall, prairie grass waving golden in the late afternoon sun; and riotous sunsets splashing wild, radiant colors across the western horizon. Her favorite moments were spent strolling among the sunflowers collecting purple-headed teasels and watching multicolored butterflies flit from flower to flower.

The young woman leaned her forehead against the warm oak window frame and gazed out into a dense blanket of fog rolling in off the Missouri River. From Annie's vantage point, nothing moved, not even Onyx, the inn's big floppy-eared mutt of a watchdog she'd known since a pup.

Annie dreamed of her own secure, little cabin where she'd plant lilacs by the front door and honeysuckle by the back. Her cabin would have a big eastern-facing window to celebrate the vibrant morning sun. The window would have strong wooden shutters to bar winter's icy chill and the blizzards that swept across the vast, empty land.

Annie could imagine herself throwing open the shutters on the first day of spring and inhaling the fresh clean prairie air once again. She would sit before her window, spinning yarn and weaving fabric for her family's clothing. She would create her delicate needlepoint artistry by the warm glow of the afternoon light.

In her home, she would hold quilting bees and canning parties for the Negro women of her fiancé's congregation. And on her cast iron stove, a pot of vegetable stew would always be bubbling for the occasional guest or wandering stranger. A fragrance of peace and happiness would pervade Annie's home just like it had Miz Pownell's.

A gentle smile spread across Annie's flawlessly smooth, honey brown face. Her dream would soon come true, thanks to the tidy sum Charity Pownell had bequeathed each of her faithful servants. Annie would receive her legacy on her twenty-first birthday or on her wedding day, whichever came first.

Now, a month before her twenty-first birthday, the young woman's dreams were about to come true on both counts. Engaged to marry freed slave, Ned Ward, a former dock worker and lay preacher in the colored communities throughout Western Missouri and Eastern Kansas, Annie's future was bright.

The thought of the muscular six-foot, four-inch ebony-skinned man sent a delightful shiver down her spine, followed by a ripple of fear. Annie knew her beloved was somewhere out there in the darkness, shepherding a group of poor, terrified souls to freedom. While she believed in her people's cause, she couldn't help experiencing envy for the peace that the average white man and woman enjoyed.

"Annie?" Serenity gently touched the young woman's shoulder. "Annie? Are you with us?" Serenity and Annie had grown up as sisters after Serenity's wealthy mother rescued the eight-year-old, raven-haired moppet from her cruel slave owner and then did the unthinkable. Charity Pownell purchased Annie from her captors, legally setting her free, and then brought the young girl into the family circle.

Annie learned to read and figure side by side with Serenity, but the greater lessons Charity taught the former slave girl were those performed with a needle and thread. Annie would be stitching the Bible text on a delicate wall sampler long after Serenity tired and ran outside to play.

Charity recognized a rare talent in the girl and encouraged her. In time, few could equal her exquisitely detailed artistry. Along with the needlework, the lovely Charity instilled in the little girl's mind dozens of promises found in the Word of God.

***

"I love thee with an everlasting love . . ." Annie mumbled, barely aware that she'd spoken aloud.

"Do you see him? Is Ned out there?" Serenity asked.

"Huh? Oh, not yet." Annie blinked. "Doing a little wool gathering, I guess." She glanced over her shoulder at her friend and smiled. The inn's dinner guests had done serious damage to the blackberry-buckle-and-whipped-cream dessert Serenity had made. The men had retired to the parlor to talk while the women put the children to bed.

The whitewashed walls of the kitchen and dining area were part of the original sod structure of Serenity Inn, which the Cunards owned. The parlor and newly appointed guest rooms were part of the wood frame structure Serenity and her husband Caleb had recently added. Throughout the summer the inn had been filled to overflowing with families heading west to the goldfields of California and to the rich farmlands of Oregon.

Serenity tenderly brushed a stray curl from her dear friend's neck. "Did Ned say when he expected to get here? I saved him a couple bowls of venison stew and some dessert, which wasn't an easy task, I might add. I had to fight my dad and Caleb away from Ned's food with a fireplace poker." She laughed.

"Thanks." Annie turned to face her friend. "I'm sure Ned's fine. He'd hoped to be back from the Kansas border by nightfall. Something unforeseen must have come up." She didn't know if she was trying to ease her friend's concerns or her own. "It's funny, when I was conducting runaway slaves in New York, I never thought about the concern of those who loved me. It's different now that I'm the one waiting at home."

Serenity gave Annie a hug. "I'm sure Ned is fine. He can take care of himself." A giant of a man, with muscles strengthened by hoisting bales of hay and crates of cargo, Ned could handle most men, regardless of the situation.

Serenity continued, "As much as I know it frustrates Caleb not to be active in the Underground Railroad since Sammy was born—and I know it's selfish—I'm so glad he's here every night and no longer wandering about in no man's land."

No man's land was the area along the Missouri/Kansas border where the "border ruffians" patrolled, looking to collect runaways for the bounty posted by their southern owners. Once a runaway crossed the border into Kansas, he was beyond the jurisdiction of the state of Missouri, and theoretically, the ruffians could no longer touch him.

However, getting to Kansas could be dangerous. And while the fog unnerved Annie, she was grateful for the protection it afforded Ned and his charges. Outlaw gangs calling themselves pro-slavers patrolled the borders, from Stringfellow's bunch in St. Joseph to Quantrill's renegades near Carthage.

Annie turned slowly from the window and heaved a heavy sigh. As usual, there was nothing to do but wait. She gazed about the inn's warm, lantern-lit kitchen and dining area, inhaling the peace the room evoked in her. A bouquet of dried grasses in a pewter pitcher sat in the middle of the long gleaming oak trestle table. In the stone fireplace, the flames danced above the bed of hot coals. An afghan of reds, golds, and greens lay sprawled across a weathered mahogany rocker.

The candles in the tin chandelier hanging from the open beamed ceiling had been extinguished. The dinner dishes had been washed and put away. It was a time for peace, yet worry agitated Annie's heart.

"Come on, let's go into the parlor with the other guests," Serenity urged, taking her friend by the hand. "Josephine has been boasting to Miss York about your exquisite needlework. I already showed her the embroidery on the baby dress you made for Sammy and the lovely cut work on the silk shawl you gave me for my birthday. She wants to talk to you about doing some work for her."

Annie blushed. "Me?" A nervous flutter stirred the quiet woman as she ran her scarred hands over the sides of her head, pushing stray curls back from her face. While the Pownells and the Cunards treated her with love and respect, she didn't fool herself into thinking other whites tolerated her presence as easily. Annie knew her place.

"Of course, you!" Serenity tapped Annie's upper arm with her forefinger. "And why not? Your work is as good as any I've ever seen, better than most, including exquisite handiwork imported from France and Ireland."

The former slave girl scrunched her eyes closed for an instant at the thought of confronting the formidable Miss Margaret York. If the truth be known, Miss York intimidated the majority of women and a good number of the men in the region as well.

A feisty, diminutive redhead with an intellect and knowledge of the law that would put most learned men to shame, Margaret York traveled with her father, the circuit court judge, Benjamin York, as his law clerk and personal secretary.

Rumor had it that Miss York knew more about the laws of the state of Missouri and the Supreme Court of the United States than did her father or any other legal expert in the region. This hadn't gone unnoticed by her father, the former state assemblyman and lawyer Samuel Pownell, or his partner, Felix Bonner.

Annie knew that the snappish young woman could unnerve the most formidable opponent with one well-turned phrase, or by lifting one derisive eyebrow, and she certainly unnerved Annie. But then, if the truth be known, Annie feared a lot of people and a lot of things with little reason to do so. She knew that her unreasonable fears frustrated her fiancé, a man who'd seldom shown fear himself.

The former slave girl reluctantly followed Serenity into the newly added parlor. The dark-stained gleam of the hardwood floors caught her eye. After Caleb and his brother Aaron finished laying and sanding the new floors, she and Serenity had polished them with beeswax, on hands and knees. A multicolored area rug, imported from the Orient, filled the space between the cluster of gold-and-sage-green chintz upholstered furniture. Serenity had accented the sage green by adding slubbed-silk sofa pillows of the same shade.

In the middle of a walnut sofa table, a pewter coffee pot overflowed with sunflowers. Beside the pot of flowers sat a magnificent mahogany-and-brass kaleidoscope, a wedding gift to Serenity and Caleb from Mr. Bonner. Whenever she had the chance, Annie spent hours gazing at the variety of vibrant colored patterns inside the brass tube. Occasionally she would sketch one particularly impressive pattern to reproduce on fabric in the future.

So much had changed at the inn in a year. No longer would guests from the East be horrified by whitewashed sod walls and pressed earth floor. Wallpaper with scenes of fox hunting and English estates covered the walls of the parlor, a housewarming gift from Serenity's father and stepmother. A fire crackled behind the cast iron filigree grate in the marble fireplace.

Annie's gaze ran to the linen table scarf, embroidered with white satin daisies and forget-me-nots that she'd designed for her friend. As shy as she was, Annie was also truthful. Her creations were finer than any she'd seen. Every French knot and every blossom had to be perfect before she would be satisfied with her work. Admitting to her skill with a needle caused her to straighten her spine and lift her chin.

"Miss York, you wish to speak with me?" Annie asked as she entered the parlor.

"I should say so. Mrs. Pownell has been telling me about your talent with a needle. And what I've seen . . ." She held up the infant dress Annie had embroidered. "You are remarkable. Have you ever thought of going into business for yourself? I know women from here to St. Louis and beyond who would pay top dollar for your artistry."

Annie blushed and mumbled, "I'm happy working for the Pownells. Miz Josephine treats me very well."

"I'm sure she does." Miss York turned toward the smiling Mrs. Pownell. "Josephine, dear, you have no right to keep this young woman under wraps."

Josephine Pownell, pregnant with her first child, laughed at Margaret's hyperbole. "Actually, I'm hardly keeping dear Annie under wraps, as you put it. She does fancywork for many of the women in my literary book club, of which she is an enthusiastic member, I might add."

"Really?" Margaret York's eyebrows disappeared into the neat fringe of bangs on her forehead. Meeting a woman who reads was rare indeed, and to be colored as well, was highly unusual. "What authors do you enjoy, Miss Annie?"

The nervous young woman thought a moment, then answered, "Hawthorne and Shakespeare are two of my favorites. And of course, Edgar Allen Poe is tantalizing to read late at night, don't you think?"

"Yes, yes I do," the judge's daughter nodded, her face filled with amazement.

Annie's nervousness dissipated as she warmed to her favorite subject. "I find Jane Austin's characters quite frivolous, but delightful as well."

The legal assistant smiled and nodded. "What do you think of Charles Dickens's commentaries on modern life in England?"

Annie paused and frowned. "Realistic, I would say. People of any color can be enslaved by evil individuals."

Miss York glanced in surprise at her hostess, then back at the shy, young woman. "You are quite insightful, Miss Annie."

Annie's eyes softened. "Life does that to one sometimes, doesn't it?" She was relieved to hear Onyx begin barking behind the inn. She leaped to her feet. "Please excuse me, Miss York. I think my fiancé might have arrived."

As she fled the room, she overheard Josephine tell Miss York about Ned and their upcoming nuptials. Annie ran through the kitchen to the pantry and flung open the back door. "Ned?" she called, Onyx barking at her heels.

"Go inside, Annie." It was the voice of her beloved, but it was unfamiliarly stern. "Please go inside."

"Where are you? I can't see you." She peered into the darkness while the dog continued barking. "Onyx, be quiet!" she ordered. "Ned, are you all right?"

She searched the area where the dog had bounded from sight. The animal's low growl caused the hairs on Annie's neck to stand on end. Whatever was threatening Ned also had Onyx upset. Ned called out again, "Please, go inside, Annie. I . . ."

"Hey, is that your sweet Georgia peach, Ward?" A gruff voice snarled from the dark shadows beside the inn. "Or is she a runaway you decided to keep for yourself?"

"Badger Oberon, I should—"

Annie heard a scuffle. "No! Ned. Don't!" She cried, running to the end of the house. As she rounded the corner of the inn, what she saw terrified her.

"Whoa there, big guy!" A short, wiry man, with a scarred face and beady eyes shining in the light from the torch he held in his left hand, grinned at Ned through picket-fence teeth. His right hand wielded a long Bowie knife. "I wouldn't want to carve you up now, would I? Might bring down the price on your head."

Ned glared at the man and snarled at him through clenched teeth. "There's no price on my head, you maggot-infested varmint!"

Two other men stood directly behind the man called Badger Oberon, each with a torch in one hand and a six-shooter in the other. One man, Jim Lair, looked like a younger version of Oberon, except for his fiery red hair and full mustache.

The third man didn't fit with the others. Rakishly handsome and dressed in an English-cut wool suit, Mortimer Cranston carried himself with an air of refinement. Originally from Canterbury, England, the dapper Jack-o'-dandy was well-known in Western Missouri for his skills at the poker table and his single shot lever action Sharp's rifle. This night, he held a revolver in his hand.

Along the central Missouri border, Mort Cranston was also known for his lack of human compassion for runaway slaves and their conductors. "The gambler would as soon hang a man as look at him," was the popular belief. As yet, he'd operated within the law, or so it seemed.

Since the repeal of the Missouri Compromise of 1830 and the passing of the Runaway Slave Act, no person of color was safe from the likes of Cranston and his men. A flimsy piece of paper declaring a man or woman free could only go so far.

Fortunately, Ned was well-known in the area, so Cranston knew to tread softly. The gentle giant of a man had built up good will among the merchants and peoples of the area and Ned was protected as long as he wasn't caught transporting runaways. Should that happen, both he and Annie knew the tide of popular sentiment would turn against him.

Ned's face remained expressionless as he straightened to his full six-feet, four-inch height. "I am a free man, Cranston. My fiancé, Miss Hawkins, is a free woman. And you men are on private property. I suggest you turn around and head back to wherever it is you came from." A muscle in his jaw flexed as he stared down the three border raiders, all measurably shorter than he.

Behind Ned's left knee, Onyx bared his teeth in a snarl. The youngest of the bounty hunters aimed his pistol at the animal.

"Shall I plug him, boss?" he asked. The dog curled his upper lip. An angry rumble rose from the beast's throat.

"No, Onyx. No!" Annie yelled, attempting to silence the animal, but her words fell on deaf ears. The inn's watchdog sensed danger when he saw it, and he wasn't about to back away from it. "Go!" She stomped her foot at the animal. "You obey!" Grudgingly, Onyx retreated around the corner of the house, growling his protest at being sent away.

With the dog out of sight, the wiry little man calling himself Badger swaggered toward Ned and poked the black man's chest with the point of his ten-inch Bowie knife. "Boy, the law says I can go wherever I want when pursuing a runaway, and for all I know, you is harboring just that! There've been rumors, you know."

The leather vest and canvas pants worn by the ruffian were as filthy as the teeth through which he grinned. Stringy brown hair poked out from under the man's worn and misshapen Stetson.

Ned lowered his gaze to the offending blade, then slowly lifted his eyes to meet the bounty hunter's sneering face. "I strongly suggest, Mr. Oberon, that you remove your knife from my shirt button or I will remove it for you."

An instant of fear darted through the smaller man's eyes as he stared into Ned's fiercesome eyes. Annie breathed a sigh of relief when, with only a moment's hesitation, the hand holding the knife blade slowly dropped to the man's side.

With the shift in power, Mort Cranston swaggered to Oberon's side. "Just tell us where you dumped your cargo, Mr. Ward, and we'll move on as you suggested." The man's clipped British accent added undeserved authority and import to his speech. "Or else we might need to take this pretty little fiancée of yours in exchange. My employer won't care whether or not I got the right 'lady of color,' as long as I bring him a pretty one."

Cranston's sarcastic sneer set Annie's teeth on edge. Memories of the kidnapping in New Orleans by another gambler sent waves of terror up and down her spine. She began to shake uncontrollably. As if he sensing her fear, Ned's arm slipped protectively around her waist, drawing her close to his side. "Over my dead body!" The man's tightly controlled anger rumbled through his body.

"As you wish, Mr. Ward." Mort Cranston aimed his pistol at the black man's chest while the other two bounty hunters tensed and inched closer, temporarily blinding Ned with their torch light.

Cranston waved his gun at Annie. "Just move away, Missy, and you won't get hurt," he growled. "We don't want you. We want those runaways."

When she started to obey, Ned tightened his hold on her waist. Annie burrowed her quivering body under Ned's protective arm and rested her head on his chest. She could feel the sweat beading on her forehead. When dots began to dance before her eyes, she bit her tongue so as not to faint. *Vapors!* she silently scolded herself. *You're hardly the type of female to have a fit of vapors!*

The Englishman curled his lip and snarled, "I said, move girl, or else!"

Before she could reply, a new voice boomed from behind the armed men. "Or else what? Do tell, sir."

Cranston and his men whipped about to find themselves staring down the barrels of two rifles and a customized blunderbuss of a shotgun resting in the hands of the sober-faced judge Benjamin York. The ruffians' torchlight accentuated the man's gray-flecked, bushy eyebrows and his piercing black eyes. The three intruders gasped in unison.

Every man in the region knew the circuit-riding magistrate at a glance and each one knew to steer clear of his displeasure.

The three members of the Cranston gang lowered their weapons. Mort Cranston broke into an engaging smile and extended his right hand in greeting. "Judge York, I'm glad you're here. This colored man is protecting a runaway slave. My boys and I are just doing our duty by taking her back to her owner in Texas."

"Oh, really? This young lady?" The judge's left eyebrow arched sarcastically.

"Yes, sir." Cranston's confident smile waned.

"That's interesting, since I and my daughter have been here at the inn with the Cunards and the Pownells as well as Miss Annie Hawkins all evening. Of course, you are familiar with Miss Annie's personal lawyer, Mr. Bonner."

Determined to justify his accusations, Cranston charged, "Likewise, Judge York, my men and I have been following this man, Ned Ward, all evening, him and two escaped slaves, a man and a woman. We lost them for a while in the fog. And then, what do you know? This boy returned here to Serenity Inn."

"You mean Mr. Ward, I presume." The judge removed a pair of wire-rimmed spectacles from his vest pocket. Adjusting the glasses on the end of his nose, he peered at the gambler. "And have you found your runaways, other than Miss Annie, of course, whom, by now you've guessed, is a free woman with papers to prove it?"

"Uh, no sir. But we will sir." Cranston sent a hate-filled sneer toward Ned. "Mark my words, we will get this man and his buddy, Aaron Cunard."

Judge York slipped his spectacles into his vest pocket. "Until you can prove your allegations, Mr. Cranston, I suggest you vacate the premises immediately. You are not only trespassing, but you are interrupting a pleasant dinner party as well."

"Say what you will, Judge, but the pro-slavers of Missouri won't cotton to a judge with abolitionist leanings," Cranston warned.

The judge gave each of the gang members an intensive once-over, then turned, and strode around the corner of the house. Grudgingly, the leader of the gang pocketed his weapon. His two sidekicks did the same.

Samuel Pownell, Felix Bonner, and Caleb Cunard hovered nearby as Cranston snarled a last threat at the stone-faced Ned. "We'll get you, boy. Sooner or later you'll slip up, and the law will be on our side then. Just you wait and see." The three border raiders swaggered to their waiting horses, mounted them, and disappeared into the night.

Ned held Annie in his arms long after the night swallowed the light from the men's torches and their rescuers returned to the inn. "It's all right precious one. They're gone. It's all right," he encouraged as she wept on his tan suede vest.

"Will we ever find peace?" she sobbed.

"On this earth? Honey, God is the only source of true peace. Peace comes from within, not from without." He tilted her chin upwards and gazed into her eyes. "I have an errand I must do. I need you to go back into the house and wait for me. I'll be back in less than an hour."

She looked at him in surprise. "What? Do you mean your cargo was on the property after all?"

"They are in the barn. Aaron is with them." Caleb Cunard's younger brother, Aaron, was Ned's point man in their segment of the route from the South to Nebraska and freedom. The two men had been working together to transport runaways from the South since the Cunards first settled in Missouri.

While Aaron's lifestyle had changed drastically since he found God and married Lilia, his dedication to the cause had only become stronger. No thug from England was about to weaken Ned's resolve to transport as many slaves as possible to freedom.

Before her terrifying experience in New Orleans, Annie had felt the same intense passion for the cause. Since then, she craved security. Ned supplied that, first by his immense size and second through his unswerving faith in God's promises. Whenever he was near, her faith was solid. But when he was gone . . . She wished she had a faith that could see her through the lonely times, but it wasn't there.

Seeing the progress on the honeymoon cottage out beyond the Cunards' blacksmith shop encouraged her. To have her very own home was a dream come true for the bride-to-be. Then she would feel safe. Then her world would be secure.

Caleb and Aaron were helping Ned finish the sod structure before the wedding. Bought and paid for by Ned's earnings on the docks, the proud young man refused to use money from Annie's trust. When he explained, he said, "Maybe it's pride, but I want my hands and my sweat to go into our first home. As a slave, I dreamed of building my own home, not with my wife's money, but with my own. Don't be offended; let me see this dream through."

Annie had agreed to Ned's wish, of course, though the money in her trust from Charity Pownell would have made it possible to finish the structure a month or two sooner. The bride-to-be was thrilled that she'd be a neighbor with Serenity and Caleb. Knowing that her best friend in all the world would be living so close reassured her growing sense of security.

Later that night, after the Cunards' guests had left and Caleb had retired for the night, Annie sat in the big dark oak rocker beside the fireplace and Serenity sat curled up on the sofa. "Thanks for inviting me to stay over tonight," Annie said. "How'd you know I needed to talk?"

Serenity laughed and tilted her head to one side. "Annie, I've known you since we were kids. And whenever you begin rubbing your pinkie finger with your thumb, it's a sign that you're upset and probably need to talk. I think I'm the only person who knows you that well."

Annie glanced down at her left hand, and sure enough, she had been rubbing her pinkie finger with her thumb. "Your mama knew about me too."

A wisp of a smile drifted across Serenity's face as she nodded gently. "Mama was very perceptive that way." She took a deep sigh, then asked, "So? What is it? Your nightmares coming back?"

The young woman leaned her head back against the chair and closed her eyes. "I don't know what to do, Serenity."

"About what?"

"Ned and the Railroad."

Serenity eyed her friend with surprise. "What do you mean? You transported runaways back in upstate New York."

"Yes, and I still believe in the cause, but, oh, Seri, I'm so frightened." Annie rubbed her forehead with her right hand.

"You've heard the men talk about the violence going on—the murders, the arson, the lynchings. I'm terrified that one day a messenger will ride up to the house and tell me Ned's been strung up by some gang." She took a deep breath before continuing. "I just want to live a peaceable life. Is that so much to ask?"

"I don't know what to say." Serenity gazed at her friend through misted eyes.

"Sooner or later there won't be a Judge York around to rescue him. You should have heard those men tonight, Serenity. I can't stand the thought of what might happen."

"It's true," Serenity admitted. "So far, God has protected our men through this nightmare."

"Our men?" Annie's lips tightened. "Your man is no longer involved, remember?"

Serenity pursed her lips for a moment. "That's not entirely true, Annie. Caleb provides a station for the runaways. He just doesn't conduct them any longer from one station to the next, not since Sammy was born. If he were to be caught, he could be strung up along with the others."

A tear slid down Annie's cheek. "I-I-I'm sorry. I didn't mean to . . ."

"It's all right, Annie. I understand what you're saying, but I refuse to live in the fear of what might happen. If I did, I'd be afraid to walk outside my kitchen door for fear of being bitten by a rattler or attacked by wasps. I'd never allow my son to crawl in the grass for fear of injury. I'd never . . ."

"I know . . ." Annie frantically rubbed her pinkie finger.

"And if my guess is right, Ned won't stop conducting runaways across the border when you marry him. You know that, don't you?"

"Uh-huh." Annie cast her gaze toward the dying embers in the fireplace.

"If you can't deal with his involvement in the cause, you'd better tell him before the wedding. It's only fair."

Annie swallowed hard. "You're right. I know you're right."

–2–
Annie's
Wedding Day

A CORNFLOWER-BLUE, POLISHED-COTTON gathered skirt with white silk and embroidered daisies splashed across the white organdy bodice—Annie gazed at the wedding gown she'd created. Her hand knew every stitch. She'd copied a similar gown from *Goedy's Ladies' Book,* but the silk handiwork design was all her own.

After Ned's visit each evening, Annie would work with yards and yards of the fine cotton fabric spread out on the Pownells' ample kitchen table and sew the fine seams. Then she would sit before her floor model embroidery hoop and craft the delicate flowers onto the mutton-sleeved bodice. The dim lamplight strained her eyes, causing painful headaches, but as she examined the finished garment, Annie decided it had been worth it.

The young couple had conducted much of their courtship in Josephine and Samuel Pownell's spacious kitchen, except on Sundays, when they worshiped with Ned's local congregation of twenty-five adults and fifteen children in an abandoned shed on property owned by one of the parishioners. After the service, they either had Sunday dinner with church members or shared outdoor potluck dinners.

On weeknights Ned would arrive at the Pownells' house in time to help Annie put away the last of the supper dishes. Dory would take Ned's arrival as her cue to head on home to her own family. And each evening, Annie would insist he finish off the leftovers. "The Pownells don't mind," she would assure him. "More often than not, they throw away the remaining food." Annie suspected that Dory made extra on purpose.

There in the fine Victorian kitchen, stocked with the finest of everything, they would sip tea and weave their dreams by the open fireplace. Hours later, the reluctant Ned would kiss his beloved Annie goodnight and slip out the kitchen door into the night. With all the time they spent together, Annie found it difficult to bring up the subject of the hated Underground Railroad. And because Ned sensed how his activities made her unhappy, he too, avoided the subject.

***

The long-awaited wedding day arrived with beautiful, azure blue skies to match Annie's gown. A bright October sun would shine on the couple's union. Serenity and Dory, the woman who'd mothered Annie through her pain and peril, arrived at the Pownell estate early to help the bride dress for her big event.

"Stand still," Serenity scolded. "Everything is going to be all right, Annie, you'll see. You're as tense as a cat poised to pounce on a dragonfly." The matron of honor fastened the last of the tiny, whalebone buttons down the back of the gown's bodice. "Please hand me the sash, Dory."

The ebony-skinned woman obliged, then stepped back to watch as Serenity tied the wide blue satin sash around Annie's waist and into a voluminous bow at the back. "You make a beautiful bride, Annie Hawkins," the older woman breathed. "You're going to knock your young man's socks off when he sees you."

"You think so? You think he'll like it?" Annie's face shone with excitement and delight as she twirled first one way, then the other before the free-standing mahogany mirror in the Pownell master bedroom. The abundance of skirt and petticoats swooshed about her tall, willowy form as she turned.

Dory, long-time housekeeper for the Pownell family and the closest person to a mother since Charity Pownell died, dabbed at her eyes with a lace-edged, linen handkerchief, a Christmas gift from Annie. With her free hand, the older woman reached in her reticule and handed the bride a pair of white, wrist-length, crocheted gloves. "Here's something new for you to wear today. I hope you like them."

Annie's eyes widened in surprise. "You made them for me? They're beautiful, Dory. Thank you." The young woman was overcome with emotion. While she was always making special gifts for her friends, seldom did her friends make gifts for her. "So that's what you've been hiding whenever I came into the kitchen." She slid the first glove over her scarred left hand. "It fits perfectly. Thank you so much." She leaned forward and planted a kiss on Dory's pocked cheek.

Dory demurred with pleasure and her eyes misted with tears. "Like you, I learned how to crochet from Miz Charity." She glanced toward Serenity. "How your mama would have loved to be here today. It wasn't fair that she missed your wedding day, the birth of little Sammy, and now, Annie's special day."

"Her memory is always with me," Annie admitted, sniffing back her tears. "I miss her so much."

"Me too." Serenity's eyes filled with tears. "But, while Josephine can never take my mother's place, she's certainly a precious gift from God, isn't she?"

The two other women nodded. It was Josephine and Samuel Pownell's largess that arranged for Annie and Ned's wedding and reception. An invitation to the wealthy Pownell estate on the outskirts of Independence was the envy of the local garden club members, the book club members, and every other ladies' social club for a fifty-mile radius. No one would dare miss a tour of the newest and finest estate in the area.

"Something old, something new, something borrowed, something blue," Serenity recited the familiar bridal quatrain as she removed from her summer green silk purse a small midnight blue velvet jewelry case. "Your gown is blue and the gloves are new. You still need something borrowed and something old. Here, these should work for both." Serenity placed the velvet covered jewelry box in Annie's hands. "They were Mama's. I know she'd want you to wear them today."

Annie opened the lid to the box and gasped. It was Miz Charity's antique, three strand, pearl necklace and earring set. The exquisitely matching pearls glistened in the afternoon sunlight that flooded through the open window. "O-o-h, they're beautiful." Her eyes filled with tears.

A soft smile wreathed Dory's face. "I remember the night your father gave them to your mother, Serenity. He was returning from a special session in Albany. He said he bought them from a ship captain from the Orient. The captain told him the set was more than a hundred years old."

Serenity smiled. "I remember that night too. I'm so thankful they weren't lost in the fire. They would have been, but Papa forgot to bring them home with him from the Albany town-house after Mama died."

Dory lifted the necklace from the box and draped it around the bride's neck. "Miz Charity loved these so much."

Annie dabbed at her eyes. Serenity, sharing the moment of loss, tenderly kissed Annie on the cheek. "Having you wear the pearls will be like having a special remembrance of Mama at the wedding."

As Annie fastened a pearl earring to her left lobe, she cast a concerned glance toward Serenity. "You don't think Josephine will feel badly if I wear them, do you, being your father's second wife and all?"

"No, not in the slightest." Serenity laughed at the idea. "In fact, she's the one who suggested I lend them to you today. She said they'd go beautifully with your gown, and she was right."

Serenity's stepmother had been as close to the first Mrs. Pownell as had Dory and Annie. Indeed, Josephine would have been upstairs helping Annie dress for the wedding if she weren't busy supervising the finishing touches in the garden. Choosing to have a garden wedding the first week in October was risky, but September's good weather had held, bringing with it a rush of Indian summer. And Josephine's famous roses had held their blossoms.

When it came to parties, Josephine Van der Mere Pownell had a knack for making every event memorable. And while Annie would always be partial to the first Mrs. Pownell, Josephine herself thought of the girl as the closest to a little sister she'd ever know. The woman's blond hair and blue eyes were but a twist of fate from a fickle blend of blood lines.

Serenity carefully arranged the last, cascading curl along the left curve of Annie's glowing face. Then she carefully pinned the wreath of daisies and dried baby's breath atop the bride's head. A bevy of slender loops of white and blue satin ribbons cascaded down the back from the wreath. Annie watched as her friend lovingly untangled them one at a time.

"Have you seen Ned today?" Annie caught Serenity's eye. At the mention of her beloved, Annie felt heat rising in her face, though her dusky complexion hid her blush from everyone else.

"Now don't go worrying about him. Caleb and Aaron will take good care of your groom," Serenity assured her. "Lilia offered to care for little Sammy during the wedding and to fix the men a light meal before the ceremony. We don't want dear Ned swooning from hunger during the wedding, do we?"

Dory giggled at Serenity's joke. The image of Ned Ward swooning over anything was inconceivable.

"You laugh," Serenity interjected. "It's been known to happen. At the Warner wedding last year, Pastor Rich had to steady poor Jake at the altar. He caught him just in time before he toppled into a basket of lilies."

When a moment of fear crossed Annie's face, Dory hastened to assure her, "That was a church wedding with all the trimmings and in the middle of July. Yours will be downstairs in Josephine's rose garden, God's cathedral. So don't worry. With all that fresh air, no one's going to swoon, especially not Ned."

"I'm sure you're right, Dory." Serenity glanced from one dark face to the other. "I didn't mean to set you to worrying, Annie. I just wanted to assure you that Lilia will take good care of Ned, that's all."

Annie's smile returned. "It's all right. I appreciate Lilia's concern too."

The women paused as the first notes of "Amazing Grace" wafted up through the open bedroom window from the veranda below. Grandpa Ellis, the patriarch of Ned's local congregation, could make his harmonica sound as if he were accompanying an angelic choir. His rendition of "Amazing Grace" brought more than one sinner to his knees.

Annie strode to the window and peered down at the carriages and wagons parked in front of the house. She spotted the Madisons, friends of the Pownells and members of Independence's burgeoning upper class walking toward the house. At the same time, the Hensons, a large family that attended Ned's cottage meetings south of Independence, were climbing down from their buckboard.

What a strange mixture of whites and coloreds, men free by birth, and others, freed by conscience, Annie thought. *Who would imagine in a place like Western Missouri, and at such a turbulent time, this miracle could occur?* A sense of warmth passed through her, causing her to wrap her arms about her waist. *A miracle of love between two people brought them together. Will there ever be a time,* she wondered, *when such social intercourse will be as natural as breathing?*

While Annie was accustomed to being loved and accepted by the Pownell and Cunard families, regardless of her skin color, Ned felt decidedly uncomfortable around a large gathering of white people. *The poor man,* Annie thought. All the folderol over a wedding was foreign to him. However, Annie had grown accustomed to European etiquette and protocol while living with the Pownells. It had taken some doing to convince Ned to go along with local customs.

The African custom of "jumping the broom" was much simpler. She'd seen it done many times as a small child growing up on a plantation. Of course, she and Ned would do that in honor of their heritage. Ned had insisted on observing other

African customs, such as hunting a large animal to present to the bride's parents. In their case, the animal was a deer he presented to the Pownells since they'd insisted on footing the bill for the reception. Dory had helped Josephine prepare several African dishes for the reception, some Annie had never before tasted.

"It's time . . ." Dory stepped behind Annie and placed her hands gently on the bride's shoulders. "I think all of your guests are here."

Annie slowly turned to discover that she and Dory were alone in the room. "Where's Serenity?"

"She went downstairs a few minutes ago." Dory rearranged a stray loop of ribbon on Annie's headpiece. The woman smiled pensively as the delicate ribbon slipped from her fingers. "I haven't thanked you for letting Abe and me play Papa and Mama today." The woman's eyes glistened with tears. "I couldn't be prouder than if I truly were your mama. I'll never forget . . ."

Tears threatened to overflow Annie's luminous, round, copper brown eyes yet again. *Why must every momentous occasion be a blend of the bitter and the sweet,* she wondered.

Dory dotted at Annie's eyes with her ever-present handkerchief. "Be happy, my darling. I promise you that if you and Ned are half as happy as Abe and I have been these last twenty years, you will have a wonderful life."

"Thank you," Annie whispered, her voice suddenly trapped in her throat.

"We'd better go," Dory urged. "Abe is waiting in the hallway to escort you to the garden."

Annie nodded. The fear in her heart caused her hands to tremble. She frantically rubbed her left pinkie with her thumb. Her thoughts must have registered on her face for Dory shook her head gently. "It's all right, sweetheart. Every bride is nervous on her wedding day. You'll be a wonderful wife, and one day, God willing, a loving mother."

Annie swallowed hard as the older woman took the bride's gloved hands in hers and bowed her head. "Dear Father God, mighty King of the universe and our Savior, bless this precious daughter of yours as she joins in marriage with your worthy son, Ned. Give her the courage to face whatever life may bring, good times and bad, knowing you are the vital connection between this woman and her man. Amen." Silently the two women hugged, then, arm in arm, they strode to the bedroom door and opened it.

Upon seeing the bride, big strong Abe, former slave and overseer of the Pownell estate, stood slack-jawed. "Annie, I don't know what to say. You are absolutely beautiful . . ."

Annie grinned shyly, tipping her head to the side and shrugged one shoulder in embarrassment.

"Wait until Ned sees you!" he announced, whistling through his teeth. "Why, that poor boy won't know what hit 'em."

Annie swatted his muscular forearm lovingly. "Oh, Abe, you're such a kidder."

"Hmmph! Believe me, I'm not kidding!"

"Didn't I tell you?" Dory interjected. "Didn't I tell you how beautiful you look today?"

The three made their way down the stairs where Serenity handed Annie an armful of daisies and late-blooming pink roses, tied together with pink satin ribbons. She then pressed her lips against the bride's cheek and whispered, "Be happy, dear sister. I love you."

Annie nodded, her throat constricted with emotion. Straightening her shoulders, the dazed bride glided through the hallway to the veranda door where she paused for an instant. A hush fell over the assembly as she stepped outside into the brilliant autumn afternoon light.

Without warning, the haze from Annie's senses lifted, and the radiant young woman came alive. The familiar strains of the Negro spiritual "Swing Low, Sweet Chariot" triggered tender memories in her mind of her real mother humming the tune as she rocked her to sleep as a child.

Annie paused for a moment to take in the scene opening before her. Guests, high-born and low, seated side by side on wooden benches and on the stone wall surrounding the Pownells' garden as well as on the grassy lawn within, gaped at the vision of beauty standing beside the graying Abe.

Regardless of the late growing season, the rose bushes had responded to the tender care Josephine Pownell had been giving them for weeks preceding the nuptials. An abundance of red, pink, yellow, and lavender blossoms brightened the festivities. The air was filled with their rich perfume.

A smile spread across Annie's face as she gazed over the heads of the wedding guests, and into the compassionate and confident eyes of her beloved Ned. Any butterflies she'd felt earlier had been replaced with an abundance of love for this gentle man God had placed in her life. As she walked toward him, she lost sight of the audience of friends and well-wishers. Like brides from generations past, all Annie could see was the acceptance and love in her intended's eyes.

***

The blend of European, American, and African wedding customs created a unique charm for the proceedings. After the bride and groom repeated their vows, the couple "jumped the broom," thus sealing their union before God and before their people.

Immediately following the shared kiss, the solemnity of the service dissolved into a grand American celebration with cheers, dancing, and laughter. There were jokes about kidnapping the bride and about holding a shivaree that night outside their cabin. Frank Pierce and Henry Chase drew their violins out of their cases, joining the harmonica and filling the late afternoon air with "Comin' through the Rye."

With a nod from their hostess, the guests filed into the Pownells' exquisitely appointed dining room for refreshments. Candlelight from the wall sconces and silver candelabras lining the white linen-covered, fourteen-foot table reflected off the mirror-lined walls.

The table groaned from the abundance of food. The koki, African cakes made of black-eyed peas, spinach, palm oil, and exotic spices, were a hit with the guests, as was the luwombo, chicken rolled in banana leaves in a rich white sauce. The Pownell cook had to use grape leaves in place of the banana leaves, since bananas were a rarity in Missouri at any time of year.

After the meal, the swirl of laughter, pretty skirts, and dashing men in western garb filled the garden with celebration. The evening air rang with dancing and song. At one point while Annie was greeting their guests, Ned slipped away from her side to ask the musicians to play a song he'd sung to her during their courtship, "Black is the Color of My True Love's Hair."

It wasn't until he began humming the melody in her ear that she recognized it above the din. She paused to listen and wondered if she could ever love her powerful man of God any more than she did at that very moment.

The final arc of the ruby red October sun was setting in the west when the night air was suddenly filled with the sound of thundering horses and men whooping and hollering. Shots rang out from every direction.

Women and children screamed. Mothers grabbed their children and ran toward the house as the gang of thirty or more border ruffians, their faces covered with red bandanas and their wide-brimmed hats pulled low over their foreheads, galloped around the circumference of the house and garden, shouting, shooting their weapons in the air, and brandishing torches.

In front of the mansion, horses harnessed to their wagons snorted and reared in terror. Samuel Pownell and several other wedding guests ran for their guns. Caleb, Abe, and Felix Bonner didn't wait for backup. The three men leaped onto the stone wall and shook their fists at the ruffians. Felix drew a sidearm from his holster and shot over the ruffians' heads.

Annie rushed into her husband's arms and begged, "Don't go. Let them take care of it. I need you."

Gently Ned eased her out of his arms. "I can't do that, my sweet. Please don't ask me to." With that he raced toward the wall where the three men stood together. As he passed Grandpa Ellis, the old man handed the groom a pistol that he kept in his boot.

"Here, you'll do better with this than I," the old man said. "I can't hit a pumpkin six feet in front of me."

"I can't . . ." Ned began to protest.

"Nonsense. Take it—my wedding gift to you, Pastor."

Ned glanced at his enemies, then at his new bride. Without further consideration, the young preacher grabbed the weapon from the old man and dashed toward the wall.

Terrified for her husband's safety, Annie stood frozen under the arched trellis where she'd, minutes previously, taken her vows. Before she knew what was happening, Dory and Josephine gathered Annie in their arms and whisked her inside the house. She'd barely cleared the doorstep when Annie broke free and whirled about to watch the happenings.

She watched as Ned joined Caleb who shouted at the armed male guests lined up along the stone wall. "Hold your fire, men, till we hear what they have to say or until they fire. And when they do, plug the leader first." Then Caleb turned to face the leader of the mob. "What do you want?" he asked.

"Git those colored folk out of Independence. They don't belong here!" A man with a thick Southern Missourian accent hollered back.

Felix Bonner's usual stoic visage and gracious aplomb dissolved into a fiery rage. Annie had never seen the man so angry. The scoundrels fell silent at his command. As a defense attorney, the man's face was familiar to the riffraff of the community.

"You men are the ones who don't belong," the lawyer shouted. "This is private property and a private party. You'd best get out of here before I set the sheriff and his posse after you for trespassing."

With a sudden leap, Samuel Pownell scaled the wall like a man twenty years younger. Staring into the face of the man who appeared to be the mob leader, he gestured toward the men behind him. "My guests are aiming their rifles directly at you, sir. If you so much as flick your little finger, they will shoot, and you will be the first to die! I suggest you and your disgusting band of hooligans vamoose as our friends to the south of us would say."

Before the leader of the mob could respond, an all-too-familiar man wearing western garb designed by eastern tailors and without a bandana over his face, sided his horse up to the group's leader. "Mr. Pownell, all of Independence knows where your loyalties lie regarding the aiding and abetting of legitimately owned slaves in their flight to freedom, as you call it. And we know why you left New York, former Assemblyman Pownell." He scanned the gun barrels pointed in his direction, then pushed the brim of his hat back from his face. A rakish curl fell on his forehead. "We're here to deliver a friendly warning, sir. We won't tolerate lawbreakers in Missouri. Do you understand?" The man's clipped British accent almost gave credibility to the mob's mission.

Samuel Pownell threw back his head and laughed. "Mortimer Cranston, not you again. Don't tell me you failed to learn your lesson the last time we met?"

"The name is Mort." A lazy grin crossed the border ruffian's face. "By the way, I learned all right. Instead of facing down four men, you're looking down the barrels of forty. By the way, where's your friend, the judge? Down Carthage way conducting a trial for a horse thief?"

"Does it matter?" Samuel redirected his aim at Cranston. "It will take only one bullet, sir, to ruin your day."

Inside the house, Josephine gasped at her husband's bravado. "No, Samuel, don't shoot him," she whispered. "Please don't shoot the man."

Tears streamed down Annie's face as she watched the unfolding drama. "Oh, dear God, please don't let this happen, not today . . ." The same prayer was on the other women's lips as they watched and waited. For several seconds no one moved or breathed on either side of the stone wall.

Then, an imperceptible move of Cranston's left shoulder, and the horsemen backed away. "Do not think this is over," the gambler snarled. "We will meet again, sir. As I told you before, the law is on our side."

"Oh, really?" Aaron Cunard shouted. "Aren't you the side-winder that Sheriff Lawson ran out of Fort Smith last spring?"

Cranston pointed his leather-gloved index finger at Aaron. "And you, sir, and Mr. Pownell, weren't you run out of New York State?" With that, he turned his horse and signaled to the others to leave.

None of the wedding guests moved until the thunder of hooves faded into the distance. Beginning slowly, then growing to a frenzy, the wedding guests fled for their homes. The party was over. The festive mood had been destroyed.

Josephine turned toward Annie who was cowering in the protection of Ned's arms. "I am so sorry this happened, but you have to admit, it was a great wedding."

Annie bit her lower lip and tried to smile. She felt sallow and old, her mind haunted by the old painful memories.

"It's not your fault, Mrs. Pownell," Ned reminded as he ran his hand up and down Annie's arm. "You and your husband have done so much for us—and the Cunards and so many others. All I can say is, thank you for everything." Ned kissed the top of his bride's head. "Cranston and his ilk can't harm us. Our cause is just and our God will be with us."

"Maybe you should stay in town for the night. You can stay here, in fact, in the guest room," Josephine urged. "Those men may be waiting along the road for you."

Ned shook his head. Annie could feel his arms tightening about her quaking body. "Thank you for offering, but Annie and I are eager to spend our first night as husband and wife in our own little soddy." He gave Annie an extra hug. "We can't live our lives in fear, Mrs. Pownell. You, of all people, know that."

The look that passed between the wealthy dowager and the young conductor said all that needed to be said. It wasn't so long ago that she and Annie risked their lives to aid runaways in New York and Louisiana.

Caleb stepped up behind Ned. "How about we return home in caravan, neighbor? Serenity is bundling Sammy even as we speak. Imagine, he slept through the wedding and the noise."

Josephine smiled softly. "Ah, the innocence of a child."

"I would be much obliged," Ned replied. "And thank you again, Mrs. Pownell."

"My name is Josephine, remember? We're family. And don't worry about packing the gifts. I'll have Abe bring them to you in a few days."

"Er, yes, ma'am. Keepin' in mind that you're of mixed color is difficult," he admitted. "Nature sure does pull her pranks, doesn't she?"

Josephine laughed aloud. "And the joke is on the local pro-slavers, isn't it? The way some of the wealthy dowagers of Independence fawn over me because of my husband's money and prestige. Imagine their shock if they could see my colored blood beneath my blond hair and blue eyes." Ned and the woman shared a conspiratorial laugh.

Annie listened to the exchange between her husband and Josephine, but her heart continued racing with fear. The last thing she wanted to do was to spend the night in the sod cabin they'd built on adjacent lots with the inn. Ned hadn't asked her how she felt before he turned down Josephine's offer to stay in town. Even with Serenity and Caleb living within easy shouting distance, what could two men, regardless of their body strength, do against thirty armed ruffians? Annie quivered with terror and with more than a touch of irritation at her new husband.

Before leaving the house, Serenity draped Annie's shoulders with a white wool crocheted shawl, then kissed her on the cheek. "Put this behind you; be happy," she whispered.

After of bevy of kisses and well wishes from the Pownells, Abe, and Dory, Ned scooped his bride into his arms, lifted her onto the buckboard seat, then climbed on board their wagon. The groomsmen had decorated the rough, seasoned sides of the wagon with a garland of red and white roses. The seat had been draped with yards of white satin and appointed with daisies and pink rosebuds. Annie gathered the creamy white, hand-made shawl about her shoulders as if a cold breeze had suddenly swept through the valley.

Sam Pownell placed Annie's camel brown leather satchel into the wagon bed and stepped back beside his wife, Abe, and Dory.

Behind the bridal wagon, Caleb helped his wife and son into their enclosed carriage. The young blacksmith had tried to convince Ned to switch vehicles for the event, but the groom held firm. The couple would begin their life together as they would live that life—honestly. To Ned, that sense of honesty included his humble mode of transportation, something Annie didn't quite understand. She'd lived a life surrounded by luxury. *Is Ned worried that I might not be able to adjust to a more primitive existence?* she wondered.

***

They'd never talked about her past, or about his, for that matter. She knew he'd been kidnapped by warring tribesmen while hunting far from his home village in West Africa. They'd sold him to the captain of a Dutch slaver, along with hundreds of other captured young men, then transported to the Caribbean to be resold to a sugar cane plantation owner. But he'd been reluctant to talk about the details.

One summer day when he'd been shirtless, working on the docks in the hot sun, Annie had seen the deep purple scars on his back, left from a slave dealer's whip. When she asked about them, he deftly changed the subject before she realized he'd never answered her questions.

***

A quarter moon hung in the eastern sky, glinting off the side of her husband's shiny face. She couldn't help but wonder about the man she married.

Ned urged the mismatched team of horses forward with one hand while he slipped his other about her shoulders and drew her closer to his side. Out of the corner of her eye, she gazed up at him. *You are a complicated man, Ned Ward,* she mused. *Will you ever let me into that secret area of your life?*

— 3 —

Haven of Peace

SERENITY AND CALEB FOLLOWED THE WARDS to their front door. Annie sat huddled on the wagon bench while Ned and Caleb checked out the interior of the cabin. When light from an oil lamp glowed from the window, she knew all was well.

To be cautious, the two men also checked the area surrounding the cabin. Again, all was clear. Ned strode over to the wagon where Annie sat while Caleb climbed aboard his carriage.

"Good night, neighbor, and thanks," Ned called as the Cunard carriage turned toward home. "Signal with your lantern when you reach home," he added.

The couple watched as the light from the two lanterns attached to the rear of the Cunard wagon grew smaller, then come to a stop beyond the blacksmith shop. The swinging light that followed assured Ned that his neighbors were home safely. Only then did he turn to face his nervous bride. The moonlight shining over his shoulder made the expression on his beloved's face unreadable.

As she gazed up at him, the thought came to her, *How well do I really know this man to whom I've pledged my life?* Had she sold her soul into slavery when she vowed to honor, love, and obey this giant of a man?

Ned held out his arms and she swung into them, pausing when her feet touched the ground. Yesterday she'd been free, free to come and go as she pleased. Standing in the moonlight before the man she'd married, she realized she'd sacrificed that freedom for "till death do us part." An involuntary shudder coursed through her body.

As if having read her mind, Ned placed his massive hands gently on her upper arms and whispered, "Bone of my bone, flesh of my flesh. I will love you and treasure you as long as there is breath left in my body." He studied her face for several seconds. "With all that is solemn and holy, I make this vow to you in the sight of my heavenly Father and his Son, Jesus Christ."

Annie knew she should reply in kind, but the words stuck in her throat. She began to tremble.

"Are you cold?" he asked, drawing her into his arms.

She shook her head. Her cheek rubbed against his rough homespun cotton shirt.

"Are you afraid, my love? I won't hurt you, my darling," he breathed into her hair. "I will never intentionally hurt you."

Annie swallowed hard. How could she tell him that she wasn't afraid, but terrified—terrified of the future, of marriage, and yes, most of all, of him? It wasn't that she didn't understand the ways of a man with a woman as King Solomon put it. She did. She'd grown up on a farm. Furthermore, both Dory and Josephine had independently taken her aside to "prepare" her for her wedding night. The afternoon Annie suspected Serenity was attempting to do the same, she told her friend not to worry, that she had been "well-prepared."

It wasn't the act of love that they would perform once they reached the privacy of their sod haven that frightened her, but the years that would follow. It was the magnitude of the vow she had made.

There was so much she didn't know about the man. Daily waking to Ned's inscrutable face, daunted by his unwavering faith in God, fixing his meals, mending his clothes, bearing his children. Annie felt overwhelmed. If she'd been a fawn, she would have bolted into the darkness, never to be seen again. But she knew she wasn't a fawn or a rabbit or a frightened colt, but a married woman who needed to "buck up" as Dory often said.

Tenderly, as a mother would carry a young child, Ned lifted her into his arms. "You are so beautiful," he whispered, his words sticking in his throat when he spoke. "I love you so much, Mrs. Edmund Ward."

Without waiting for her reply, he swept her, amid a flurry of skirts, through the open door of their one-room sod home where a fire in the gray stone fireplace had been started hours earlier. The firelight fell on the two matching oak rockers that flanked the hearth and an overstuffed sofa covered with a green flowered chintz, a gift from the Pownells. Across the back of the sofa was a cream-colored cable knit throw, a gift from Aaron and Lilia Cunard, Ned's partner in crime, as Annie had come to think of him.

As she gazed about her new home, Annie's fears faded into a quiet sense of peace and love. A bouquet of roses in a dented tin teapot graced the center of the square maple kitchen table. The couple had purchased the table and four chairs from a California-bound family who needed quick cash. It had been in terrible shape. They knew they'd paid too much for it, but the family needed the cash, and Ned had it to give—one of Ned's weaknesses, Annie had decided.

She and Ned had scraped, sanded, and waxed the warm-toned maple table to a shine. A blue and white gingham valance topped Annie's massive, multipaned kitchen window, the work of her friend and neighbor, Serenity. Annie's spinning wheel, embroidery stand, and a ladder-back straight chair sat to one side of the window, her sewing box in easy reach.

Ned gently lowered Annie to her feet. His eyes radiated love as he gently brushed a stray curl from her forehead. She followed his gaze to the opposite corner of her simple kitchen to the hand-hewed, four-poster bed with its sturdy rope foundation and mattress of downy, chicken feathers, a gift from Dory and Abe. The blue and yellow patterned crazy quilt covered the mattress ticking and the rough muslin sheets made by the ladies of one of her husband's tiny parishes south of Independence.

When his gaze returned to her face, she could feel heat rising in her cheeks. Suddenly she felt like an awkward child. In a husky voice, Ned said, "I need to bed down the horses for the night. There's hot water in the kettle on the stove, some bars of soap, and some Turkish towels in the trunk at the foot of the bed."

"Turkish towels?" She blinked in surprise.

The young husband gave her an embarrassed nod. "I ordered them from St. Louis for you."

An involuntary cry escaped her throat. She melted into his surprised arms. "You are so thoughtful." Annie had cut and hemmed several lengths of cotton flannel to use as bath towels, and later, if a baby should bless their home, as diapers and blankets.

Reluctantly he disentangled himself from her arms and tenderly kissed her lips. "I have to see to the horses, darling. I'll be back as soon as possible, my love."

A feeling of loneliness swept through her as he disappeared out the front door into the night. She'd never before felt so bereft of his presence, nor as eager for his return. Lost in thought, she closed the door and leaned against it for several moments, gazing about the room. This is my home, she reminded herself, mine and Ned's.

When her gaze fell on the stove, she noticed steam coming off a large galvanized washtub sitting in the shadows near the pantry door. She frowned. What was that doing there, she wondered as she walked across the room.

Beside the tub was an expensively etched crystal bottle container filled with fragrant bath salts and a matching bowl filled with red rose petals. Annie smiled when she lifted the wooden cover on the tub and discovered it was filled with hot water. Carefully the young bride removed one of her gloves and dipped her fingers into the water. It was a perfect temperature for a soaking bath. She groaned with pleasure. "Mr. Ward, how did you manage that?"

A note was tied to the bottle of bath salts. The message read, "Roses for my lady." Annie clutched the bottle to her chest for several seconds, her eyes misting with tears. The nagging fears she'd been experiencing throughout the day melted as the enormity of Ned's love and tenderness filled her senses.

Suddenly, remembering that her new husband would be returning from the barn at any time, Annie shed her wedding garments onto the floor, sprinkled a handful of rose petals and a cap full of bath salts into the tub, then slipped into the hot, soothing water.

The luxury of the hot bubble bath had done its job by the time Ned returned from bedding down the horses. Annie suspected that he'd taken longer than necessary, giving her time to enjoy his gift to her.

Hearing him whistling up the walkway, the modest young bride leaped from the water, wrapped herself in one of the thirsty new towels, and hid behind the door. He walked inside and hung his Sunday-go-meeting jacket on a hook beside the door. When he saw that the tub was empty, a look of fear swept across his face. He scanned the room for his bride.

Annie's giggle gave away her location. Relief filled his face. He released his breath and swept her into his arms, burying his face in her neck. "Don't scare me like that, woman," he warned. "When I didn't see you in the tub, I thought you'd run away from me."

Annie giggled softly. "I wouldn't do that."

"Well, I wasn't sure after the excitement of today."

Tears glistened in Annie's luminous eyes. "I made a vow, my darling, to love you till death us do part. And I don't take that vow lightly."

He laughed and swung her into his arms. "Thank you, Father God, for the incredible woman I married!"

Annie smiled to herself as her husband's musty aroma filled her senses, pushing away the worries of tomorrow that had previously filled her mind. All memories of yesterday faded into insignificance. Haltingly at first, she prayed, "Thank you God, for the magnificent man I married." She placed her hands against Ned's smooth, muscular chest as he carried her to their marriage bed.

***

The warm morning sun shined through the east-facing window, forming geometric patterns on the hardened earth floor of the sod house. Sunlight glistened on the recently refinished dinner table and on the scrubbed bottoms of the iron kettles hanging on the wall beside the cast iron stove. A teapot simmered on the stove's grates.

Annie inhaled the beauty of the cabin from the vantage point of her four-poster bed. Outside the window, late-season songbirds serenaded her on her first morning as Mrs. Ned Ward. Lazily she rolled over to greet her bridegroom with a kiss and found his pillow empty.

Ned? Where was he? Her imagination sprang to the most bizarre things that could have happened to him while she slept. Since the night of the fire at the Pownell home in western New York, Annie had slept lightly, fearing the worst might happen should she relax into too sound a sleep.

She threw back the bed covers and swung her legs over the edge of the bed, all the while her logic wrestling with her wild imagination. Slipping her feet into a delicate pair of white moccasins that Serenity's Indian friends had given her, Annie rushed to the front door, opened it, and peered outside toward the barn she and Ned shared with the Cunards.

Next summer they'd build their own, but for now, Serenity and Caleb had insisted that theirs had plenty of room to house Ned's buckboard, his team of horses, and their one cow. In exchange, Ned helped Caleb in the blacksmith shop during the winter months when the weather prevented Ned from traveling his preaching circuit that extended from St. Joseph to Fort Scott.

Annie heaved a relieved sigh when she spotted Ned standing in the doorway of the blacksmith shop holding a bucket in one hand. When he saw her, he waved with the other hand. She gave him an enthusiastic wave in return, then sank back against the doorjamb.

Would she react like this every time her husband stepped out of her sight? She scolded herself for being so silly as she padded to the kitchen stove. She found it loaded with wood and lit, ready to use.

She'd been trained as a chambermaid, not as a cook. If not for Dory, Annie knew she'd be in serious trouble, but Dory's instructions had given her confidence in the kitchen. She padded into the well-stocked pantry and checked out the supplies.

"I'll make hot cakes," she muttered to herself, "hot cakes, corn syrup, apple sauce, and, of course, coffee." She would save part of the cream Ned would bring in from milking their Guernsey cow, Rhody—short for rhododendron—for the cake she would later bake that day. Ned loved shortcake. Thinking about the hot buttered treat, she could almost taste the slathering of blackberry jam preserves she'd prepared last spring in anticipation of her new home and larder.

Annie set the whistling teapot on a back burner, then hurried to wash and dress before continuing with her breakfast preparation. She didn't want her new husband to find her lolling in bed in a state of undress so late in the morning. Ned was a hard worker; she would be the same.

After setting the table with their mismatched pewter dinnerware and mixing the flour, water, and eggs to the proper consistency, she retrieved Ned's Bible from the nightstand beside their bed. Tenderly she traced the gold-leaf letters on the front of the well-worn cover with her index finger. B-I-B-L-E.

Annie was so grateful that she'd learned to read and write. So many of her people were denied the privilege of reading and writing, to the point of death. Being able to read elevated her in the eyes of Ned's parishioners as well. They considered her to be "well-educated."

She had Charity Pownell to thank for that. The woman had insisted the former slave child learn her letters right alongside Serenity. While Annie had been quick to learn, the Scriptures meant little to her beyond the reading practice they afforded. It was a white man's book meant for a white man's world.

She knew that Bible reading was quite different for Ned. The young slave boy had learned to read and write in secret, under the threat of the plantation overseer's whip. Annie wondered if that was why he spent as long as he did each day reading the "Word," as he called it. Of course, being an itinerate preacher would account for his interest in the white man's book as well.

Annie remembered seeing Charity Pownell, her gracious mentor and benefactor, reading the Bible each morning and each night. Miss Charity had taught Josephine Van der Mere to appreciate God's Word as well. Later, after Charity's death, when Josephine married Samuel Pownell, the new bride had encouraged him to do the same—a strange circle of events to be sure.

Since Annie moved from New York to Independence, Serenity had replaced her mother as Annie's inspiration. Serenity and her husband seemed to have the answers for establishing a happy home. She wasn't sure if Serenity and Caleb made Bible reading a habit other than at the breakfast table. Whatever was the source of their happiness, the bride-to-be wanted to begin the same custom in her own home. Besides, Bible reading seemed like such a civilized way to begin and end the day.

As Annie transferred her husband's Bible to the breakfast table, a piece of parchment paper fluttered to the floor. She picked it up and read the first line. "On the fourteenth day of March, in the year of our Lord . . ." As she scanned the rest of the document, Annie gasped in surprise. In her hands was Ned's writ of freedom! She'd never seen the document before, and she had no idea how he came to be set free. In fact, as she thought about it, she didn't know much of anything about her new husband's past. Now that they were married, Annie was determined to remedy that situation in the near future.

Annie kept her own writ of freedom in a walnut jewelry box topped with a padded needlepoint lid, along with the expensive steel needle set Josephine had given her and Annie's only piece of valuable jewelry, a peach cameo locket suspended from a slim gold chain, a gift from Serenity and Caleb on Annie's twentieth birthday.

Also stored in the jewelry box was the legal trust Charity had bequeathed her. According to the official-looking paper, she, Annie Hawkins, was heir to a modest fortune. At least to her it was a fortune. While she didn't understand how the trust worked, she knew the money was hers because she knew and trusted the woman who'd willed it to her.

She placed the Bible beside Ned's place at the breakfast table and smiled to herself. As she spooned the batter onto the hot griddle, a catchy tune she'd learned as a young child slipped unbidden from her lips. Sweat from the heat of the stove beaded her forehead as she sang the familiar words. "Kum-ba-ya, my Lord, kum-ba-ya. Kum-ba-ya, my Lord, kum-ba-ya. Kum . . ."

". . . ba-ya, my Lord, kum-ba-ya . . ."

Annie whirled about in surprise at the sound of her husband's deep baritone voice harmonizing with her. "Oh," she gasped, "you startled me."

"Sorry, sweetheart." He set the bucket of milk on the broad shelf beside the sink. "Keep singing, beautiful. We sound good together. We should sing for the people come Sunday." He strolled over to her and crushed her to his chest. "M-m-m, you feel so warm and inviting." He kissed her eager, upturned lips. "Have I told you yet this morning how much I love you?"

"Uh-uh." She gazed at him through round and love-filled eyes.

"Please, let me correct that error immediately, Mrs. Ward. I love you more than life itself." He blew a stray curl from her moist forehead. "You are so beautiful. I'm so thankful that God gave you to me to love."

Forgetting the hot cakes simmering on the griddle, Annie rested her head against his pounding chest. She was the grateful one. She felt safe in his arms. Whenever he was near, her fears and doubts and questions vanished. She snuggled closer, holding him tighter.

"Whoa!" He shoved her from his arms and grabbed the pancake turner from the rack above the stove. Smoke billowed from the griddle. He flipped the first burned hot cake. "We don't want burnt offerings, do we?"

"Oh! Sorry." Annie grabbed a hot pad and moved the griddle off the grate. She eyed the scorched food through a veil of tears welling up in her eyes. "I wanted everything to be perfect this morning. And now, look what I've done, burned your breakfast." She turned her face away from him.

"Hey, it's all right, darling," he coaxed.

Her hands flailed the air in defeat. "But today of all days." She reached into her apron pocket for a cotton handkerchief, then blew her nose.

"Don't cry, my love. It wasn't your fault. I distracted you, remember? Besides, you will have thousands of breakfasts to redeem yourself with." He laughed and drew her into his arms once again. He gently kissed the places on her face where her tears had touched. "Maybe breakfast can wait." His voice was husky with emotion. "This is our honeymoon, you know."

She laughed and pushed against his chest. "Mr. Ward, you are the only person I know who can turn a near disaster into a delight!"

*   *   *

The outside world stayed away from their little patch of heaven for three days. Then the poisonous apple dropped into their perfect Garden of Eden in the form of Aaron Cunard. Annie had been sitting by the window, darning a hole in one of her husband's socks when she spotted a buckboard rounding the corner of the Cunard's barn and heading for their home. Ned was cultivating the soil near the pantry door where her lilac bush would be planted.

After dropping her darning ball and the sock into her sewing basket, she rose from the rocker, slipped her shawl about her shoulders, and opened the front door.

The driver of the buckboard waved. "Hello there, Mrs. Ward." Aaron Cunard's grin was infectious. "Mrs. Pownell insisted I deliver your wedding gifts to you."

At that moment Ned rounded the corner of the house. "Well, hello there. I thought I recognized your voice. Good to see you again, my friend."

Aaron hopped down from the buckboard and walked to the back of the wagon. "You folks made a real haul." The man laughed as he lifted a loaded gunnysack from the wagon bed. "Everything from fancy dishes to a slab of dried meat and a sack of spuds, which I'll carry to the storm cellar later."

"Everyone has been so nice to us," Annie hurried to add. "Just bring the rest into the house." She didn't like thinking of their wedding gifts as a "haul." To her it sounding grasping and greedy, something she never wanted to be.

"Here, let me give you a hand." Ned reached for the second of the five overstuffed gunnysacks while Aaron carried one of the three wooden crates. "So, what's happening along the line? Did you hear any more from those ruffians?"

Aaron shook his head. "Not a word. I think they went into hiding after the wedding, but that doesn't mean they're not busy spreading their poison elsewhere. I do need to talk with you, though, Ned."

By the look on Cunard's face, Annie knew the topic they would discuss. Not wishing to hear what the younger Cunard wanted to tell her husband, she hurried into the house. The link between the two men was and always would be the Underground Railroad, and to the young bride, that meant trouble. A shiver coursed her body. She drew her knitted shawl tighter about her shoulders and prayed, "Oh dear, God, don't let this be what I think it is."

She'd barely uttered her prayer when the two men entered the soddy and dropped the gunnysacks on the dinner table. The anticipation she'd felt upon first seeing the gift-filled gunny-sacks dimmed upon recognizing the distant look in her husband's eyes.

Aaron quickly begged his leave. Annie assumed he could sense that she was unhappy with his presence. Ned walked Aaron out to the buckboard. Annie watched quietly from inside the house as her husband stood talking with him for several minutes.

Ned watched Aaron's rig disappear around the corner of the barn; then he strode purposefully in the same direction. Annie squeezed shut her eyes. A throbbing ache had begun in her head. Her burn-scarred fingers gripped the edges of her shawl until the blood left her knuckles. Like it or not, the cold, evil world had sneaked in and snatched her cozy little paradise from her, which she knew she'd never find again.

***

Ned harnessed the horses to their wagon and drove it around to the cabin. Annie didn't hide the fact that she was upset with him.

"We'll talk later," he said when he tried to kiss her lips and she turned her head away from him. "I'll be back by morning."

Frightened, hurt, and frustrated, Annie moved about the kitchen slamming pots and pot covers as she went. "How could he leave me?" she shouted, breaking the oppressive silence of the soddy. "How could he do such a thing so soon after our wedding?"

She couldn't bring herself to open the sacks and examine her wedding gifts. Instead, she threw herself onto the bed and cried into her pillow. The humble little home that had brought her so much joy and pleasure over the last few days felt cold, empty, and frightening. After hiccuping several times from her sobbing, Annie drifted into a restless sleep.

She awakened several hours later to a darkened room. The sun had gone down. The world outside her window was black as midnight. A chill had settled into the one-room soddy. Only scarlet embers remained in the fireplace.

Her joints ached as she crawled off the bed and lit the lantern on the nightstand. The warm glow from the oil lantern's flame pushed the darkness back from her as she crossed the room and closed the window shutters for the night. As the metal latches fell into place, holding the shutters closed, Annie realized that as Ned's wife she would experience many nights alone while he shepherded to safety those whom he called his "lost sheep."

"Oh Lord, what have I done?" she wailed. Grabbing her shawl from the back of the rocker by the fireplace, she flung the wooly garment around her shoulders, grabbed the lantern, and bolted out the front door. A cool October breeze out of the west caught her skirts and swirled them about her ankles. Above her head, stars shone brightly in the moonless night. The night had blanketed the prairie, shrinking its vastness to the lantern's tiny halo of light.

A glow of light from Serenity's Inn lent a grayish hue to the prairie grass beyond the corner of the barn. *Serenity*, Annie thought. *I need to talk with Serenity.* With one hand hugging the shawl to her chest and the other hand holding the lantern aloft, she headed for her friend's house.

-4-
Learning to
Trust

"I CAN'T DO IT, NED. I JUST CAN'T DO IT!" Annie swung a heavy skillet onto the stove, then disappeared into the pantry. When she emerged, Ned hadn't moved from his position at the head of the table. "Serenity was right. This was something we should have discussed before we were married." Tears welled up in Annie's big brown eyes. "But I was so afraid of losing you that I told myself I could, but I can't."

Ned gestured helplessly with his hands. "I don't understand. You knew I was committed to the Underground Railroad before you married me, and I thought that once, you were too."

"I know. I was . . . before New Orleans." She nervously rubbed the pinky finger on her left hand with her thumb.

Ned rose from the table and strode to the stove. He removed the skillet from the flame and took Annie's hands in his giant callused ones. "We need to talk—now."

She allowed him to lead her to the sofa where they sat down side by side and stared at the oval rag rug under their feet. "Annie, you know that I've dedicated my life to freeing my brothers and sisters from the chains of slavery. If you love me, don't ask me to quit."

"I know." She slipped her handkerchief from her apron pocket and dabbed at her eyes and nose. "My heart is proud of what you do, but I'm so scared . . ." A sob burst from her unbidden. She doubled over, burying her face in her lap.

Ned gently lifted her onto his lap and silently caressed the back of her head and shoulders. She burrowed her face into his chest until her sobbing dwindled to uneven breathing.

Softly, he brushed a stray curl from her face. "Honey, tell me about New Orleans."

She blinked in surprise. Where had that come from? And how could she tell him about the horror and humiliation she'd experienced in "The Bloody Nail"? How could she put into words the repulsion she felt when the half-drunken gamblers leered and pawed at her? She could feel heat rising in her face as she remembered the drunks drooling on her neck and face as they groped her body. How could she speak of the terror-filled nightmares that had haunted her since?

Sensing her reluctance, Ned began his story. "All right, I'll go first. I was on my 'spirit quest' when the slavers captured me. A 'spirit quest' is a time when the boys of my tribe go alone into the jungle to prove themselves brave enough to be accepted as one of the adult men in the community." A far-away look appeared in his eyes for several seconds. Then, abruptly as it had come, Ned shook his head and returned to telling his story. "I was stalking a male lion when three men from a neighboring tribe jumped out of the bushes and grabbed me. Our tribes had been warring for several generations. I had let down my guard." He flexed a muscle in his left cheek. "I fought with all my might but couldn't break free."

He tightened his arms about her. "They stuffed a gag in my mouth, tied my hands and feet with hemp rope, threw me over the back of a donkey, and headed west. I knew because I could see the sun setting. We passed my village within calling distance, but I could do nothing more than watch my home disappear behind me."

Annie straightened. Her deep brown eyes welled with a new wash of tears, not for herself, but for the man she'd married. Gently she caressed the side of Ned's ebony face as he continued his story. "I rode slung across the back of that animal all night long. Every muscle in my body ached, and I thought I'd die of thirst.

"As dawn broke behind us, I lifted my head and could see, for the first time, a vast body of water like I'd never imagined before. I learned later that it was the Atlantic Ocean." The muscle in his cheek began twitching again.

"When we arrived at the docks, my captors dickered with a sea captain, speaking in a language I'd never heard. When they'd come to an agreement, money exchanged hands and my new captor ordered that I be stripped to the waist and chained by my hands and my feet to a long line of black men. Some were as young as seven; others were much older, graying, in fact. All looked as terrified as I felt."

Annie's heart ached as she read the agony on Ned's face. "Darling, don't—"

"No, there can be no secrets between us." His eyes glazed over once again. "Life aboard a sailing ship was anything but living. We were marched into the ship's hold where we were laid out on long wooden planks, one next to the other like the keys on a piano—chained, ankle to ankle, wrist to wrist. The heat and the fetid odor of fear was . . ." His voice dropped to a whisper. "At times, when I'm surrounded by too many people, the memory of that stench returns." Ned paused to take a deep breath. "Several perished during the crossing, including a ten-year-old boy chained to the space beside me. He'd injured his leg while fleeing his captors and received no care. The gaping wound became infected. Some nights his screams still ring in my ears."

Tears trickled down Annie's cheeks as she saw the agony on her husband's face. "Oh, Ned, don't—"

"No, Annie. I want you to understand why I'm driven to help my people, why I can't stop, even for you." His eyes filled with pleading. "Aboard ship, we were fed once a day, a gruel of some sort. Terrible tasting stuff, but when you're hungry, you eat. They brought us out of the hold once a day for exercise. More than one slave leaped overboard into the ocean, preferring death to returning to the ship's bowels. When one got away, the rest of us suffered by random beatings." He took a deep breath.

"As for me, I vowed to live. I would have my revenge against my captors!" A strange smile crept across her young husband's face. Annie shuffled off his lap, snuggling close to her husband's side. He barely noticed, so intent was he in retelling his story.

"It was a rough crossing, many storms. Massive waves tossed our ship about like a twig in a water-swollen stream. Both the sailors and slaves became seasick. As for me, I was too frightened to think about being sick to my stomach.

"Following each storm, my captors brought us out of the hold to attend a worship service on the deck. They sang hymns and prayed to a God they believed to be stronger than they were. Having always had a bent toward the spiritual—I'd been in training to become our village witch doctor—I listened as they read from a black book. I vowed I would one day steal that book and discover the magic that could bring these wicked sailors to their knees."

Ned leaned forward, resting his elbows on his knees and his chin in his hands. He seemed to be staring at the rag rug on the floor in front of the sofa. "I thought things couldn't get worse than the beatings and the chains aboard ship—until they took us ashore, removed what clothing we still wore, and herded us naked, into cattle pens. There the plantation owners and their wives would come through and 'inspect' us—prodding us with sticks, forcing open our mouths to check our teeth, and examining and squeezing our body parts at will."

Annie felt a shudder pass through her husband's strong body. Slowly, he returned to his story. "One by one, we were marched out of the holding pens into the New Orleans blinding sunlight. They paraded us onto the auction block, men and women alike, naked for all to view. I'll never forget the sound of that hammer coming down and the auctioneer shouting, 'Sold!'" His words caught in his throat, coming out broken with emotion. "I remember the stark terror in one woman's eyes when a particularly filthy specimen of a man bought her. To insure that she understood his dominance over her, he yanked her from the auction block by the hair of her head. A moan of fear passed through the captives waiting to be sold."

Annie massaged Ned's massive back and shoulders. Raised purple scars inflicted by his captors' whips crisscrossed the man's back.

After a few minutes of silence, he uttered a soft chuckle. "At the time, I had no idea what my heavenly Father had in store for me. What a marvelous God! Only an all-powerful Supreme Being could work through a practice so evil to bring one home-sick slave into the knowledge of His love. Isn't He amazing?"

Annie couldn't honestly answer. The furthest thing from her mind at that moment was uttering words of gratitude or praise.

Her heart ached with a web of sorrow and pain for this man she'd married.

Silence hung between them for several seconds before Ned continued his story, his voice less strident than before. "I was purchased by the owner of a large tobacco plantation in Kentucky. Massa' Dorchester's younger brother, Harold, a schoolteacher from Connecticut, made the trip back to the plantation with us." Ned straightened his shoulders and threw an arm around Annie's shoulders and pulled her close to his side. She snuggled close, drawn by the warm beat of his heart.

"On the trip from New Orleans, Harry, as he asked me to call him, introduced me to a God who loved me. For the first time since my capture, I wasn't afraid. Then without his brother's knowledge, Harry taught me the rudiments of reading from the magic Book."

"Did Massa' Dorchester find out?" Annie's eyes were wide with fear.

A smile spread across Ned's face. "Not before I'd also learned to read and do figures as well."

"What did he do when he found out?"

Ned chuckled. "He was furious. He threatened to sell me to the first taker until Harry mentioned that my worth had tripled now that I could read and figure. Harry reminded him that he'd been complaining about needing someone to keep the plantation books and to deal with buyers. Harry said, 'This boy will make an outstanding plantation overseer someday, given the right instruction. And on top of that, look at his size. This boy will be able to whip his weight in polecats!'"

"An overseer?" A shudder shook Annie to her soul at the thought of the cruel man from the cotton plantation where she'd been born. "How did you get free?"

Ned shrugged. "God's hand was in that as well. I was at the tobacco plantation seven months. During that time, Harry tutored me in everything from speech to the Word to advanced algebra. My favorite subject was astronomy—made me imagine I would make my way home someday."

"Would you return to Africa if you could?" This was a new and frightening thought to Annie.

He laughed aloud. "No, probably not now. God has shown me that my home is with Him, regardless of where I am; and now, my heart is with you, my love." He gave her an extra squeeze.

"So, how did you get free? I've seen your papers in your Bible." She sided around to face him.

"In God's time. . . . What happened was Massa' Dorchester and his brother took me to Pennsylvania with them to purchase a carriage from the Conestoga Company. On the way home we were crossing a frozen lake. The ice broke beneath the horses and carriage." He glanced down at Annie, her eyes wide with fear. "Neither of the Dorchester brothers knew how to swim. I did. I pulled both of them to shore at the same time. As a thank you for saving their lives, Massa' Dorchester granted me my freedom papers."

"Then?" The palms of Annie's hands tingled with excitement.

"I stayed on the plantation for two years as their accountant until I'd saved enough money to make my way to New Orleans where I still hoped to settle the score with my captors. But God is full of surprises." Ned gave her another hug. "During a violent rain storm, I detoured north into Illinois. There I found shelter in a Negro gathering where the people were worshiping and praising God. It was during that service that the group's patriarch, a field hand bent over with arthritis, prayed for me to lay down the heavy burdens that were 'bendin' me low.' And I knew it was time to let go of my hate."

"How did you get to Missouri?"

"I hired out to a riverboat captain and headed west on a paddle wheeler, eventually ending up on the docks here in Missouri."

Annie was too disturbed with what she'd heard to speak. Her story would wait for another day. As she prepared the evening meal, her heart ached for this kind, gentle man who'd been through so much. If nothing else, she knew she could never again stand in his way of fulfilling his God-given mission with the Underground Railroad.

For several days, she mulled her husband's nightmarish experience. When she heard his singing as he chopped wood or as he scythed down the prairie grass outside their sod house, she wondered how he maintained his cheerful demeanor and his gentle spirit after such an ordeal.

Surely he felt bitter at times, she reasoned, especially when the border raiders made their intimidating threats. She didn't want to think about what would happen if the likes of Mort Cranston and his gang caught Ned transporting runaways.

Ned hadn't asked her to tell her story. She was glad, for she wasn't ready. During the day, while she puttered about her perfect little home—to her it was perfect—and Ned labored in the blacksmith shop with Caleb, the young bride could almost forget about her past. And each evening there was no room for her age-old nightmares when she slept securely in her bridegroom's arms.

With winter coming on, there was much to do. Together Annie and Serenity picked wild apples from a nearby abandoned orchard and preserved apple jelly. They stocked a root cellar Ned had dug for them that also served as a place of refuge when a twister might hit. The two men helped their wives when it came time to preserve the venison that Serenity's Shoshone friends, the Blackwings, shared with the Cunards before the tribe headed further south for winter.

One afternoon the two women each carried a basket of freshly dug potatoes to the storm cellar. Standing in the middle of the cellar, Annie gazed at the barrels of apples, flour, grain, and pickles they'd preserved, and crackers they'd baked and dried. Butternut squash from Serenity's garden filled a portion of the shelves. Shiny jars of fruit and vegetable preserves completed the vast array of color on the wooden shelves.

Serenity stood to one side beside the slab of preserved venison hanging on a hook from a wooden beam in the ceiling. Behind the venison, several bags of salted beef hung from the rafters as well. Outside they could hear Onyx pacing back and forth in front of the storm shelter's stairwell, anxious for the women to emerge from the cavelike darkness.

"Beautiful, isn't it?" Serenity whispered.

"Yes, it is." Annie nodded. "Such abundance."

"I know." Serenity hugged herself. "We've enough here to feed the five of us and anyone else who might wander by. As long as the cows keep producing milk, Sammy will be happy." She chuckled aloud.

"Serenity, I-I-I think . . ." Annie smiled at the thought of Serenity's young son. She'd been waiting for the right moment to speak with her friend. "I think I'm pregnant."

Serenity whipped about to face Annie. "Really? Oh, how wonderful! Are you sure? How does Ned feel about it?"

Annie shook her head. "I wanted to be sure before I . . . He so wants children, you know."

Serenity blinked in surprise. "How far along are you?"

"I think six weeks or so. I was sick this morning . . ."

Serenity giggled with delight. She grabbed her friend by the arms, dancing up and down like a child of five. At the top of the stair, Onyx barked excitedly.

"I am so happy for you," Serenity gurgled. "You can't imagine how much a baby changes your life. Having Sammy was the most terrifying, yet the most fulfilling experience of my life."

Doubts crossed Annie's mind. "I'm not sure that I'm ready for . . ."

"Are you kidding? I'm ready to try for another. Sammy needs a little brother or sister. Wouldn't it be fun being pregnant together?" Serenity's eyes sparkled with enthusiasm.

Annie tipped her head from side to side. "I admit I was scared when I first suspected I might be pregnant. Maybe that's why I haven't said anything to anyone."

"Oh, honey . . ." Serenity squeezed Annie's slight shoulders. "Don't be afraid. All thoughts of fear and the pain for childbirth fades when that beautiful baby is placed to your breast for the first time. You'll never be the same again."

"I know." Just that morning, she'd battled nausea as she cut up the vegetables for the evening stew. A battle raged within her. She didn't worry about the fact that her life would change having this child, but would Ned's?

The fear of losing Ned and being left alone with a child to raise had been haunting her sleep since she first suspected she might be carrying his child. She wanted to beg him to give up conducting slaves, yet she knew that was out of the question. Wasn't it enough that the inn was a station where the runaways could hide? Couldn't he let someone else transport them over the border into Kansas and freedom? "I'm scared." A tear slid down Annie's cheek.

Serenity slipped her arm about Annie's shoulders. "I understand. I was too. I'd heard too many old wives tales about childbirth."

"No, I'm not afraid of having a baby, but of losing Ned," Annie sniffled.

"Losing Ned?" Serenity looked dumbfounded. "I don't understand."

"The Railroad. What if he's caught by the ruffians? What if he's hanged? I couldn't survive alone, let alone with a child to raise. I know I couldn't."

Serenity stared at her friend. "Annie, haven't you settled this issue yet? Life is risky. There are no guarantees for any of us, short of eternity with our God."

Annie frantically rubbed her pinky with her thumb. "Please stop. I've heard it all before—several times. Ned is always quoting one Scripture or another about God being with us and all that. I don't want to hear it again!"

"All right. I'm sorry, but it's true, you know, every word of it." Serenity busied herself rearranging the jars of jelly on one of the shelves.

"Please don't be mad," Annie begged. "But I just can't accept the conditions of God's promises. For instance, why did He let your mother die? And your home burn? And allow me to be k-k-kidnapped . . ." The woman dissolved into tears. Serenity gathered her into her arms. "Sh-sh, it's all right. You're safe now. You have a cozy little home and a man who loves you dearly. Doesn't that show God is looking out for you?"

Annie squeezed her eyes shut. "You cannot understand! I love you like a sister, but when it comes down to it, I'm a colored woman and you're white, and that makes all the difference. If Caleb were caught harboring runaway slaves, he'd be fined and possibly do jail time, but if Ned's caught, they'll string him up on the nearest oak tree."

Serenity stepped back from the onslaught of Annie's fury. "You are not necessarily right. From what I hear, the border raiders are indiscriminate murderers."

Annie shrugged as if she hadn't heard her friend's protest. "I understand why he needs to do it, but I can't stop thinking about losing him. And now with the baby . . ." She could feel pain developing in her head. "Worse yet, that Cranston gang knows where we live. What if they come out here to cause trouble sometime when Caleb and Ned are gone? What happens to us and the children then?"

Serenity touched Annie's shoulder. "Aren't you creating problems where they may never be? Anything can happen, that's true. But will it? God says not to worry about tomorrow, that today has enough troubles of its own."

Annie glanced over her shoulder at her friend, her agony spilling out of every pore in her body. "Somehow that's not very comforting."

Serenity laughed aloud. "My mother used to say, 'If you spend your life worrying about the future, you'll miss all the good things happening in your life today.'"

Annie nodded and began to smile. "I remember her saying that many times. Back then, you were Miss Worry Wart and I was Merry Sunshine, remember?"

"All too well." Serenity grew solemn. "After Mama's death, Caleb's mom helped me. She helped me see God as a loving God who cares about every little detail of my life, despite the tragedy that comes from living in a world of sin. As a result, I've learned to trust Him, which allows me to be at peace wherever I am."

A quirky grin widened Annie's face. "Did you know that you are becoming more and more like your mama?"

"Thank you. That's the nicest thing anyone's ever said to me. Yes, Mama had that kind of faith, but I was too young to see it, I guess."

"She'd be proud of the woman you've become," Annie added.

Serenity's eyes misted. She sniffed and dotted her nose with a handkerchief from her apron pocket. "I'd better get back to the shop and rescue Caleb. He's been watching over Sammy for me this morning."

Annie started for the stairs. "Thought I'd make some sweet potato pies for dessert tonight. Would you folks like one too?"

"Sure. Caleb especially loves your flaky pie crust." Serenity rolled her eyes toward the ceiling. "One of these days when you have time, you'll have to teach me to make pie crust like you do."

"It's easy, really. A gentle touch is all you need, so Dory always told me."

The two young women stepped out of the root cellar into the warm sunlight. With a bucket of sweet potatoes in her left hand, Annie shaded her eyes with her right. "Isn't it supposed to be cold sometime soon?"

"Isn't it beautiful?" Serenity's skirts billowed as she twirled about in a circle, lifting her hands to the sky. "I can't believe it's already late November!"

Annie envied Serenity's spontaneity. Lately Serenity seemed much younger than Annie, despite being the mother of an active toddler. "I know. I keep thinking I'll wake up to a frost."

With Onyx a few steps behind, Annie strolled with Serenity toward the blacksmith shop where Caleb and Ned were working and Baby Sammy was playing with small scraps of wood. The roar of the bellows and the clash of a hammer striking metal accosted them before they reached the shop door.

As Serenity opened the door, Annie placed her free hand on Serenity's forearm. "Please don't say anything to Ned about the baby. I want to be sure I am really pregnant before I tell him."

Serenity's eyes twinkled; her laughter trilled in the clear, morning air. "I wouldn't be surprised if he doesn't already suspect, but I promise I won't tell anyone but Caleb, and I'll swear him to secrecy."

"Thanks. I appreciate that." Annie heaved a deep sigh. "This afternoon I'll dig up the last row of carrots left in your kitchen garden and put them in the cellar."

"You don't have to do that. I'll get to them before the end of the week," Serenity assured her. "But since you want to . . ." A snicker escaped Serenity's lips. Both women knew the young mother didn't enjoy gardening.

"No problem. I'll be glad to." Annie whirled about, almost skipping toward her sod home while Serenity disappeared into the blacksmith shop. The dog bounded ahead of her.

After retrieving an empty basket from her pantry, Annie returned to the inn's garden and began at the nearest end of the row of wilted carrot tops. Halfway down the row she straightened to nurse a kink in her back, then resumed her harvesting. Memories of working in the cotton fields as a child, taking water to the grown-ups, haunted the corners of her mind. If it hadn't been for the Pownells . . . She shuddered at the thought. How well she remembered that day, when as a girl of eight, she tripped on a root and spilled the bucket of water she'd been carrying to the field workers. The overseer, a brute of a man, shouted at her. Lifting her and shaking her by the scuff of her neck, he dragged her to the edge of the field and threw her into the scratchy cotton plants. The man lifted the whip over his head, only to have a fancy carriage stop beside the road and a stranger leap out of the vehicle and grab the overseer's wrist.

Right there in the field, Mr. Pownell bribed the overseer not to beat Annie. The stranger and his wife took her to the plantation house and purchased her on the spot. Annie remembered how stunned she was to leave the plantation, her only home. Annie remembered thinking that maybe the kind couple would take her to her mother who'd been sold to a nearby plantation when the little girl was five.

Annie didn't remember her father. He'd been sold to a plantation owner in South Carolina before she was born. Annie returned to the task at hand with renewed vigor, trying to dislodge the ugly memories. The basket of carrots filled quickly. As she yanked the last carrot free in the row, she sensed someone breathing heavily behind her, his hands reaching out toward her.

Thoughts of the plantation overseer, of the New Orleans gambler, of Mort Cranston and his dirty, filthy men popped into her mind. Terrified beyond words, Annie's blood-curdling scream pierced the silence of the morning. Onyx, who'd been sleeping a few feet away, scrambled to his feet, yipping, barking, and running in circles around the frightened woman.

Annie whipped about and shoved the basket of carrots into her attacker's chest. Carrots flew every which way, but she didn't care. Run! Run! Her brain screamed at her. Onyx, in a high state of excitement, suddenly cut in front of her, causing her to trip over her skirts. Flat and facedown on the ground she stopped screaming long enough to hear, "Honey! Honey!"

Ned ran to her and lifted her to her feet. "Are you all right?" He held her at arm's length. "It's me, Ned, your husband."

Annie stared in horror at the man she'd mistaken for an attacker. "You . . . you . . . you!" She burst into tears, buried her face in her Mother Hubbard apron, and sobbed. By this time, Serenity, carrying Sammy, and Caleb, carrying a shotgun, appeared around the corner of the inn coming to her rescue.

Ned tried to coax a smile out of her. "Honey, I'm so sorry. I didn't mean to scare you. I just wanted to swing you in my arms and kiss you. Honest. Please forgive me."

The distraught Annie scooped up her skirts and fled to her home, stumbling over dirt clods and rocks along the way. Onyx bounded behind her, thinking the woman was playing a game of tag.

~5~

Secrets Revealed

ALL THOUGHTS OF CARROTS AND SWEET potato pie had vanished from Annie's mind, leaving only mortification in their place. By the time Ned strode into the one-room soddy, she was sprawled facedown on the bed, sobbing into her pillow. Of all the stupid reactions! She scolded herself repeatedly as her confused husband crossed the hardened, dirt floor to her side to comfort her.

The bed ropes creaked as he seated himself on the edge of the mattress beside her and began gently rubbing her back and neck. Sobs wracked her body. "I really am sorry I startled you. Please forgive me, darling. I didn't mean you any harm."

His apology produced a fresh wail of tears. The man brushed his hand across the back of her neck. "I don't know what to say, sweetheart. Please talk to me. Tell me what is wrong."

"Oh, Ned, I'm so sorry. I feel so silly. I'm the one who should apologize," Annie cried, lifting her face an inch from the pillow. She rolled over and looked up into her husband's anxious face. "My mind was elsewhere, and I thought you were . . ." She paused and closed her eyes in pain.

"Who, darling? Who?"

"It's too long of a story . . ."

"No!" Ned gently shook her by the shoulders. "That's what you always say. This time it won't work. You need to talk to me honestly. No more evasions."

Annie ran her right hand over her forehead and squeezed her eyes shut. She knew he was right. He'd shared his past with her; she must do the same. She rolled over and extended her arms toward him. "Hold me . . ."

Willingly, he slid onto the bed beside her and gathered her into his arms. Annie snuggled down into the warm security of his embrace. A new rush of tears burst from the woman's exhausted body, brought on by the love she felt for this man and for his incredible patience with her. She tried to speak, but her words came out in a series of hiccups.

"Sh-sh," he whispered into her ear, caressing her back as he spoke. Carefully he removed the hairpins and combs from Annie's hair, allowing her thick black curls to tumble freely onto the snowy white pillowcase beneath her head. Running his fingers through the curls, he added, "There's no hurry. We can cuddle like this all day if you need to."

"I feel so foolish," she wailed.

"No, no. I love you, remember? No matter what."

With his "no matter what," Annie whimpered and sniffed. "You say that now, but you don't know . . ." She couldn't bring herself to finish her thought.

"Nothing you can say will alter my love for you." He continued to caress her until her sobs subsided.

"I've told you about how the Pownells purchased me and set me free and how they took me to their home in Western New York, then brought me up alongside Serenity." Annie fell back against the pillow. Ned draped his arm across her waist and lay back against his pillow, giving her whatever time she needed to tell her story. She gazed at his profile through the corner of her eye, wondering whether or not she could trust this man enough to reveal her most repulsive secrets. "And you know about the fire and my hands getting burned."

Ned picked up her hand, turned it palm up, and traced the scars with his forefinger. "Your hands are beautiful to me," he whispered, kissing her fingertips one by one. She glanced unbelievingly at her husband. The compassion she saw in his face encouraged her to continue.

"Living in New York with Josephine after the fire was like being a part of an exciting adventure with an older sister. As my hands began to heal, I joined her in her escapades as a conductor for the Underground Railroad. We actually had great fun eluding the authorities and the bounty hunters. When we returned to her townhouse, she and I would share stories about our hapless pursuers and laugh about how we 'skunked' them.

"I don't believe I considered it as dangerous as it was until we boarded the ship for New Orleans. The 'mystery man in black,' who turned out to be a friend of Sam's, added spice to our exciting adventure. Then on board ship, I met Tad, and he needed me. Have I ever told you about Tad?"

Ned shook his head. She continued, "Tad was a ten-year-old, former slave who played the flute like I've never before heard. Josephine bought him from the captain of another ship." Annie laughed. "I wonder what that ship's captain would have thought if he knew he was selling the boy to a woman of color? I've never seen anyone pass into the white world with as much ease as Miz Josephine."

Again Ned nodded. "Yes, I would never have guessed when I first met her. She told me a while back when I was waiting for Aaron to deliver a shipment."

"Can you imagine being a blue-eyed blonde and having African blood in you? Josephine told me that sometimes she feels guilty being able to pass herself off in the white man's world, like she's denying her heritage, or something." Annie paused. "I told her she shouldn't. She didn't do anything wrong being born with porcelain white skin. And look at how she's helping her people, in ways you and I can't."

Suddenly Annie fell silent.

"And?" Ned asked.

"And what?"

The young man chuckled. He was used to Annie rambling from the point of her story. "What happened with you and Tad?"

"Oh, sorry. Tad and I were kidnapped the night before the ship docked in New Orleans. While Josephine was dining with the captain and his officers, two men burst into my sleeping quarters where Tad was staying, put gunny sacks over our heads, dragged us onto deck, then lowered us over the railing into a small rowboat." Annie smiled to herself. "I took a bite out of my captor's hand before he subdued me. He yelped in pain, then tied my hands behind my back, stuffed a rag into my mouth, and lashed my ankles together."

"Oh, my poor darling . . ." Ned drew her closer to his side. "I hate the thought of anyone being unkind to you."

"The worse was yet to come." Her voice was flat, void of emotion. "They loaded us from the boat and into a waiting wagon where they threw a dirty blanket over us. Above the rumble of the wagon wheels, I remember hearing the sound of out-of-tune pianos playing bar tunes, so I knew we were riding past the saloon district. I tried to remember the turns the wagon made should I escape. I have a good sense of direction, but it was hopeless.

"Tad lay weeping in the wagon next to me. The child was terrified. I wanted to reach out to him, to assure him we'd be fine, but I couldn't guarantee him that." Annie shuddered. "After a convoluted route, the wagon stopped. Our captors hauled us out of the wagon and into a musty-smelling building. That was when I first recognized one of the men's voices—Peter Van der Mere, Josephine's awful stepson. That's when I really became afraid."

"My poor baby." Ned caressed her cheek and forehead. She cleared her throat, trying to remove the lump of fear. "First they carried us up a flight of stairs to a filthy, dusty room where they left us hog-tied for several hours. At one point, the second man returned and gave us water to drink and allowed us to relieve ourselves in a chamber pot. "I was surprised to discover he was Quincy Gatlin, the man who had been romancing Miss Josephine during the voyage to New Orleans. The man kept repeating, 'I'm sorry. I would help you if I could.' But I didn't believe him. He was a spineless toady for Van der Mere."

A bitter edge crept into her voice. "Toward evening Van der Mere returned with a handful of clothing for us to wear— a green velvet jacket and knee-length trousers braided with gold for Tad and an English barmaid's home-spun skirt and soiled cotton blouse for me. Feeling I would be less vulnerable in anything other than my night dress, I cooperated when he ordered me to put it on. The gathered skirt was hiked up on one side and the blouse barely covered my, er, nakedness." Annie turned her face away only to have Ned gently turn it back toward his.

"I love you, Annie. Nothing you say will change that, remember?"

The woman nodded her head with a high degree of uncertainty. "Perhaps you'd better hear the rest of my story before you make such a claim." She didn't wait for him to declare himself again. "They took me to a bar and gambling room called 'The Bloody Nail.'" Annie reached into her pocket for her handkerchief and blew her nose.

"At first Peter Van der Mere made me sit beside him 'for good luck,' as he claimed, while he gambled away the Pownells' money that he'd stolen. When the money ran out, he lifted Tad onto a neighboring table, jammed the boy's flute into his hands, and ordered him to play something for the customers."

Annie began to shake. Her teeth began to chatter; her words came in short gasps as she fought to hold reign on her emotions. "Nobody bid on Tad, so Van der Mere set me on the edge of the table and offered me to the highest bidder. I became his ante in the next game." She lowered her eyes from Ned's. She couldn't bring herself to look him in the eye.

"The neck of the blouse I wore was held in place with a silk drawstring. He-he-he-he untied the string and . . . I can't go on!" She wailed, turning to face the wall.

"It's all right, my love. I understand your humiliation, darling. I understand." Ned cuddled up to his sobbing wife and held her in his arms. "It wasn't your fault. None of it was your fault. Remember, I've been in similar circumstances."

"But don't you see? I let him. I should have fought him off, but I just sat there and let him do . . ." She couldn't complete her thought. "The front of my blouse . . . and, and, and he was . . ." Her words came in short hiccups. "When one of the gamblers sitting at Van der Mere's poker table leaped to his feet and waved his side arm in the air, he found an extra ace of diamonds in Van der Mere's last hand. He demanded Van der Mere give me to him in payment for cheating during the last game."

Annie took a deep breath. "Van der Mere drew his gun. In the mad scramble to avoid possible gunfire, Gatlin whisked me from the tabletop and carried me, half dressed, out of the bar into the alley where the wagon was parked. Fortunately, Tad had enough sense to follow us and hop into the wagon before Gatlin tossed me onto the wagon seat, hopped up beside me, and shouted at the horses to go.

"Move, they did, at full tilt through the crowded streets of New Orleans while I struggled to cover my shame as the wagon bounced over the cobble stones. Mr. Gatlin returned me to Josephine. I am still mortified at having that man's hand touch . . ." Her lower lip quivered as she averted her gaze.

"No, no, my darling." He rested his giant hand on her waist and on their unborn child. "You came to me as chaste as a baby chick, regardless of what happened in New Orleans. Before God and before me, you are innocent of any wrongdoing. And both of us love you very, very much."

Annie shook with emotion. "It was there, in that ale house that I lost my trust in God. Why would a loving God allow that man to . . ." Tears of anger welled up in her eyes. She ached to punch something, anything!

"But he didn't, don't you see? You prayed for rescue, and your heavenly Father sent it in the form of this Gatlin fellow," Ned reasoned. "God answered your prayer."

"No! A loving God would have prevented Van der Mere and Gatlin from kidnapping us in the first place. A loving

God wouldn't have wanted those whom he loved to go through one minute of that kind of humiliation!" Fire burned within her.

"Oh, darling . . ." Ned caressed her tear-stained face. "That isn't the way it always works. Even God's Son hung naked on a cross for us, remember? He hasn't asked any more of you and me, has he?"

He warmed to his subject. "We live in God's time, not ours. Remember the story of the crippled man at the Gate Beautiful? The Master passed that gate many times during his ministry on earth, but the cripple's healing didn't come until Peter and John passed by, perhaps as long as five years later. Was that fair to force this man to live an extra five years as a cripple?"

"Hardly," she snapped.

"As a result, two thousand people learned of Jesus Christ through the man's healing. We're on this earth to bring glory and honor to God. The cripple fulfilled his destiny that day. Do you understand?"

Annie shrugged. "Yes, but I still don't like it."

Ned laughed and wiped a stray tear from her face. "The only thing we have to remember is that God said, 'I will never leave thee nor forsake thee.'"

The young bride paused a moment. She remembered hearing those words from Charity Pownell, many times in fact. Yet, Charity had died, never seeing her daughter marry or the birth of her grandson, or Annie's own wedding day. Annie closed her eyes and pressed her fingers against the bridge of her nose to equalize the pressure from the throbbing in her head. "I don't want to talk about it anymore."

"That's fine, sweetie. Just close your eyes and rest here in my arms for as long as you like."

As she drifted off to sleep, a strange, new contentment washed over her like she truly was an innocent child once again. Knowing Ned loved her, despite her nightmare, had released her from her self-inflicted imprisonment. For the moment, her husband's love allowed her to sleep like a child once again.

When she awoke, Ned was gone. Annie sat up and swung her feet to the floor. She smiled when she spotted two wooden buckets in the middle of the table, one filled with carrots and one with sweet potatoes. Though the sun was past its zenith, she decided she still had enough time to make those pies for her hubby, plus one for Serenity and her family.

Annie's heart seemed lighter as she blended the flour, salt, lard, and water in the large yellow ceramic mixing bowl, a gift from one of Ned's parishioners. Despite the embarrassment of retelling her story, it felt good to share her hateful burden with the man she loved.

As she slipped the bib of her blue gingham Mother Hubbard apron over her head and tied the strings behind her waist, Annie recalled the startled look on Ned's face when she fired the bucket of carrots at him. Remembering the events of the morning brought a grin to her face, followed by a chuckle, then a genuine belly laugh. By the time she regained her dignity, her sides hurt.

Gently, she rubbed her still-flat stomach. "That's one story I'll be sharing someday with you, little one."

"Oh, them golden slippers . . ." Annie's laughter bubbled into singing as she rolled out the pie dough on the wooden table top. ". . . golden slippers to wear, because they look so . . ." She didn't know about owning a pair of golden slippers, but she did know that for the time being life was sweet.

With flour up to her elbows and clumps of pie dough coating her fingers and the front of her apron, Annie lifted her face heavenward. "All right, Mr. God, wherever You are, I don't want any of that Thee and Thou stuff between us. If You love me like You said, I think You'll agree. What I want to say is thank You for today and for giving me a godly man to love."

The rest of the baking, along with the remainder of the afternoon, slipped by uneventfully. With the pies in the oven, Annie sat down in her favorite rocker by her window to work on the holiday dress Josephine had commissioned her to embroider for her.

The deep blue taffeta swirled about the seamstress's feet as she embroidered matching silk calla lilies and fancy scrollwork to the bodice and down the front of the skirt. No one would guess from the style of the dress that the wealthy young matron was with child. Recalling Josephine's condition, Annie's thoughts returned to the tiny button of a human growing within her, and she smiled a contented smile.

Annie loved her window view. From her rocker, she'd seen animals, small and large. She loved watching Onyx chase off all four-legged intruders. Indians from the neighboring tribes often passed by the window on their way to the inn where Serenity would barter with them, exchanging garden produce for their day's hunt. A rabbit or a couple of squirrels added much needed variety to the pioneer diet.

As for the new bride, Annie preferred to view these untamed and unpredictable people from behind her twenty-four-paned window.

After almost an hour of stitching, Annie glanced up from her work and stretched. The tantalizing aroma of sweet potato pies wafted from the oven. Setting her fancywork aside, she hurried to remove two of the pies from the oven to the cooling ledge Ned had built for her outside the pantry's small window. She placed the third pie on a back burner. It wouldn't cool as quickly as the other two, but it would taste good by morning.

She covered each pie with a dinner plate, grabbed the bucket of carrots, and hurried to the storm cellar. Annie dreaded being caught outside the soddy once the night fell. To her, even a trip to the outhouse after dark was a frightful event. She'd willingly empty and wash their porcelain chamber pot to avoid leaving the protection of her home once the sun set for the day.

She added the carrots she'd picked earlier to the mountain of carrots already in storage. Noticing a brown spot on one of the carrots, Annie began inspecting the vegetables individually, dumping the bad ones back in the bucket. "I'll clean these and boil them for supper," she mumbled to herself.

She paused and listened when she heard a startled bark coming from outside the cellar. Onyx must have found a rabbit to chase, she mused. Gathering her skirts in one hand and the bucket of carrots she'd culled in the other, Annie climbed the six steps out of the cellar and closed the wooden doors behind her.

The sky was ablaze with the oranges and reds of evening by the time she reached the front door of her soddy. Aromas from the cooling sweet potato pies lingered in the air as she pushed open the cabin's heavy oak door. She hurried to light the lanterns and add a few logs to the fire in the fireplace.

As she replaced the poker in the cast iron stand beside the fireplace, she paused to appreciate her home once more. She was satisfied. Everything looked homey and inviting. All she had left to do was to put the carrots in the pantry, stir the vegetable stew simmering on the back burner, and set the table.

"I think I'll use the red-and-white gingham table cloth tonight," she muttered to herself. "It's so cheery. Hmm, I'd better bring in those pies first." Annie hurried through the pantry and out the back door. She stared in horror at a bare shelf. Beneath the shelf was one empty pie tin and Onyx taking his last licks from the other.

"Bad dog! You are a bad, bad doggie!" She scolded, shooing the surprised animal away from his booty. "I can't believe you did this, you naughty creature. You should be ashamed of yourself." She shook her finger in his face, then rescued the two surprisingly clean pie tins.

The animal gazed up at her with his big, innocent, brown eyes, licking his chops and wagging his tail. "You go home! Bad dog." She looked at the empty pie tins and groaned. "Now what will I do? I promised Serenity a pie." She heaved a giant sigh and walked back inside the house. "I guess I'll have to give her the only pie I have left."

Out of the corner of her eye, she spotted the shadow of a man passing her window. "Good! I'll ask Ned to take the remaining pie over to the inn." She hurried to the door and flung it open to come face to face with a tall, older Indian holding a young brave by the scuff of his neck.

Startled, Annie screamed and slammed the door in the Indians' faces. Her heart pounded louder than the man's fist as he banged on the door. "Go away!" she shouted in response. "Mrs. Cunard, at the inn, will give you whatever it is you want."

The pounding continued. Annie pressed her back against the door, frantically glancing about the cabin. "Where is Ned's rifle when I need it?" she wailed. "Under the bed! I'll bet it's under his side of the bed!"

She ran to the bed and tossed aside the bedding. She pawed about in the darkness, but her hand contacted nothing but empty space. About ready to give up, her fingers suddenly touched something cold and smooth. She hauled the object out where she could see it, then groaned. She'd located his left Sunday-go-meeting boot.

Exasperated, she fell back onto her haunches. "That gun's got to be here somewhere! Oh, dear God, I need that gun!" She dropped the covers over the edge of the bed and cast about the room looking for other places where he might have the weapon stored.

The pounding on the door continued. Annie's hands flailed the air. "God, where are you when I need you? It seems to me that you always manage to be helping someone on the other side of the world somewhere, perhaps in Italy or Japan."

As abruptly as it had started, the pounding on the door stopped. Annie watched in horror as the door slowly inched open. "I may not be able to defend myself with Ned's rifle, but I won't go easily," she vowed. "Not again."

Clutching the boot in both hands, she lifted it high over her head and scooted to the space behind the opening door. The instant the top of a head poked around the edge of the door, Annie bellowed and swung. Before her weapon could strike its target, a massive black hand caught her wrists in a life-and-death struggle, or so it seemed to the screaming woman.

"Annie! It's me! What are you trying to do? Kill me?" Ned shouted in his wife's face.

Annie's eyes widened in surprise. Her scream caught in her throat. "Ned?"

"Yes. Is this the greeting I can expect whenever I return home?" He sounded miffed. "We have guests, Running Fox and his son, Black Hawk. Running Fox wanted to speak with you."

Turning to the waiting Indians, he invited them inside the cabin and introduced them to the quaking woman. When Ned finished, Running Fox squared his shoulders. "My son has something to tell you."

The boy, uncomfortable with embarrassment, stared down at the braid rug beneath his moccasins.

"Go ahead, Black Hawk." The father's face remained impassive.

"Ma'am," the boy began in perfect English. "I ate your pies, and I'm sorry." He extended his hand toward her. Grasped in it was a dead rabbit. "I want to pay you for the pies."

Paralyzed, Annie stared at the dead animal, then at the uncomfortable youth. Finally, Ned accepted the boy's gift. "Thank you very much Black Hawk. I'm sure my wife is grateful for your generosity. I hope you enjoyed the pies."

A smile brightened the young man's face, then disappeared as quickly as it had appeared.

"Won't you come in and enjoy a bit of supper with us?" Ned added. "My wife always makes more stew than she and I can finish in one meal."

Annie watched as Ned led the two men to the table.

"Is dinner ready, dear?" he asked after seating the Indians across from each other at the table.

"Yes! Yes." She scurried to the pantry and returned with soup bowls and spoons. She trembled as she filled the bowls with hot stew, then placed them before the men. Then she quickly escaped to the pantry and returned with a loaf of yesterday's bread and a jar of blackberry preserves.

Seating herself across from Ned, Annie looked questioningly at her husband. He smiled, then indicated to his guests, "It is my wife's and my custom to join hands for grace." He extended his hands to each of the Indians.

Once the three men were joined, Annie had nothing to do but take the Indian men's extended hands as well. Once linked, Ned bowed his head and closed his eyes. "Heavenly Father, Creator of all mankind, we invite You to our table today. Thank You for the bounty, this delicious smelling stew, and for the lovely wife who prepared it. Amen."

Running Fox grunted his approval. Before releasing Annie's hand, the older man turned her hand over and inspected her scars. "My wife has an ointment that could ease the pain you feel from the stretched scar tissue."

Annie looked at him in surprise.

"I will send some to you tomorrow with Black Hawk when he delivers the second rabbit for the second pie," the man assured her, eyeing his son as he spoke.

"Oh, that won't be necessary, Mr. Running Fox. The one rabbit will be enough for tomorrow's stew," Annie urged. The last thing she wanted was to have the young thief skulking around the soddy a second day.

"No." The father was insistent. "He must make amends for his sin."

"Sin?" Ned lifted his head in surprise.

"Yes, Mr. Ward. I am a God-fearing Christian, thanks to the Cunards and their weekly meetings in my village. My life has changed since I learned about Jesus and His love for me. My son is still learning, I fear. But then, aren't we all?" A hint of a smile teased the corners of his lips.

"Your speech, you speak English so well," Ned admitted.

"Joseph Blackwing and I were taken from our people as children. We were both raised by traders. His captor was French and mine was English." The man gave an imperceptible shrug. "For me, it was learn English or suffer the results." He lifted his right sleeve and revealed a long narrow burn scar.

Annie gasped.

"I refused to clean my captor's boots once—only once." The proud man lowered the sleeve of his garment over the wound.

Ned shook his head in amazement. "Yet you accepted the white man's religion?"

The man gave a slight smile. "It isn't the white man's God I serve. My God is bigger than skin color or race. He's bigger than man's petty prejudices."

Ned nodded. "You're right, my friend. I sometimes forget." Turning to Annie, he gestured toward the pie on the stove's back burner. "We have a third pie, gentlemen."

Neither Annie nor Ned had missed seeing the enthusiasm with which Running Fox's boy devoured the bowl of soup. Ned gestured toward the stove. "Would either of you like a second helping of stew first? There's plenty."

Her guests' eyes lit up at the prospects.

"This is good stew, Mrs. Ward," the Shoshone father said.

Taking her husband's cue, Annie refilled the bowls, including Ned's and her own. She smiled to herself as she carried them to the table. *A good scare does wonders for the appetite,* she thought to herself.

As the men finished the last spoonfuls of soup in their bowls, Annie glanced at the pie still on the back burner of the stove, then at her husband. She'd promised the sweet potato pie to the Cunards, but these were her and Ned's first guests in their little home.

Without stopping to reconsider, Annie leaped to her feet, gathered the empty bowls from the table and returned with the pie, a pie server, and four dessert plates. She'd planned to serve the pie with whipped cream, but hadn't had time to whip up the luscious topping. By the looks in the three men's eyes after taking their first mouthfuls, she doubted it would be missed.

— 6 —

To the Road

ANNIE AND NED WALKED THEIR GUESTS TO the top of the hill and waved good-bye. Before returning to the house, Annie gazed about the tiny cemetery where the inn's former owner and several of her babies had been buried. The grieving wife had sold out and headed back East to her family. Serenity and Mrs. Doran had kept in touch. In Mrs. Doran's last letter, the woman informed her that she'd remarried, to a young pastor for that matter, a Reginald Wiles. They were expecting their first child, and so far, all was going well.

Caleb and Serenity cared for the tiny cemetery as if members of their own family had been laid there to rest. Serenity had planted daffodil, crocus, and iris bulbs at each grave as a reminder that death is not the end, only the beginning for a new and glorious spring.

During their courtship, Annie and Ned often strolled up the hill together. It afforded them a modicum of privacy, but was public enough to be proper for a courting couple. While resting on the large rock at the top, they would share their hopes and dreams. From her vantage point, Annie believed she could see forever. Now, to stand by Ned's side, no longer as his fiancée, but as his wife and the future mother of the babe within her body, caused her to flutter. She basked in the security she experienced whenever she felt the weight of Ned's arm around her shoulders. She thrilled to the warmth of his massive hand on her arm, despite the presence of her shawl and sleeve.

A brisk breeze rolled in from the west, promising to bring with it colder temperatures and, by the looks of the clouds on the horizon, a blustery storm. The hazy ring around the half moon affirmed the prediction.

Annie snuggled beneath the crook of Ned's arm as if she needed protection against the pending storm and whatever it might bring. "I'm so sorry I acted so badly this evening. I don't know what's gotten into me. I've never thought of myself as a flighty woman, but lately . . ."

Ned caressed her arm lovingly. "It's entirely normal, so I've been told, for a woman in the early stages of pregnancy to be skittish."

Annie started in surprise.

"You are pregnant, aren't you?" he asked.

She swallowed hard. "Uh, yes, but how did you know?"

A furrow deepened in his forehead. "Darling, I love you. You are bone of my bone and flesh of my flesh. I know everything about you."

"But, how? How?" Suddenly she felt foolish for asking such questions. The man did understand the fundamentals of the female body. He was hardly a naïve schoolboy. She tried to redeem herself. "But I wasn't even sure until just recently."

"I know. That's why I didn't say anything sooner. Pregnancy is a sacred female trust. I felt you needed to come to the realization in your own time."

She'd married a perfect man, Annie had no doubt. He was so gentle, sensitive, and kind. Shyly, she tipped her head to one side and smiled up at him. "So, are you as happy about the baby as I am?"

"Yes and no."

Annie frowned. His response startled her.

"I'm thrilled about beginning our family so soon, but the timing complicates the plans Aaron and I've been making these last few months."

Warning bells clanged in her brain. Anything to do with Aaron spelled trouble. "Plans? What plans? You haven't told me about any plans."

"I didn't want to upset you." Shadows of evening covered his face. She couldn't read his expression.

"Upset me?" A note of irritation crept into her voice. "How are your plans going to upset me?"

"I've been going to tell you, but you've been preoccupied . . ."

"Tell me what?"

Ned cleared his throat. "Several of our stations along the Missouri-Kansas border have closed due to the raids. We need to scout out new ones, especially on the Kansas side. Runaways need a place to go to rest before beginning the trek north to Canada."

"So?" Annie urged.

"So, Cunard and I have come up with a plan that would allow me to travel back and forth across the border without suspicion." By the note of excitement in her husband's voice, Annie could tell the plan had gone far beyond the empty exchange of ideas.

"Yes?"

"I'm pretty good with animals, as you know, and I pastor several small Negro communities between here and the Arkansas border. It would be natural for me to visit these communities on a more regular basis." He warmed to his subject. "Being a circuit-riding veterinarian, I could get to know the ranchers and farmers in the area as well. Learning their politics would help Aaron and me to establish safe routes for our freight."

Annie stared at the pebbles on the ground by her feet. "You would be gone for weeks at a time?"

"Probably so."

"And when did you plan to tell me about your grand scheme to rescue the world? The day you hopped into your dream wagon and sailed west?"

"Almost." He dropped his head. "The wagon comes tomorrow. Of course, the main project won't get underway much before spring, but if I could have the routes mapped out before the snow falls . . ."

Annie shook herself free from her husband's grasp. "I don't believe you! You're a married man and only months from becoming a father! And you plan to traipse off to no-man's land without me?"

"Annie . . ." Ned heaved a deep sigh, then continued, "I thought you understood my dedication to this cause. We talked about it, remember?"

"We never talked about you leaving me alone for weeks at a time." She folded her arms across her chest and began rubbing her left pinkie finger with her thumb. She fought back the tears springing up in her eyes. "Have I been such a bad wife that you would want to escape so soon after our marriage?"

"No, no, it's not that way. I love you dearly, but I have a mission to accomplish for our brothers and sisters. I can't let that go!" He reached out to touch her, but she snapped away from him.

"Oh? And what about your mission for your unborn son or daughter?" As her fury grew, Annie's foot began to diddle. Even as she spoke, she knew she was being foolish and unfair, but she couldn't stop herself. "But then, I suppose everyone else's children will always come first with you."

"That's not fair."

"And I suppose you are being fair?" She whirled about, running and stumbling down the hill, her billowing skirts whipping about her legs as she ran. Annie's angry words had carried through the night air, but she didn't care. Let the whole world know what a perfect husband she'd married—perfectly horrid!

Inside the house, Annie gazed at the room through blurred vision. Hot coals simmered in the fireplace. Earlier she'd rinsed the dinner dishes in the cast iron sink. The light from two oil lanterns glistened on the waxed tabletop. Tossing her shawl on the back of the rocker by the window, she whipped across the room to the stove. She had dishes to wash and tasks to accomplish.

Even as she bustled about the cabin, she could hear her husband shouting her name. She waited until she heard the door squeak. Then, picking up the tin of half-eaten sweet potato pie, she hurled it at Ned's surprised face, the rim of the pan catching him on the bridge of his nose.

Blood spurted from Ned's nose. Horrified at what she'd done, she ran to his side. "Oh, darling, I'm so sorry. I didn't mean to hit you. Sit down."

Equally stunned, the young husband sank into the nearest chair—Annie's rocker. Annie ran to the sink and poured cold water from the bucket onto a drying dishcloth she'd earlier draped over the edge of the sink.

"Here, this should stop the bleeding." She placed the moist cloth on the bridge of Ned's nose. "I'm so sorry. I didn't mean to hit you with the pie tin, honest."

Without a word, he held the cold compress in place while she flitted to the sink and prepared a second cloth. "Please, honey, say something. Say something."

"What do you want me to say? I forgive you?" It was obvious that in addition to the cut on his nose, his left eye would blacken as well. "Fine, I forgive you. Does that make you feel better?"

Annie's heart sank further at the lack of emotion in his voice. What had she done? Would he, could he ever love her as much after she'd done such a heinous thing? When she tried to speak, her words refused to come. She placed the cloth on his nose. "You should lie down," she whispered. He allowed her to lead him to the bed where he could lie down until the bleeding stopped.

A slab of meat—beef! The remedy for a black eye popped into her head. Would preserved venison do the same thing? She didn't know, but it was worth a try. Grabbing her shawl from the rocker and a lantern from the table, she dashed out of the cabin and down the narrow pathway to the storm cellar. She set the lantern down on the ground outside the cellar, lifted the heavy wooden doors, and let them fall back against the earth.

She picked up the lantern and started down the stairs into the cellar when she heard a sound, a baby's whimper. Annie stopped and listened for several seconds. Outside she could hear the wind whipping through nearby oak trees, a prairie dog call to its mate, and Onyx, in the distance, barking and chasing some nocturnal creature. Then she heard it again, coming from the darkened cellar. It was the mewling of an infant.

Shining the light into the dark hole, Annie gasped in surprise at spotting the face of a woman close to her age holding a baby in her arms. One of Annie's wedding quilts lay crumbled on the floor, a gift from Pastor and Mrs. Rich.

The terrified woman shrank against an apple barrel at the rear of the cellar, clutching her small babe to her breast.

"Sh," Annie whispered, regaining her composure. "I just came for a piece of venison. It's all right. You're safe."

Relief flooded the mother's tear-stained face. "Oh, thank you, Missy. I heard shouting and a dog barking. I thought the hunters had followed us here."

Annie hung her head in embarrassment. "Sorry. It was my husband and me. We're newlyweds, you see."

A twinkle of understanding appeared in the runaway's eyes. "I understand," she said.

Annie extended her arms toward the baby. "May I hold your baby?"

The woman nodded.

"How old is he, or is it a she?" The child snuggled down into Annie's arms, resting its tiny head in the crook of her arm.

"It's a he. Benny is six months old. He's why we ran, my husband and I. We heard rumors that Massa' George planned to sell me and my son to a neighbor. Ben, my husband, decided we had to do something before we became separated forever."

Annie glanced quickly about the root cellar. "Your husband?"

"Yes, he escaped a week before me. We were supposed to meet in St. Louis, but something went wrong. Ben left word for us to meet him in Kansas. How big is Kansas?"

"Whew." Annie blew a stream of air through her pursed lips. "Kansas is a pretty big place, but I'm sure my husband and the conductors along the line will see that you find each other."

Annie noted a tinge of pride in her voice as she assured the frightened young woman.

When the child began to fuss, Annie handed him back to his mother's eager arms. "There you go, sweetheart," she cooed, tucking the baby's thin blanket of summer flannel under Benny's double chin. "Back to mommy. I wish I could offer you a more comfortable bed, but it wouldn't be safe for any of us to have you found inside our home."

Remembering her mission, Annie hacked off a piece of cured venison with the knife that hung on the wall behind the door. "If you get hungry . . ." She gestured about the room. "Help yourself. And keep the quilt for the baby, my gift to you."

"Thank you." The woman reached down and drew the yellow and blue wedding-ring-patterned quilt around her and the child. "You are so kind."

Annie blinked back a sudden rush of tears. She'd been anything but kind. "Sleep well. And don't worry, my husband is one of the best conductors in the west. If anyone can transport you to safety, he can."

As she turned to leave, the runaway added, "You're a lucky woman. You married a good man. Not many would risk their lives to save the lives of strangers."

"I know," Annie whispered. "I know."

The storm clouds seen earlier on the horizon swirled in the sky above her head as Annie made her way back to the cabin. Yet, in her mind, the skies were clear. Meeting that young woman and her baby hiding in the root cellar hadn't been an accident, or happenstance, she decided.

For the first time she understood what Ned meant whenever anyone spoke of luck. "There's no such thing as luck for

God's children," he would say. "Just as an earthly parent doesn't leave the guidance of his offspring to chance, so our loving heavenly Father doesn't guide His children by the fickle finger of fate."

Annie knew that she had an apology to make to her husband, one that went far beyond her clipping his nose with a pie tin. "All right, Father, if you want my husband to fulfill this mission, I will help and encourage him in every way possible, even if it means I have to be . . ." Annie couldn't bring herself to utter the word, alone. "After all, I wouldn't be totally alone. Caleb and Serenity live within shouting distance of me."

The word "shouting" brought heat to Annie's cheeks. How much of the argument had the other couple overheard? Probably she would never know, and certainly she would never ask.

By the time she entered the house, Ned was asleep in bed. She checked his nose. The bleeding had stopped. And yes, his eye was darkening, though the contrast between his injured skin and his regular complexion was minimal.

Annie crossed the room to the pantry to put away the slab of venison. As she passed the table, she spotted the unopened Bible. Every night since their wedding night, they'd worshiped together—every night except this one, when they needed the healing most.

She considered waking him. As she studied his peaceful face in the lamplight, she decided to let him sleep. She would serve the venison for breakfast with scrambled eggs. Thanks to the Cunard's generosity, the Wards were sharing their chicken coop until spring when Ned would build a coop for their own flock. Digging the root cellar before the ground froze had been more important.

Annie and Ned's five hens had immediately claimed their roosts in their new digs. The Cunard chickens hadn't objected, or so it seemed.

Long after the fire in the fireplace dwindled to ashes, the troubled bride kept watch over her sleeping husband. As the first streaks of morning appeared in the east, Annie awakened, surprised to find herself sitting in her rocker by the window. However, all was not lost. During those long hours of wakefulness, a plan was born, one that would meet Ned's needs and Annie's as well.

In the morning, neither Ned nor Annie mentioned the previous night's scuffle. When he left to do the morning chores, she leaped out of bed and quickly dressed. Soda biscuits were already in the oven by the time he returned with milk and eggs for breakfast.

As he set the bucket of milk on the dry sink, Annie greeted him with a kiss. "And how are you this morning?" She winced when she examined the bruise beneath his eye. "Ooh, that must hurt."

He grunted and strode into the pantry to deposit the basket of eggs on the shelf. She paused when he called, "The covered wagon is arriving today. I plan to head out tomorrow morning after Aaron helps me outfit it properly."

"That's nice, dear." Annie smiled to herself. "Did the mother and baby get off all right last night?"

Ned stuck his head around the pantry door. "You found them?"

"Of course."

"Aaron moved them during the night."

When she thought about it, Annie remembered seeing shadows drift past the window during the wee hours of the morning. "And this wagon of yours, it will be here today?" She sounded like a sprightly girl of twelve.

Ned frowned. She could read the confusion in his face. "You're not upset about it?"

Annie widened her eyes innocently. "Why, no, dear. I think the idea is splendid. I presume there's a false bottom in the wagon for hiding the runaways?"

Ned blinked, his face wreathed with consternation.

"Can our team of horses pull such a heavy load?" she asked, batting her eyes at her bewildered spouse.

"Uh, no. I traded them for two draft horses."

"My," she cooed, "what a lovely surprise. When were you going to tell me?"

His brow narrowed into a frown. "Is this the beginning of another brawl?"

"Why, no, my love. Nothing like that. After all, you need to do what you must do . . ." Her words hung heavily on the morning air. "And I must do what I must do."

"I'm not sure I know what you mean."

Annie shrugged her shoulders and grinned. "That's all right, dear. A good wife knows her place. And I do so want to be a good wife."

Grabbing the hot pads, she removed the soda biscuits from the oven. "M-m-m, don't they smell good? Why don't you sit yourself down and read the Good Book while I mix up a batch of eggs and a pan of gravy. Breakfast will be ready in no time."

They were halfway through breakfast when Ned spoke again, other than the blessing he'd offered at the beginning of the meal. "I'll be going into town to stock the wagon this morning. I should be back in time for our midday meal."

"That's fine, dear. I have several projects myself today." Annie dropped her gaze to her plate to keep from laughing at the confused look on her husband's face. She raised her head slowly to meet his stunned gaze. "Do you have any clothes you need washed before you leave on your journey? I'll be washing the sheets this morning."

"Why, yes, as a matter of fact, I do." He twisted his mouth to one side and narrowed his eyes. "I'd appreciate it if you could launder my canvas overalls, my red plaid flannel shirt, and my socks, of course. Aren't you going to ask me how long I'll be gone?"

"I'm sure you'll come home when your business is done, dear." She lifted a forkful of biscuit laden with gravy to her mouth, then licked her lips, savoring the flavor. "I decided it would be easier to do the laundry before the first snow falls. If you think of anything else that needs laundering, lay it at the foot of the bed before you go."

Ned drank the last bitter dregs of coffee, then lowered the cup to its saucer without reply. He opened his Bible to read a morning text. "We were reading from Ecclesiastes yesterday— er—since we skipped our Bible reading last night, I'll pick up where we left off." He avoided her gaze.

"Yesterday morning you read verses five and six about the dead knowing nothing," she reminded, her hands folded modestly in her lap.

"Er, yes. I'll begin with chapter nine, verse seven. 'Go thy way, eat thy bread with joy, and drink thy wine with a merry heart; for God now accepteth thy works. Let thy garments be always white; and let thy head lack no ointment. Live joyfully with the wife whom thou lovest all the days of the life . . .'" Ned lifted his gaze to meet Annie's. His eyes glistened with compassion. "I do love you, darling."

A gentle smile tweaked the corners of her mouth. "I love you too."

"I'll miss you terribly," he added, continuing before she could respond. "You know that I don't want to be gone from you, don't you? I wish there were another way, but I believe this is God's will for me right now."

To Ned, his wife's silence implied her consent, but to Annie, her silence was a matter quite different, a characteristic of hers that he would learn in time. *I may be pregnant,* the silent woman reasoned, *but I am far from stupid!*

***

The morning flew by quickly as Annie completed the tasks she'd set out for herself. By noon, when Ned and the heavy-duty farm wagon with its white canvas cover rumbled to a stop in front of the house, clean sheets on the line were waving in the nippy breeze, along with Ned's overalls, shirts, and socks. Sitting in her favorite rocker and darning a pair of Ned's socks, Annie glanced out of the window at the two stocky mares hauling the wagon. The animals appeared to be up to the challenge.

The aroma of bubbling stew and bread baking in the oven accosted Ned as he opened the front door. A cheery fire danced in the fireplace. Except for a pile of clean clothing stacked on the bed, all was orderly and inviting.

"Welcome home, darling." She set her darning on the seat of the rocker and hurried to his surprised arms. "Did you have a successful morning? Did you accomplish everything you set out to do?" she asked. "The team looks quite strong. I think they'll serve us well. Bertha and Cora could never have handled the load."

By the delighted grin on her husband's face, she knew the homey tranquility of the moment had impressed him. She decided not to disillusion him until after he had his fill of homemade bread, freshly churned butter, and applesauce.

As he spread a layer of applesauce on the last piece of bread, Ned announced, "After I eat, I need to take Brownie, one of the horses, to Caleb to see what's wrong with her left rear shoe. Then, except for my clothes and a few supplies from the root cellar, I'll be ready to leave."

This was exactly the moment for which Annie had been waiting. She struggled to hide her delight.

Ned gazed slowly about the cabin, his face drawn and grim. "I'm going to miss all of this, but I'll be back home before you know it."

"Yes, dear." Annie smiled sweetly. "Have you packed cargo in the hold of the wagon yet?"

"No, not on this trip. I want people to get used to seeing me traveling through the area before I risk transporting runaways."

"Good!" She whispered to herself. Her smile broadened as she carried the dirty dishes from the table to the dishpan. "How long do you expect it to take for you and Caleb to repair the shoe?"

Her husband rose to his feet and stretched before answering her question. "I don't know, an hour or two perhaps."

"Well, take your time. If you leave the wagon here, I'll load the clothes and cooking supplies you may need while you're gone."

"That's nice of you." He looked at her in surprise. "Thank you, sweetheart. You are certainly taking this better than I thought you would."

"What did you expect me to do? Cry? Stomp my feet and pout?" Annie shrugged dramatically. "I can tell that your mind is set, my darling. It wouldn't help to kick and scream; you've made that quite clear. So what else can I do?"

He crossed the short distance to his wife and slipped his arms about her waist. "What a beautiful and understanding woman I married. Do you know how much I love you?"

She slid into his protective embrace, resting her head on Ned's massive chest. "I am sorry about losing my temper last night. I didn't show you the respect you deserve, and I'm sorry."

"It's over and done with, remember?"

She nodded. "Hope you always forgive my impulsiveness so graciously."

"Of course, I will. What a silly goose you are. You take care of the little one while I'm gone, you hear?" He patted her tummy lovingly. "What a blessing it must be to carry a life within your body; what a God-given trust."

For a moment Annie wavered. *Perhaps I am being impetuous and foolish,* she thought. Biting her lip, she considered scrapping her entire plan.

Unknowingly, Ned didn't give her time. "Well, gotta' go. Things to do." He rubbed his hands together in eagerness. "I have to admit I can hardly wait to hit the road."

When her smile melted into a scowl, he added, "Of course, not a day will go by that I won't miss you. By the way, if at any time while I'm gone, you need help, Serenity promises to be here for you."

Her eyes flashed with determination. Her jaw hardened; her lips tightened. Her mind was set, regardless of how angry her husband would become. Calling upon every ounce of self-control within her, Annie pasted a smile on her face and rose on her tiptoes to kiss him good-bye.

"I'll be back as soon as I can," he assured her. "But you know how these repair jobs often take longer than one imagines."

"No problem, darling," Annie cooed, cast-iron determination lurking behind her widening smile, "I'll be right here waiting, your faithful little wife."

Cupping her face in his hands, Ned kissed her lips tenderly. "You don't know how grateful I am that you're taking this so well. I don't deserve you."

Annie wrinkled her nose in a little girl fashion. "No, you really don't."

He shot her a startled look, but before he could ask any questions, she gently pushed him away and gave him a love pat on his bottom. "Go. Do what you have to do and leave the packing to me. Just remember how much I love you."

A sigh of relief escaped her lips as she watched her husband unfasten the harnessed horses from the wagon and lead them toward the blacksmith shop. He gave her a cheery little wave as he passed her window. She did the same.

She watched until he disappeared into the blacksmith shop, then turned the tranquility of the cozy little soddy into a tornado of activity.

~7~

Throwing Sheets to the Wind

WITH THE FURY OF A CYCLONE, ANNIE whipped between the cabin and the canvas-covered farm wagon. If the wagon was going to be her home for the next few weeks and months, she would make it as livable as possible. Since they'd be carrying no cargo for the Underground, she decided to use part of the space under the wagon to store her bolts of fabric and extra blankets should the weather turn colder. She packed extra food and extra fuel for building campfires, and her sewing basket. She would finish the fancywork on Josephine's party dress while on the road and possibly have time to stitch a few Christmas gifts for her friends as well.

After dragging their mattress on board the wagon, she rescued the sheets she'd washed that morning from the line and made the bed—for two, then ran into the cabin for another necessity, her window rocker. She had no intention of roughing it completely.

Returning to the cabin, Annie checked the stew. It was bubbling hot and smelled delicious. *Now to the Bible,* she thought. "I know it's in here somewhere," she mumbled as she turned the book's onion-skin pages. "Ah, ha!" She squealed with glee.

A knock at the door broke into her delight. She left open the front door. "Serenity," she exclaimed. "Come in. Come in."

Serenity glanced about in confusion at the sparse cabin. "Uh, hi. Did I come at a bad time?"

Annie bounced to her feet. "Quite the contrary. I'm so glad you came. I was about to visit you, in fact."

Serenity smiled through her look of concern. "I just thought you might be needing company, what with Ned . . ."

For a moment the young bride frowned, knowing she'd been the topic of discussion among Ned and their friends. Annie hated the thought of people talking about her as if she were a nonperson, or as if she were a child incapable of dealing with life as an adult.

"In fact," Serenity continued, "I came to invite you to come stay with us while Ned's gone. We won't have any paying guests till spring, so we have lots of empty rooms at the inn."

Annie struggled to be gracious to her friend and her gesture of kindness. "That's so nice of you to offer—"

Before she could finish, Serenity interrupted. "With you being pregnant and all, it wouldn't be good for you to be here by yourself. Besides, Ned would worry about you constantly if you were staying alone." Serenity grinned and grabbed her friend's hands as she had when they were children. "We will have so much fun being together again. I can hardly wait. And I know Sammy will love having his favorite Aunt Annie to play with every day."

"Wait, wait, wait. Slow down. I agree that I would hate being alone here in the soddy without Ned. And I appreciate your offer. You and Caleb do so much for us, and I appreciate it . . ."

Serenity's eyes narrowed. "Why am I hearing a *but* coming on?"

Annie laughed. As children, she and Serenity had joked about how grown-ups used the word *but* to ease the pain of their nos. They'd say, "I'd like to let you go, but . . ." or "I would have made the cake I promised, but . . ."

"People and their buts!" Serenity would say. "They never seem to put them in the right places. Why can't they say, 'I didn't think it would be possible for you to go, but . . .'"

"That's because one is coming." Annie glanced out the window in time to see Ned coming from the blacksmith shop leading the horses with Sammy straddling one of them. Caleb strode beside the horse carrying his son, an ever-present, concerned father. Realizing she had no time to play word games with her friend, Annie whispered, "I'm going with him, Serenity. I've decided to go along with Ned."

Serenity's eyes grew wide with surprise. "Annie, you can't do that. You're pregnant, remember?"

"Yes, I remember, but a wife belongs at her husband's side— that's what the Good Book says, you know. So as a good wife, I intend to stay right by Ned every mile of the way!"

"Annie! That's totally unacceptable!"

Before Annie could reply, Caleb and Sammy popped inside the cabin. Outside, Ned was harnessing the horses to the wagon. "Wasn't too much wrong with the horse's hoof, a small cut from a burr. Ned took care of it with some salve. We thought we'd have to reshoe the poor animal." He sniffed the air. "Smells good—the last supper, huh?" He laughed at his own joke. The two women dropped their gazes to the floor. "I came over to help you take some of your things to the inn, Annie," Caleb said. When the woman didn't respond, he continued, "Of course, we can make as many trips as you need, our place being so close and all . . ."

Annie crossed the room to the pantry. Serenity sent a worried glance toward Caleb. "Annie's not coming to stay with us," she whispered.

"What?"

"She's not coming to the inn."

"What she gonna' do? Stay here alone?"

"Sh!" Serenity scolded as Ned entered the cabin. By the satisfied look on his face, the man hadn't discovered his wife's plan as yet. He glanced around the room in surprise.

"Has Annie moved her stuff over to your place already?" he asked Serenity. "She took her rocking chair too?"

Serenity reddened with discomfort. "Uh, well, uh, we've got to be going, Ned. I, uh, have bread in the oven."

"Yeah," echoed Caleb. "I've worked up a gigantic appetite this morning. Come on, Sammy, let's go home." He scooped the little boy into his arms and onto his shoulders. "You have a great trip. Our prayers will be with you." Under his breath, he added, "More than you know . . ."

Serenity poked her husband in the ribs and called to Annie, "We gotta' go, honey. I'll be praying for you."

Ned scratched his head in wonder as his friends exited the cabin. "Annie? What was that all about?"

Annie stepped out of the pantry carrying soup bowls, silverware, and two tumblers filled with milk. "Hi, darling." Her heart pounded with fear. *What if he gets angry? What if he refuses to take me along? What if . . .* She didn't know what else could happen to her carefully executed plan. "Are you hungry?"

"Yes . . ." Caution filled his eyes, like a prisoner facing sentencing. "What's going on here?"

"Why, what do you mean?" she asked, placing the dishes on the table and disappearing into the pantry once more. "Just make yourself comfortable, sweetheart, while I slice some bread for our meal."

When she returned with the bread and a crock of honey butter, Ned was seated in his place at the table. She carried the pot of hot stew to the table and handed her husband the ladle. "Here, help yourself." Then she slipped into her chair across from him and watched as he dished the steaming hot stew into his dish and offered to do the same for her.

"Thank you." She smiled. "That would be nice."

Except for the clinking of spoons against soup bowls, silence hung heavy over the couple. When Ned finished his last spoonful of stew, he placed his spoon in the empty bowl and stared across the table at Annie. "All right, what is going on here? Do you intend to punish me for doing what I'm about to do? Is that it? The silent treatment?"

Anger simmered deep in his ebony eyes, so much that Annie feared what might happen next. Taking a deep breath, she gave him a loving grin, leaped up from the table, and handed him his Bible. "What silent treatment, darling? Here. I was reading from Genesis this morning." She gathered the empty dishes and carried them to the dishpan of hot water she'd prepared earlier. "Perhaps you'd like to continue where I left off—Genesis 2:18?"

Ned's face was filled with questions. Annie hurried back to the table, slid onto her chair, and gave him the sweetest smile she could manage. Beneath her breath she was praying, "Dear God, help him to see the wisdom of my decision. Please Lord, I don't want to stay here alone, and I don't want to live with Serenity and her family, no matter how much I love them."

Ned cleared his throat before beginning. " 'And the LORD

God said, 'It is not good that the man should be alone; I will make him an help meet for him.' And out of the ground . . .'"

Annie smiled to herself as her husband read through the next five verses, only partially listening until he came to verse twenty-four. "Therefore shall a man leave his father and his mother, and shall cleave unto his wife: and they shall be one flesh—"

"That's far enough," Annie interrupted.

Ned looked up in surprise.

"God said it isn't good for man to be alone, so he made woman, and they were made one flesh!" The triumph in her voice surprised even Annie.

"Yes . . ." Ned answered cautiously.

"God Himself said that, right?" Annie tilted her proud little nose slightly upward. "And we should always do what God tells us to do, right?"

"Right." Ned drew out his answer slowly.

"God wants me by your side . . ."

Ned closed the Book and rose to his feet. "Annie, we've been through all this. I believe God has called me to do what I'm doing. Don't ask me to go against what I believe is right."

Annie grinned, and her eyes sparkled. "I'm not. I've decided to go with you."

He planted the palms of his hands on the back of the kitchen chair. "You've what?"

"I've decided to go with you!" She jumped to her feet and took the empty stew pot to the dish pan. Swooshing the dishes in the hot soapy water, she continued, "I've decided it would be wrong for me to do anything else. I belong with my husband. That's what our wedding vows were all about, remember?"

"Annie, this is ridiculous! You're pregnant."

"So? How many women have you seen heading west who were further along in their pregnancies than I am but didn't let that stop them from staying by their men? And it won't stop me."

Ned shook his head. "Annie, Annie, Annie, you don't know how rough it can get. Who knows what will happen when the weather turns? It will be cold, uncomfortable, lonely . . ."

Annie glanced over her shoulder to see why her husband paused. He'd discovered that the mattress was missing from the bed. Then he whipped about to notice that the rocking chair was no longer in front of the window. The fire in the fireplace had been stoked, and Annie's two dresses that usually hung from the peg beside the bed were gone.

"Annie! What have you done?"

She placed the last washed dish on the wooden drainer and dried her hands on her apron. "I think I thought of everything. If you'll close the shutters, I'll grab my shawl and carry your Bible out to the wagon."

"What? You loaded everything you own into the wagon? It will take me hours to unload . . ."

Annie straightened to her full five-feet, seven inches. Ned still towered over her by a good ten inches. "You will not unload one stitch of my personal items. You are following God's commands. So am I."

In mortal conflict, Ned stared at her, his jaw flexing from anger. Annie's determined gaze didn't waver. Finally, after several seconds, Ned's eyes flickered. Taking that as a sign of victory, the young woman snatched her shawl from the back of the sofa and her sunbonnet from the peg behind the door. She giggled, then waltzed out of the soddy calling over her shoulder, "You'd better hurry, darling; we want to cover as many miles as possible before the sun goes down."

Annie sat on the wagon bench looking as prim and proper as any pastor's wife should when Ned lumbered out of the soddy. She watched patiently as without a word, he secured the shutters and padlocked the front door, then boarded the driver's seat of the wagon. His arm brushed against her shawl, but he stared straight ahead.

Ned shook the reigns and clicked his tongue. The two new draft horses stepped lively at his command. Annie waited for him to speak, but he kept his eyes focused on the road ahead. He slowed the horses to a stop at a shanty at the edge of the river, the home of the owner of the river raft that would ferry them and their wagon to the other shore. A tiny wisp of smoke from the rock chimney indicated that someone was home.

The scraggly dressed owner with a head of bushy red hair and an even bushier beard stepped out of the one-room shack. Chewing on the stem of his corncob pipe, he eyed the couple and their wagon as Ned climbed down from the wagon.

"Hello there," Ned called, waving his hand in a friendly gesture.

"Ha-ope'," the man replied without removing the pipe stem from between his teeth.

"Beautiful day, isn't it?" Ned smiled broadly, extending his hand in greeting.

The river man glanced at the black man's hand and stuffed his own hands deep into his jacket pockets.

"We're here to cross the river, my wife and I. How much do you charge to take a wagon and two passengers to the other side?"

"Depends . . ." The man squinted up at the towering preacher.

"On what, sir?"

Annie gazed out over the water. It seemed so calm despite the bite in the afternoon breeze. In a few weeks it could be snow-covered, and soon after, the ice could be thick enough to cross at any point along the shore.

"Well," the man strolled over to the wagon and peered under the canvas, then circled the vehicle, checking out the wagon and its contents, "depends if'n you're runaways. I don't cotton to breaking the law."

Ned smiled between gritted teeth. Annie could hear the anger in his voice. "Sir, my wife and I are both free Negroes." He reached into his pocket and removed two official-looking documents and showed them to the man.

"What's your business in Kansas, anaways?" he asked.

"I'm an itinerate preacher, visiting my flock."

"Hmmph! Never did cotton to preacher men and their damnation sermons." From the way the river rafter studied the parchments, it was obvious that he couldn't read a word written on them, but he seemed impressed with the shiny gold seals and the embossed emblems on the base of each sheet. "Well, looks official to me. I'll take you across for . . . My, you sure are a pretty thing," he said, resting his hand on the wagon's cast iron arm rest. "Preacher, ya' got yourself a real looker here. Sturdy too. A good breeder. She'll bear ya' strong sons."

Annie glared at the raft owner. The man smirked and patted the horse on the right. The animal snorted at his touch.

"Well, let's get a goin'. Time's a wastin'," the man said as he strode toward the river and loosened the rope. "Just guide 'em on board and I'll push off."

Ned led the horses and wagon on board. Once he'd received the all clear, the rafter shoved off from shore with his long-handled oars.

Annie remained in her seat aboard the wagon while Ned chatted with the raft attendant as they glided across the river. The longer Ned went without speaking to her, the more nervous the young woman became. She began to doubt the wisdom of forcing her will on her husband. She thought of Dory and Abe, the Pownells' housekeeper and head groom. They'd taken over as her parents after Charity Pownell died. As forceful as Dory was, she always deferred to her husband's good judgment.

Further, as charming and winsome as Charity had been, the elegant and gracious lady had always discussed her decisions with Assemblyman Pownell. Even Serenity sought Caleb's advice before she made any major decisions. Of course, she also knew of husbands who beat their wives and abused and treated them worse than they did their favorite horses, but that wasn't the case with any of these men. And it wasn't the case with Ned. He'd been anything but cruel. He treated her with the utmost respect and tenderness.

Annie tightened her lips into a pout. *He did buy the horses and the wagon without talking it over with me,* she fumed, *knowing how I feel about the Underground Railroad. He did do that,* she argued with herself. *Yet if God is really in this venture, if Ned seriously believes this is what his heavenly Father wants him to do . . .*

Overhead, two crows chased each other, squawking, dipping, and nipping at each other as they flew. After a short time, the birds returned to a large willow tree growing alongside the river, their problems apparently settled. Annie laughed. "Thank you, God," she whispered, "for showing me how Ned and I must look to You."

Knowing she would have to apologize once Ned returned to the wagon, Annie steeled herself for the humiliation of admitting she'd been wrong. Again she thought of the couples she admired and wondered if they did stupid things to each other and had to apologize. Knowing the people involved, the woman doubted any of them would act so foolishly.

Annie cast an admiring glance at her husband's sharply chiseled profile. It had been that strong and manly chin she'd first noticed about him the day she arrived at Independence on the riverboat. He'd been working on the docks then. The massive muscles in his back and upper arms caught her attention as well. But it was the way he stopped unloading cargo to help a small girl catch her runaway kitten that first attracted her to him. He'd been so gentle with the sobbing child.

Then the girl's father, who'd not seen what had happened, shouted at the ebony-skinned giant for daring to "touch" the little girl's face. Ned wiped away a tear from the little girl's cheek after he returned the kitten to her. Annie had cringed in fear, expecting trouble. With little effort, the giant of a man could have crumpled the arrogant father into the size and shape of a Spanish lady's fan. Instead, the dock worker smiled, tipped his hat at the irate father, and strode away.

How can a man be stubborn, yet humble? she wondered. *Is Ned humble only to the white man, or is humility part of his nature?* Suddenly Annie realized how little she knew about this man with whom she had linked her life.

According to the laws for white women, a husband could beat his wife for disobedience, take as his own any earnings she might make, and banish her from her home and her children should he so desire. He could even kill her if he suspected adultery. A woman couldn't stay in a hotel overnight without a note of permission from either her father or her spouse. A married woman's inheritance went directly to the man she married, regardless of her wishes.

According to the laws of the land, Ned could pocket the trust Charity Pownell had left Annie, but he didn't. Instead, he did the opposite. He refused to use any of it on building the house, or purchasing of the covered wagon or horses. At first this decision had pleased the new bride, but with his arbitrary decision-making regarding this trip, Annie wasn't so sure the pride she admired in Ned was well-placed.

The woman stared at the backsides of the team of horses Ned had purchased. She noticed how well they worked together. Sooner or later she and Ned would have to learn how to pull together too. And, she realized, she needed to take the first step and apologize for her morning's behavior.

On the Kansas side of the river, Ned led the horses and wagon onto the bank, climbed on board, and turned toward Annie, his serious face more solemn than usual. "Annie," he said, "I have thought it over and will allow you to travel with me this time, but don't ever pull a stunt like this again to get your way."

With that, he shook the reigns, and the horses strained to pull the loaded wagon up the slight incline of the riverbank and onto flat land again.

Annie bit her tongue. Heat flamed in her face and fury in her heart. Even as a servant for the Pownells, Annie had not been scolded in such a demeaning manner, at least not since she had reached her late teens. *This isn't over, Ned Ward,* she muttered in her heart as her lips tightened into a pout.

"Can I have your word on that?" he asked.

She inhaled sharply. His question hung in the air between them for several seconds. "Well?"

"Yes, I give you my word that I will never do such a thing again . . ." Then she paused a moment before continuing her thought to measure her words carefully, ". . . as long as you never, I mean never, make such a monumental decision that affects us both without at least mentioning in passing before you act. Is that asking too much?"

He was startled at the force with which she spat out her ultimatum. His face revealed his surprise. Annie was known by their friends as a sweet, docile, woman, not one to have a personal opinion of any kind, especially of such a magnitude. "B-b-b-but, I can't promise you such a thing. A man's business is a man's business. You are out of line, woman!"

Annie snatched the reigns from her husband's hands. "Whoa there!" She turned her face toward Ned's hardening face. "I was born a slave just like you and I lived the last twelve years as a servant. But as much as I love you, Ned Ward, I am not your hired servant or your purchased slave! I will stay with you only as your wife, bone of your bone and flesh of your flesh, like our marriage vows say."

His brows tightened as he stared deep into Annie's cold, hard almond-shaped eyes. "Are you thinkin' you'll drive the team now? And I suppose you'd like to wear the pants too? Think you're big enough, woman, to wear a pair of mine?" His deep voice boomed across the empty prairie. "When I courted you, I never took you for a suffragette from back East!"

Annie shoved the reigns at his balled fists. "I don't want to drive the team, and I sure don't want to wear your britches, Mr. Ward. But I do want to be treated as if my opinions matter in this marriage. Married or not, I'm a free Negro! And free, I will always be."

Violently, he shook his head. "No! You gave up your so-called freedom to become my wife. 'Till death do us part,' that's what our marriage vows said."

When Annie's mouth flew open, no words emerged for an instant, but then the dam broke. "That's what you believe? That I am no longer a free Negro now that I'm your wife? You think I would have sacrificed my precious freedom for the likes of you?"

Without warning, the woman swung her legs over the side of the wagon and leaped to the ground. "I am not going one step further with you, Mr. Ned Ward, either in this wagon or in this marriage."

Ned wrapped the reigns around the brake handle and dropped to the ground beside his wife. "Come on, Annie, this has gone too far." He touched her arm, but she whirled away from her reach. "Annie, I'm sorry. Maybe I got a little heated back there and said some stuff I shouldn't have said. Though how's a husband gonna' react when his wife tries to usurp his God-given authority?"

She whipped about to face him. Her arms tightly folded across her chest and her eyes blazing with anger, she snarled, "Don't touch me!"

"Annie, be reasonable. Get back in the wagon, will you? I know that women sometimes grow testy when with child, but I didn't know—"

"Testy? You want testy?" She turned and strode toward a barn in the distance.

Ned started after her. "Annie? Come back here. Where are you going?"

"Leave me alone!"

"What are you going to do, stay out here on the prairie alone?" He called from behind her.

"Yes, in fact, that's what I intend to do. I'll hire out as a servant while I wait for Serenity or Josephine to send someone for me. If I hire out as a servant to some farmer's wife, I'll at least be paid something beyond my room and board!" Annie strode purposefully toward the distant barn. Someone would be there, she reasoned. Someone would help her, a pregnant woman, right? The further she walked, the more she realized that no one would help her by coming between her and Ned. That would be against the law just as much as hiding runaway slaves. Pride or no pride, there was nothing she could do but return to her husband. And if he should choose to beat her for her indolence, she had no protection, no recourse.

Annie began to tremble inside as she thought about the consequences of her decision to marry Ned. She'd been frightened of Peter Van der Mere and his cronies. She had been afraid of Mort Cranston and the animals that traipsed after him. But nothing matched the sudden wave of fear she had toward Ned Ward. For the first time she realized how final her decision had been to marry Ned. There was no escape. This man could treat her however he desired, and as far as the law was concerned, she could do nothing about it. Spots of red, blue, and gold danced before her eyes as she ran. The world began swirling; her eyes wouldn't focus.

Stumbling over a clod of dirt, she struggled to stop her fall, but to no avail. Her forehead struck a large rock. For a minute, Annie couldn't figure out where she was or what had happened. When she regained her reason, she found herself facedown in the prairie grasses. As she fell, a capricious gust of wind whipped her bonnet from her head and sent it soaring into the air.

Suddenly warm arms engulfed her. "Darling, are you all right?" Ned asked as he felt her head, then her arms and ankles. "Did you break anything?"

"Uh, I'm not sure." She clung to him as he lifted her into his arms. "Where are you taking me?"

"Back to the wagon." He strode over the dirt clods and through the grasses, carrying her as tenderly as possible. "I want to make sure you and the baby are all right."

Pulling back the canvas tarp, he placed her inside the wagon on the foot of the mattress. She watched silently as he removed her boots and checked for injuries. Except for the bump growing on her forehead, she felt fine.

When he suggested she lie down until they stopped for the night, Annie protested. He touched his fingers to her lips. "Sh-sh-sh, darling. It's for the baby, to make sure the fall didn't injure our little one."

Annie had to admit that he made sense as she crawled onto the mattress and Ned covered her with one of their wedding quilts. As he tucked the quilt beneath her chin, a tear trickled down Annie's face. "I-I-I'm sorry for the trouble I caused. I'm so selfish! I didn't even think of any danger I might cause our tiny one."

"Sh . . ." He tenderly kissed his wife's forehead. "We can talk about this later. In the meantime, you rest and I'll drive the team to the Tylers' place. All the colored folk in the area come to their place each Sunday to worship. They're expecting me, er, us."

Annie nodded, choking back a rush of tears burning her eyes. How foolish she'd been, she realized, risking the life of her unborn child over what, she wondered. Just what had they been arguing about anyway?

~8~

Before the Winter Winds Blow

ANNIE COZIED THE MUG WITH HER HANDS AS she sipped the hot soup Ned had brought her for breakfast. It was a portion of the starter soup she'd brought from home, and it tasted so rich and warm. Both Ned and Annie were reluctant to bring up the subject of their disagreement because they didn't want to ruin the beauty of the moment.

Overnight the weather on the prairie shifted from late Indian summer to a seasonal chill. Annie had awakened in the night cold shivering, despite the warmth of her soft flannel nightie.

"Where did you put the extra quilts?" Ned asked. He, too, was shivering despite having wrapped his body around his wife's.

"In the well. There are several there," she added. They'd taken to calling the secret compartment under the floorboards of the wagon "the well."

Ned climbed out from under their one quilt, turned back the mattress, and lifted one of the floorboards.

"They're stacked toward the front," Annie directed. "You can't miss them."

After a mumbled litany of complaints, Ned spread two more quilts over the first one and crawled inside the cocoon of warmth they'd created. He slid his arm around his wife and placed his hand on her growing waist. She loved the sense of well-being she received from him each time he did that.

"How long will it be before we can feel the child's movement?" Ned asked.

A smile came to Annie's face. "I'm not sure, but I think it will be a couple of months at least." What did she know about having babies? She'd never been around them much, except Serenity's son, Sammy.

Annie fell asleep with Ned's arm resting about her waist. When she awoke, he was standing over her, smiling and holding a mug of hot stew. "I would have made grits, but to tell the truth, my grits taste horrid!"

"Thank you," she murmured. "The stew is delicious. It's just what I needed this morning."

Ned turned to leave the wagon. "We'll be at Billy Tyler's place before the midday meal. Billy's wife, Jess, is one great cook, and she will fuss over you like you can't imagine." He hopped down from the wagon. Annie watched from inside the wagon as he tightened the canvas. She could hear him banging around pots and pans as he stored the morning's dishes.

Annie closed her eyes and fell back against the stack of pillows Ned had stacked for her comfort. Before long she could hear the harnesses jangle and felt the wagon lurch forward. *It will be good to get to where we're going,* she thought.

When Annie dressed, she noticed a small spot of blood on her undergarments. Fear gripped her spirit. "Oh, please, dear Lord, forgive my headstrong pride. Keep my baby safe." She fell asleep repeating her heart-wrenching prayer, the prayer of millions of expectant mothers throughout time.

An hour later Annie awakened when the wagon slowed to a stop in front of a two-story, unpainted, clapboard farmhouse. She peered out from under the canvas at a fierce-looking, yellow dog the size of a small colt that bounded toward the wagon.

"Lilly-bell! Lilly-bell! Go back to your babies!" A woman with a complexion as black as Ned and equally as tall, stepped out onto the farmhouse's side porch. Wiping her hands on her red-and-white calico flowered apron, she touched the runabout curls about her face, the ones that had slipped from the tight yellow gingham bandana tied around her hair. "Preacher Ward! Good to see you. That dog . . ." the woman cried as she strode toward the wagon, "she's all bark, no bite! She'd lick a bandit to death if she ever found one in these parts." Her easy laugh was hearty and genuine.

Ned jumped down from the wagon and embraced the woman. A twinge of jealousy tweaked Annie's nose when she saw another woman's arms about her man, although Annie had to admit that there was nothing suggestive in their embrace.

"I have a surprise for you, Jess. I brought my wife with me." Annie had enough time to slip on her bonnet, shawl, and gloves by the time Ned rounded the wagon, lifted the canvas flap, and helped her to the ground. "Annie, I'd like to have you meet Sister Jess. Jess, this is my bride, Annie. Isn't she beautiful?"

"She truly is, Ned. Yes, she has good hips for carrying and birthing children and . . ." Annie could feel the heat rise in her face at the other woman's direct appraisal. "There's honesty in her eyes. You did good, Preacher." The woman took Annie by the shoulders and kissed both of her cheeks. "Welcome to my home, Annie Ward. Your husband insists on calling us brother and sister, but you can call me Jess."

Annie dipped her head in embarrassment. "It's nice to meet you, Jess. Please call me Annie."

"Oh, I will." The woman turned to Ned. "Billy is in the barn. You arrived at just the right time. A nag got into some spoiled hay and made herself sick."

Ned kissed his wife's cheek, then bounded toward the barn, leaving Annie to the ministrations of Jess. Annie studied the farmwife's relaxed demeanor; it was like she'd never had a care in the world. From the strands of gray in her hair, Annie would guess Jess to be at least forty-five years old. Yet her smooth complexion belied a woman ten to fifteen years younger.

The woman called Jess wrapped her arm around Annie's shoulders and led her toward the kitchen door. "So, are you excited about the birth of your firstborn?"

Annie stumbled over a dirt clod in surprise. "Excuse me?"

"Your babe." She glanced toward Annie's stomach. "You do realize you're pregnant, don't you?"

"Yes, but how did you know?"

The woman threw back her head and laughed with relaxed joy. "Honey, I'm a midwife. It's my business to know these things. For colored women on the prairie, I am their only help, me and the Almighty God, that is."

Jess paused to eye Annie again. "I'd say this one will be born the second week of July. That's good—not having to carry a full-term baby through the heat of the summer."

Lilly-bell pranced out to meet her mistress. Behind her, three golden puppies, their feet much too big for their ungainly bodies, followed, tripping and tumbling over one another to keep up with their mother.

Jess Tyler bent down to pick up the runt of the litter. "This is Biscuit. When she was born, she was as small as a breakfast biscuit, hence the name." The woman lifted one of the puppy's front paws and clicked her tongue. "By the looks of this paw, Biscuit won't stay small for long."

"Ooh," Annie cooed. "She's beautiful."

"Would you like to hold her?" Jess offered.

"May I?"

The farmwife dropped the pup into Annie's eager hands. "You precious little thing." Annie nuzzled the tiny creature with her nose. "You are just too beautiful."

Jess climbed the steps to the kitchen door. "Come on inside and rest a spell while I make you a cup of chamomile tea. You look a little peaked."

Annie looked up at the woman's disappearing form. "How does she know these things?" she whispered into the puppy's soft fur. The puppy rewarded her with a slurpy kiss in the cheek.

"Bring Biscuit with you. She's welcome in my kitchen, at least while she's small. Besides, I think I see love at first sight between you two." Jess held the screen door open for her guest.

"Oh, no," Annie protested. "Being on the road and all, a dog would be out of the question." As she protested the woman's words, her heart was wishing otherwise. "Poor Ned has enough trouble taking care of me, I'm afraid. The last thing he needs is another creature to care for."

To Annie, the subject was dropped. After seating her guest at an oak kitchen table, shiny with wax, Jess bustled about the room, preparing two cups of tea. "It is so delightful having another woman to speak with. Billy is a dear man, but he can't understand a woman's heart. Of course, you and Ned haven't been married long enough for that, have you?"

Annie smiled. "My dearest friend in the world lives next door. I do enjoy Serenity's company, I must admit."

Jess took a blue tin teapot from the back burner on the stove and poured the hot liquid into two white porcelain cups on matching saucers. "I was just about to pour myself a cup of chamomile when I spotted your wagon pulling up out front." She set one of the teacups with its saucer in front of her guest. "Careful, it's hot. There's sugar in the bowl." She pointed to the round little sugar bowl in the center of the table. "Excuse me. I'll be back in a minute with some cream."

Annie watched as the woman disappeared into a pantry off the kitchen and return almost immediately. Making herself comfortable in the chair across from her guest, Jess leaned forward on her elbows. "Now tell me, Sister Ward, how are you feeling? Are you having trouble with this pregnancy? As I said outside, you look a little peaked to me."

"I, ah, well . . ." The night previous Annie had prayed for divine help, and God had answered her prayer by leading her to Jess. Why was she finding it so hard to open up to this woman so knowledgeable in the ways of women?

Jess measured out two teaspoons of sugar into her cup and a generous droplet of cream while Annie studied the tiny pink-and-red rose pattern on the steaming teacup before her. Under the sugar bowl and creamer was a delicate embroidered doily. She traced the silk scallop edging with her right forefinger.

"I'm sorry. I can be pushy. Billy warns me about that all the time," Jess said, taking a sip from her teacup.

"No, thank you for caring." Tears tumbled from Annie's eyes as she lifted her gaze toward her hostess. "You are right. I-I-I have been spotting—no cramps, just spotting. I took a fall yesterday afternoon."

Jess leaped to her feet and set her teacup and saucer in the dry sink. "Drink your tea! You need to be flat on your back, young lady, until we're sure your baby is going to be all right."

"Oh no, I checked this morning. I think . . ." Annie's protests fell on deaf ears. Before she realized what had happened, Jess had her buttoned up in a well-worn, flowered flannel nightdress that swam about her ankles and tucked in a massive four-poster bed in the Tyler's leaf-green-and-white-stripe wallpapered guest room. "I'm really fine . . ." She tried again as Jess tucked the green, navy, and white log cabin quilt under her chin.

Her resistance was weaker this time as she snuggled deeper into the downy feather bed. Annie felt like a child of ten suffering from the sniffles. It felt good to have someone like Dory or Charity take care of her once again.

"I'll be right back with a cup of chicken broth. You need to build up your strength if you're going to carry this baby to term."

Carry her baby to term? Of course, she would carry her baby to term. Why wouldn't she? That's what women do, right? Have babies? As she stared up at the rough board ceiling, Annie remembered hearing Josephine and the women talking about Susan Thomas and the babies she'd lost, one after the other. She remembered Serenity telling about the woman named Analee from whom they purchased the inn. How many times had she and Ned paused to read the names on the tiny headstones at the top of the hill beside Serenity Inn? But that was them, delicate white women with no constitution. Surely she would have no trouble. . . .

She laid there for hours as Jess bustled in and out, bringing her broth, hot milk, and cookies. In between trips to the kitchen, the farmer's wife sat in a small, armless maple rocker by the window, her knitting needles moving at dust-devil speeds.

By midday, Annie had drifted off to sleep. She awoke to Ned leaning over her and brushing stray curls from her brow. Her eyes fluttered open in surprise at the concern she read in his face. "Ned? Where am I?"

He gently shushed her with his finger to her lips. "At the Tylers', honey. Jess is downstairs fixing you a sandwich and some tea. Shall I get her for you?"

Annie touched her husband's concerned face. "No, I'm fine, really. I don't need to be in bed," she protested. "I feel perfectly fine."

The concern in his brow deepened. "No, sweetheart, Jess says you need to lay flat for a few days to make sure our baby's safe. She knows what she's talking about, Annie."

"I know she does, but I feel perfectly—"

Ned placed a finger to her lips. "Please, for my sake and the sake of our baby, do what she says."

Annie nodded, though she felt terribly silly playing the role of invalid instead of servant. The sound of footsteps on the stairs drew the couple's attention to the doorway.

"Well, hello there, sleepyhead." Jess carried a pewter tray holding a teacup and a sandwich. She beamed with pleasure. Turning to Ned, she grinned. "It feels good to take care of your wife; it's like having a daughter."

Ned rose to his feet and helped the woman with the tray. "Sister Jess, I can't tell you how grateful I am for all you are doing for us. I know God sent us to you just when we needed you most." The man's face was creased with deep emotion.

He really cares about this baby. Annie's heart was stirred. Can a man experience stirrings of love for an unborn child the way its mother can? She'd always been told that a woman begins to love her unborn with the child's first movements, but what about the father who has no physical bonds with the developing baby? she wondered.

Jess laughed in reply to Ned's remark. "I don't know about that, but the company of you and your wife is medicine to me, too, you know. It gets mighty lonely out here, just Billy and me and the stock."

"When do you think it will be safe for Annie to get out of bed?" he asked.

"Oh, by Sunday morning if there are no complications in between." The midwife nodded her head sagely. "What we want to do is give that sweet, little infant of yours time to cozy down for the long haul."

"But," Annie protested, "I'm not some delicate hot-house flower, Sister Jess, that needs to be coddled."

The farmer's wife adjusted the blankets around her patient. "A woman can't tell what she'll be until she's pregnant. I'm hardly a Caribbean orchid, yet I never could carry a child to term."

She gazed past her guests to a far-away point beyond the lace-curtained window. "Five, we buried five out there in that empty wasteland." The woman shook her head as if to dislodge the sadness. When she turned toward Annie, her eyes were glistening with tears. "But one day, Sister Annie, one day, I'm going to gather those precious ones in my arms and dance across the prairie, if heaven has a prairie . . ." Her voice grew husky, ". . . if God's heaven has a prairie . . ."

★ ★ ★

Sunday morning couldn't come any too soon for Annie. To be out of bed for the first time in five days! She stared in the small mirror hanging on the wall behind a walnut dresser. "You do look a little peaked, m'lady," she said aloud to herself. The natural shade of peach beneath her cocoa-brown complexion had faded.

Annie picked up her ivory-handled hairbrush and drew it through her tangled curls. Her favorite dress, burgundy wool with pink roses embroidered on the matching cape, lay spread out on the bed. She'd designed the pink rose pattern from the roses in Josephine's garden where she and Ned had spoken their vows.

She pinned back her hair from her face and gathered it into a wad at the nape of her neck. One particularly stubborn curl popped out, dangling down the side of her face. "That's not acceptable . . ." She tugged the curl back into place and continued, ". . . for the wife of a preacher."

"Preacher?" Ned popped in the door. "What was that you said about being a preacher's wife?" He slid his arms about her waist from behind and gazed at their reflection in the mirror. "It's a mortal sin for you to be so beautiful." He nuzzled her neck.

"Ned, I have to get dressed for the morning service." She squirmed but enjoyed every second of it. "Aren't you supposed to be working on your sermon or something?"

"M-m-m, you smell good too—like a lily in the moonlight."

"Ned, stop it. That's just the smell of the lemon-verbena soap Jess insisted I use." She shifted about in his arms to face him.

"M-m-m, good suggestion." He gave a deep chuckle and planted a kiss firmly on her lips. "I came up to help you dress for church. Jess thought you might need some help."

"Thank you, but I can do this myself." She wriggled out of his arms and slipped two of her petticoats over her head, then tied them at the waist.

"Let's forget about church," Ned teased.

"Preacher Ward! I am ashamed of you!" She giggled and skipped to the opposite side of the bed. Outside the bedroom window, two wagons drew to a stop. The voices of the arriving parishioners drifted through the closed window. Annie adapted her best schoolmarm voice. "I can manage better without your help. Now you go down there and welcome your congregation!"

He laughed, kissed the tip of her nose, and headed for the door. "Oh, all right. See you soon, sweetheart."

She blew him a kiss and slipped the soft woolen garment over her head. After she slid her arms into the full sleeves, gathered at the wrists, she fastened the tiny, black velvet-covered buttons, then did the same with the line of buttons up the front of the bodice.

She paused before the mirror to straighten the gathered row of antique cotton lace circling the high neckline. For an instant she flinched at the sight of her scarred hands. The salve Running Fox gave her before she and Ned left home had softened and smoothed the scarred skin across the back of her hands, but had done nothing for their deformed appearance. She quickly brushed the thought aside. Ned loved her in spite of her ugly hands. She knew she could trust his love.

She smiled at her reflection. The deep burgundy hues in the soft woolen fabric brought out the deep pinks in her cheeks. The stylish little embroidered cape of matching wool added the perfect finishing touch.

Will they like me? she wondered as she slipped a pale pink muslin mob cap over her hair and a pair of crocheted gloves on her hands. *Of course they will. They love Ned, don't they?* The butterflies in her stomach were in a frenzy. She paused, took a deep breath, drew in her stomach, and glided down the stairs to meet her husband's parishioners.

In the great room below, the men, some in straight-breasted coats and high-standing collars, some in cotton shirts and farmer's bib overalls, others in wool flannel shirts and canvas pants with red-striped suspenders, gathered near the roaring fire in the fireplace. The women, wearing frocks of calico, faille, and wool like herself, chatted with Jess in the kitchen area. Courting couples huddled in small groups of two to six near the split rail fence out back while younger children dashed about the porch and front yard with wild abandon.

When Jess spotted Annie on the stairs, she called to her. "Come on over here and meet Granny Cook. She'll be eighty-one next week. Can you imagine? Granny tells the best stories about life in Africa and later on a sugar plantation in Jamaica."

Ned drew Annie aside and planted a hearty kiss on her cheek as she passed. Jess made all the introductions. Each of the adult parishioners welcomed Annie to the gathering with either a nervous handshake, a shy nod, or a warm kiss. Unlike her friend Serenity, the quiet, young woman had never felt comfortable meeting new people.

Jess drew her immediately into the female conversation. "I want you ladies to look at the fancywork on Sister Annie's cape. Isn't it exquisite? She did it herself. Quite the artist, don't you think?"

The women oohed and aahed over the delicate stitchery. Many asked if the pastor's wife ever gave lessons. Annie hadn't thought about that possibility before. As she gazed about the circle of eager women, Annie decided she was going to enjoy being a pastor's wife.

For the church service, family units gathered in the Tylers' hay barn, sitting on stacks of hay that had been arranged in a semicircle. Grandpa Ellis hauled out his silver harmonica and played "Michael Rowed the Boat Ashore," for the children. At the end of the song, someone suggested they sing a song they'd learned from the "po' white folk"—"Jesus Walked That Lonesome Valley."

Most of the parishioners had traveled great distances, doing morning chores by candlelight and leaving home long before dawn in order to worship together. As they sang full voice in beautiful harmony, Annie studied their faces. The lyrics to the song reflected their daily lives.

The isolation of the prairie was absolute, exactly what these people had sought. Young and old alike, their faces and bodies bore the scars of slavery. The babies and toddlers present were the only ones who did not hear the crack of the overseer's whip in their dreams at night.

After the hymn, Deacon Jefferson read from the Book of Revelation. His deep bass voice rang off the barn's rafters. "Revelation 22:1–2, 'And he shewed me a pure river of water of life . . .'"

The people gave a great amen.

Deacon Jefferson continued, "'clear as crystal . . .'"

Another amen followed. These farmers and their families depended on the water from the great Missouri River, which was anything but clear as crystal.

"'. . . proceeding out of the throne of God, and of the Lamb.'"

Another amen.

" 'In the midst of the street of it, and on either side of the river, was there the tree of life, which bare twelve manner of fruits, and yielded her fruit every month . . .' "

The people shouted another amen. Their lives depended on the "fruit of their labors."

Annie tried to imagine a tree that produced twelve different fruits—apples, pears, cherries, peaches—she couldn't name twelve different fruits.

" '. . . and the leaves of the tree were for the healing of the nations.' "

The loudest amen of all exploded from the hearts of the congregation. Then Ned stood to preach. "Healing of the nations. Tell me, brothers and sisters, does our nation need those leaves of healing?"

"Amen."

"Do our people long for the healing those leaves will bring? Imagine, 'There shall be no more curse.' Truly our people have been cursed by the scourge of slavery, but that curse will be lifted."

"Amen, brother."

"And we shall see his face. Isn't that right Brother Jefferson? That's what the Scriptures say. The Scripture also says, 'There shall be no night there,' no more sneaking around in the darkness, no need to risk our lives and the lives of our children to reach freedom. For God will be our light."

"Amen." The people rose to their feet and cheered.

" 'His name shall be in their foreheads.' Some of you bear on your body the brand of your former owner; most of you bear that brand in your heart." Ned removed his jacket and rolled up his left sleeve. On the tender skin of his inner arm a capital J was imprinted by the slave holder's iron. The people nodded to one another.

Ned unrolled his sleeve and adjusted the cuff at his wrist. "I wear that J in shame and humiliation. But I proudly wear, every day of my life, the name of my Lord and Savior, Jesus! I wear it on my forehead as I praise my Father for his goodness; on my hands, as I do the daily chores God has given me to do; on my feet, as I travel from place to place as he commands; on my lips as I speak his Word. I want my people to be branded as God's men, as God's women!"

The people were on their feet, clapping and cheering. Granny Cook broke into singing. "Gonna' lay down my burden, down by the riverside . . ." The others joined in.

Annie gazed at the man with whom she united her life, the father of the child within her womb, and love overflowed from her heart.

Caught up in the celebration of the moment, she barely noticed the strong winds whipping around the corners of the barn, seeping through each crack in the walls, and stirring up dust and hayseed. Her thoughts were on the man of God to whom she'd "hitched her wagon," as Dory said so often. Feelings of trust, peace, and joy filled her heart.

~ 9 ~

The First
Snowfall

WITH THE THREAT OF THE PENDING STORM, meal preparation was a hurried affair. The women rushed about in Jess's kitchen like a well-trained militia, frying chicken, mashing potatoes, and boiling the last of the season's greens. In the barn the men held an unscheduled meeting regarding possible safe houses and new routes for the Underground Railroad.

Annie was daydreaming, staring out of the kitchen window toward the barn when Betsy Forche spoke to her from behind. "Looks like it's going to be a doozy."

Annie snapped alert. "Excuse me?"

"Sure hope we all get home before the worst of the storm hits." Betsy had a way of voicing the obvious. "Packed extra blankets though, just in case."

"Thank you for reminding me, Betsy." Jess peered outside, over the shorter woman's shoulder. "I have plenty of quilts upstairs for anyone who might need to borrow some for the trip home."

"We could use an extra blanket or two." Nettie, the deacon's wife, was a shy, little creature who seldom spoke above a whisper. "I've been meaning to get to Independence to buy some wool for a coat for Little John, but well, it's been a rough summer, if you know what I mean."

The women nodded in agreement. Money was never in great supply for these farm women, and this year even less, due to a very dry summer.

"Little John needs a coat?" Beulah Witherspoon straightened after removing her apple cobbler from the oven. "Why didn't you say so? Lloyd's winter coat is hanging on a peg behind the front door. Little John might as well get some wear out of it." The woman's voice quivered for an instant, then she continued, her eyes swimming in tears. "Stop by our place on your way home today."

The buzz of conversation ceased at the mention of Beulah Witherspoon's son, Lloyd. Polly Daniels, a young mother of three, whispered an explanation in Annie's ear. "Lloyd drowned in the river during a tornado last spring. He was their only child."

Nettie rushed to Beulah and put her arms around the grieving mother. "Thank you."

Beulah nodded. "While you're there, I'll check through some of Lloyd's other things. Might as well be put to good use."

"You don't have to do that." Nettie's voice rasped with emotion.

A whistling teakettle on the stove interrupted the moment. "The water's hot for the coffee," Granny Cook announced. "And the platter of fried chicken looks ready to topple! Let's eat."

The women laughed with relief. Death was never far from any of them. Too lose a loved one after risking everything to reach the "promised land" of Kansas didn't seem fair to Annie. But as Ned said so often, "On this earth, life isn't fair."

"Let me see to those blankets," Jess volunteered. "Annie, if you'd call everyone to eat, I'd appreciate it."

Annie strode out of the house and rang the triangle dangling by a cord from the porch roof. The clatter brought children running from every direction and the men flooding out of the barn. Behind her, the women had stepped out onto the porch.

Ned bounded up the steps to her side. He raised his hands for silence. "Due to the possibility of a storm brewing in the west, the families from the greatest distance will go through the line first for their food. That means Brother and Sister Dodd and their brood will lead the way, followed by the Jeffersons and the Forches."

The group nodded in agreement. Ned continued, "All right, let's bow our heads for a word of gratitude and praise."

"Dear heavenly Father, for Your bounteous blessings, we say thank you. For Your fairness and Your faithfulness, we praise You. And for Your love, we bow in humble adoration. Amen."

"Pastor," one of the teenage boys in the back row shouted, "You forgot the food. You didn't thank him for our food."

Ned grinned and shrugged at the good-natured laughter that spread throughout the crowd. "Thank you, Ben Sample." The boy hid his face in embarrassment while his buddies chortled at his expense.

"Excuse me, Lord," the pastor began again, "We do thank you for the great fried chicken we're about to eat." A loud amen followed, along with a stampede for the food line.

"Those young'uns really like you." Annie slid her arm around her husband's waist. She liked the way his arms were always ready to receive her and the comfortable way her shoulder fit beneath his armpit.

"I hope so." There was a twinkle in the man's eyes, an easy smile on his face. "They're the future of this congregation, of any congregation, in fact."

Annie and Ned waited with the Tylers until everyone had their fill before getting their own food.

"With my business done here, and my little wife doing so much better, it's time we head back home," he said as he gave her a squeeze. "I'd hoped we'd make it as far as Ft. Scott and perhaps, Carthage, but if not, there's always next spring."

"Aw, let's not give up hope yet," Billy Tyler interjected. "This is only the first snow of the season. You could still make it as far as Ft. Scott before you return to Independence. If you could line up a few more farms of refuge on this side of the border, it would be a great help to the cause."

"Seems to me . . ." Jess folded her arms across her chest, ". . . we need more safe-way stations to the north of us. That Stringfellow guy and others of his caliber have sworn to make Kansas a slave state, on peril of their lives. These pro-slavery men are offering large rewards on the heads of several of the conductors across Northern Missouri. Billy heard it from two gentlemen from Massachusetts who attended one of their secret meetings."

"Billy told me about that, Sister Jess," Ned began, "and come spring, a few of us men intend to scout out a new route and abandon the existing line. With very little law to protect runaway slaves along the central Missouri/Kansas border, Cranston and his barbarians are wrecking havoc on the black farmers in the area, free or not."

"They'd come all the way out here? This far into Kansas?" Annie had never imagined that the band of troublemakers would dare cross the borders.

Billy Tyler shook his head in consternation. "Sheriff Maxwell and his posse do everything they can, considering how much border they are supposed to watch. So far, the lawmen in these parts have been nothing but helpful to our cause. However, that's not true down Carthage way. I expect real trouble to break out at any time, what with pro-slave sympathizers for lawmen."

A chill passed through Annie's body. She'd heard enough horrid tales to last a lifetime. Sensing his wife's discomfort, Ned pointed to the food tables. "Looks like the chow line's down a bit, and there's still a piece or two of chicken left."

Granny Cook, who'd been standing close by, wrinkled her nose and grinned sheepishly. "Don't you worry none, Preacher Ward. I saved a platter of my fried chicken for you and the missus. Got it warmin' in the oven." She glanced past the Wards toward the Tylers'. "There's plenty for you two as well."

Ned wrapped his left arm around the older woman. "Why Granny, I never worry about eating when I have you and the good Lord watchin' out for me."

The matriarch of the parish beamed with pleasure as she bustled to the oven and extricated a large platter full of golden fried chicken. Annie eyed the woman with curiosity. What was her story, this woman's tale of woe? Was she kidnapped like so many others in the assembly? Was she mistreated on some plantation? Did she once have children? A husband? Was she a runaway?

By the joy that filled her eyes, one would never guess this remarkable woman had suffered for a minute. But experience told Annie that the woman probably had as hard a life as any of the rest. Considering her age, maybe worse.

Later, after the last wagon pulled away from the Tylers'

ranch, and Jess and Annie had tidied up the kitchen, Ned invited Annie for a stroll.

"Don't overdo it," Jess warned as Ned draped Annie's woolen shawl over his wife's shoulders. "You still need to be very careful, Annie, honey."

Annie read nothing but love and concern in Jess's face. "I'll be careful," she assured her hostess. "When we come back, I'll lie down for a nap, in fact."

"Forgive me for being a mother hen, child." Jess gave the younger woman a hug. "I want that baby of yours to make it into this world safely."

"I know," Annie assured her. "And, to be honest, I enjoy your mothering. I hardly remember my mama."

"Oh, you poor child . . ."

"Oh no, I've had an easy life compared to most of the women I met today." A sad little smile swept across Annie's face. "But it would be nice to one day meet her."

"Of that you are guaranteed!" Ned interrupted.

"Amen," Jess added, her face filled with joy. "And my babies . . ."

Annie placed her hand on Jess's arm. "And your babies."

"What a great, gettin' up mornin' that will be!" Ned opened the front door for his wife. "We'll be back in a few minutes, Sister Jess. Don't worry."

***

The storm arrived around nightfall, breathing a frigid wind through its teeth, but not much snow. As the icy breezes whipped around the corners of the clapboard farmhouse, the two couples huddled together before a roaring fire, telling stories of their pasts and sharing hopes and dreams for the future.

In the morning a light blanket of snow covered the earth as far as Annie could see from the Tylers' guestroom window. The skies remained overcast; the clouds pregnant with moisture. As Annie dressed in her warmest gown, Ned led their team of horses and wagon around to the front of the house. Her stomach growled at the aroma of frying eggs and baking biscuits wafting up from the kitchen. She hoped she could keep them down this morning. Tossing her hairbrush on top of the clothing in her satchel, she snapped the case closed and hurried down the stairs to breakfast.

At the breakfast table, the topic was safe houses, places where the runaways could stay for a time until they could make their way further north into Nebraska and the Dakota Territory.

Annie listened as Jess and the two men discussed the areas along the Kansas/Missouri border where rest stops were needed.

"There's a Quaker family north of Fort Scott. I heard that they are setting up an Indian mission." Billy dabbed at a dollop of gravy that dripped from his fork onto his green plaid, wool shirt. "The Quakers are known to be sympathetic to our cause."

"What is their name?" Ned asked between mouthfuls of biscuits and white sauce.

"Herman Judd. His wife's name is Hattie." Jess volunteered. "We met them at the fall grain-market auction. While they seemed uncomfortable, like most whites around coloreds, they appeared to be devout in their faith. Maybe if you play on their religion . . ."

Ned cast her a sardonic grin. "And Sister Jess, we all know how deep and wide some white men's religion can go."

"True," Billy admitted, "but it gives you a place to start."

"You're right, and I thank you for the lead." The preacher leaned back in his chair far enough to get a good view of the overcast sky outside the kitchen window. "If we get along right away, we might be able to make it to Mr. Judd's place before dark. If not, we'll have a sweet honeymoon night in our covered wagon, won't we darling?"

The color in Annie's coffee-toned cheeks raised to a cranberry hue. "And you, a preacher of the Lord!" she hissed.

Ned grinned at his wife's discomfort. "All the more reason to set a good example to the married couples of my congregation, right?"

"Stop picking on poor Annie," Jess defended. "Don't you worry none, honey. Billy and I don't need no example. You and your little woman just worry about your own relationship with each other and with God, and the rest of us will do the same."

Ned winced at the woman's remark, causing the farmer and Annie to laugh at his discomfort.

"You might check out the Methodist mission too." Billy had returned to business. "I don't know much about 'em, but I'm sure they're good people."

"Oh, Annie, before you go, I have a quilt top I am making for Sister Nettie. She ain't tellin' no one yet, but Little John will be having a baby brother or sister come spring," Jess confided. "Anyways, I'd pay you to appliqué and embroider lil' brown cherubs on each square. You know, baby angels? Do you think you can?"

Annie brightened at the suggestion. She remembered seeing some drawings of cherubs in her *Goedy's Ladies Book* before leaving home. As she rose to help clear the breakfast table, she began to mentally sketch possible poses. "I'd love to and I'll do it for free."

"What? Oh, no, I won't have it!" Jess looked insulted.

"You've put us up for almost a week and refused to accept anything in return," Annie pleaded.

"No! You are my sister in Christ. Would you take away my blessing?" Jess argued.

Wisely, the men stayed out of the discussion.

"Wait, I have an idea." Annie arched her left eyebrow and grinned. "I will embroider the quilt for barter. In return, you will drum up future customers for me."

Jess's frown shifted into a saucy grin. "I can do that. I'll sing your praises far and wide." The woman whirled about and headed for the hallway. "I'll run upstairs for the quilt top while you finish getting packed. Forget the dishes. Billy and I will get to them after you go."

"I beg your pardon?" Billy acted indignant. "Dishes are hardly a man's job."

Annie glanced toward Ned in dismay. As she did, Jess poked her head around the doorjamb. "Don't pay any attention to him. Billy's just joshing you. He and I spend many evenings at the sink washin' dishes, and I spend many a mornin' helping him muck the cattle stalls in the barn."

Billy chuckled aloud. "Matter of fact, I wear an apron in her domain and she dons trousers in mine. Don't tell anyone. It would be scandalous. Next thing you know those ornery suffragettes will show up on my doorstep." He laughed to himself as he pushed his chair from the table. "Well, Pastor, let me help you get your bags loaded in the wagon."

Annie collected a stack of soiled dinner plates from the table. "And I will stack the dishes in the dry sink, like it or not."

Within a short time, Annie was waving good-bye to her new friends as Ned headed the team south toward Fort Scott.

The storm had helped them decide to postpone their visit to Carthage until spring.

"You may be getting yourself into more than you can manage with this sewing business," Ned warned. "What if you get too busy, what with the baby coming and all?"

Annie chuckled. "I doubt that will happen. The women I met at the Tylers are hardly in a position to pay for fancy needlework."

"I don't know." His voice sounded dubious. "Never underestimate the vanity of a woman."

"I beg your pardon!" Annie's eyebrows shot up into her hairline just as a rut in the road caused the wagon to jounce. Instinctively, she grabbed her husband's right arm and the wagon seat's iron rail. "What did you say?"

Ned chuckled. "Never underestimate—"

"That's what I thought you said!" She clicked her tongue and stared straight ahead at the wagon trail cutting through the waving, sun-dried, prairie grasses. "And men have no such vanity, I suppose?"

"Not really." He flicked the horse's reigns urging them on.

"Have you ever seen a man showing off his new horse?" She chuckled to herself knowing that Ned had held center court at the church gathering displaying his frisky new team.

Ned scratched the side of his head before answering. "Well, maybe you have a point. The wisest man who ever lived did say that 'all was vanity and vexation of spirit.'"

"Vexation of spirit, I should say! Ned Ward, you have a talent for vexing my spirit; about that there is no doubt."

He wrapped his nearest arm about her shoulders, tossed back his head, and laughed. "That's why ya' love me, right?"

She set her jaw in defiance.

"Come on, admit it. That's why ya' love me." He tickled her side. She pulled away but couldn't control the laugh lines forming at the edges of her lips.

"You are a pest, Pastor Ward, an absolute pest!"

"And I vex your spirit?" He tilted her face up toward his.

Annie could contain her laughter no longer. "Yes, you vex my spirit!"

"Good," he said, dipping his head to place a kiss on her lips. "That's a good sign."

"A good sign?"

"Absolutely, a good sign." He jangled the reigns. The horses broke into a trot, then after a short distance, slowed to a gentle walk. Feeling the cold seeping through her cape, Annie wrapped one of their wedding quilts about their shoulders and snuggled against her husband. The beating of Ned's heart and the gentle swaying of the wagon lulled her asleep, despite the bumpy road.

Along about midday Ned eased the team to a stop beside the road. Annie opened her eyes and stretched. The quilt slid from her shoulders. "Where are we?"

"Nowhere in particular. The horses need a rest," he explained. "Besides, I'm getting mighty hungry for some of that fried chicken I saw Jess pack in the basket."

Ned hopped down from the wagon, then helped his wife down. She gave an involuntary shudder.

"Are you cold? Maybe we should eat in the back of the wagon."

"Good idea." Annie wrapped her arms tightly about herself and hurried toward the rear of the wagon. The cold wind whipped through the Scottish plaid, woolen cape with a vengeance.

"You go inside. I need to give the horses a drink of water."

"All right." Her teeth chattered as she climbed aboard. Just as she started to lower the canvas flap, she heard the thunder of galloping horses.

"Ned! Someone's coming!" She shouted to Ned who was filling a bucket of water from the water barrel lashed to the side of the wagon.

"I hear 'em," he called, walking toward her. "You'd better stay out of sight till I find out who it is." He squinted down the road behind them. "Whoever it is, is sure riding hard."

Annie popped her head back inside the wagon without any argument. The sound of horses' hooves grew until they came to a halt beside the wagon. "Howdy," Ned called. "May I do something for you?"

"Hello there, stranger. Having wagon trouble?" an unfamiliar voice asked.

"Oh, no, sir," Ned replied. "My wife and I just stopped to water our team and get a bite to eat before continuing on."

"Where you headed?" the stranger asked.

"We hoped to make Fort Scott by tomorrow evening. The name is Ward, Ned Ward. I'm a preacher by trade."

"Good to meet you, Preacher. I'm County Sheriff Maxwell, and these are my boys. We've been on the look out for the Cranston gang. I'm sure you heard of 'em."

A chill skittered along Annie's spine at the mention of the bandit leader's name. *Why would they be over the state line?* she wondered.

"Yes, sir," Ned replied. "I wish I could help you, but we haven't passed a soul on the highway today. We're comin' from the Tyler place where I conducted church services yesterday."

"Oh, Billy and Jess Tyler. That woman makes the best huckleberry cobbler." The sheriff gave a hearty laugh. "As nice a folk as you'll ever meet—them's being colored and all." He paused. "Er, excuse me, I didn't mean nothin' 'cept they's good people."

"No offense taken, Sheriff," Ned replied. "Is there anything I can help you with?"

"No, sir, but if you run into those slimy varmints, they're mean as a skunk with a burr in its tail. Steer clear of 'em, you bein' colored and all."

"Yes, sir. I'll keep my weapons dry, or is it my ammunition I'm supposed to keep dry?" Ned chuckled.

Behind the canvas wall, Annie clicked her tongue in disgust. A joke at a time like this? Her husband wasn't taking the lawman's warnings seriously. Yes, Ned had a shotgun as protection against snakes and other possible threatening varmints, but she knew he'd never use it against another human being, even in self-defense.

"Well, I don't know how wise that is, as Cranston is a crack shot, and his sidekick knows how to handle a knife with the best of 'em," the sheriff drawled.

"I was just joshing, Sheriff. I'm a man of peace, not violence. My God promises to supply all my needs, even against the likes of Mr. Cranston."

"Have you been in these parts long, Preacher?" The sheriff asked incredulously.

"I've lived in Independence for a good five years now."

"Hmmph!" Sheriff Maxwell snorted. "Then you should know that a man needs to protect himself and his family from all kinds out here."

"Yes, thank you, sir," Ned agreed. "I'll keep that in mind. Seriously, I will."

"Welp, gotta' go on down the road a piece, then double back before nightfall. Good day to you, Preacher, and to your missus."

"Thank you, Sheriff. Happy hunting."

Ned sprang into the rear of the wagon as soon as the sheriff and his men headed on down the road. Annie fell into his surprised arms. "Oh, Ned, I heard everything. Maybe you should listen to the man and keep your shotgun loaded and under the wagon seat."

Ned laughed. "One good rut in the road and it would shoot the seat out from under us."

Tears welled up in Annie's eyes. "I wish you'd take this seriously."

"Seriously? Believe me, I take these border ruffians mighty seriously. They're evil men trafficking in the lives of my people, but I have no intention of matching them rifle for rifle."

"But—"

"But nothing, my sweet. Either God is my refuge and strength, or He's not. There's no two ways about it. I'm putting my money on heaven's firepower."

Realizing her battle was in vain, Annie opened the food basket and spread out on their bed quilt the carefully wrapped packages of food. Hot coffee would be nice, she thought, but she knew the winds were blowing too hard to light a campfire. They'd make do with the lukewarm mint tea Jess had insisted on including.

After Ned lit an oil lamp, its glow reflected off the wagon's canvas walls, creating a cozy atmosphere for the couple as they munched on the leftover fried chicken and buttered breakfast biscuits. Cleanup was easy since they finished every crumb. Only the chicken bones remained.

When Annie put on her cape in order to sit beside Ned on the wagon bench, he insisted Annie stay inside the wagon and sleep while he drove.

"The wind is getting worse," he argued, "and by the looks of the sky, it could snow within the hour. Besides, Jess said you should sleep as much as you can during the next few days."

"Aha!" Annie laughed as she folded the red-and-white-checked cotton napkins Jess had wrapped around the tin of chicken to keep it warm. "The real reason is Jess. I might have known. Actually, I don't need to be coaxed. A nap sounds good."

By the relieved look on Ned's face, Annie knew he'd suspected she would argue with him. This bothered her. For the next hour she questioned herself and the reasons for her negative reactions to her husband's suggestions.

"Am I too quick to disagree with my husband, Lord? Am I making his job as leader of our home more difficult by maintaining a belligerent spirit?"

The young bride had to admit to herself that she wasn't sure what the difference was between being a submissive wife and an obedient servant. How could she, at one minute, crave Ned's protection and the security his presence afforded her, and the next, demand the freedom to make her own decisions? Annie fell asleep pondering the strange conundrum called marriage.

* * *

She awakened to find herself bound by ropes. What had happened? Where was she? Where was Ned?

"Shut her up!" It was the voice of Peter Van der Mere. "Stuff this gag into her mouth and shut her up!"

Annie struggled to break free of their hold on her, but the ropes about her wrists and ankles were tied too tightly. The gag in her mouth threatened to suffocate her. Tears slid down her cheeks as she wrestled with her terror. *Be still,* she told herself. *The knots pull tighter the more you fight.*

The stench of moldy gunnysacks of corn weighed her down and made her breathing more labored. "Oh dear God, I can't breathe. Don't let me die this way!"

She struggled to open her eyes, but they wouldn't open all the way. It was as if she were peering through an out-of-focus spyglass. The laughing face of her captor appeared distorted. *No,* she argued with herself, *Peter Van der Mere is dead. I saw him die.*

She cried out in pain as the wagon lurched over a bump and landed with a thud against the hard roadway. Her left hip and thigh ached from the bruises caused by each torturous bump. To ease her discomfort, Annie tried to roll onto her back but couldn't. She seemed to be wedged between the wagon wall and a large gunnysack filled with, she knew not what. When she tried to shift onto her stomach, she couldn't turn.

Somehow, she didn't know how, Annie managed to free her hands from behind her back. She immediately yanked the filthy rag from her mouth and tried to scream, but no sound came out. Her breath came in short panicky gasps. She feared she might faint.

"Help, help me!" she silently cried. "Someone has to help me." She shot a desperate look toward the driver of the wagon and gasped. It was Ned! He looked at her and laughed, a loud bawdy laugh.

"Help me," she cried.

"Help you? Did you hear that, Van der Mere? She wants me

to help her!" Ned made an ugly, mocking face at her, threw back his head, and laughed again.

"Help me. Please help me!" she cried.

"Shut her up!" Peter Van der Mere's English accent melted into that of another Englishman's voice she immediately recognized—Mort Cranston. "Stop this wagon, boy, if you know what's good for you."

Mort Cranston was coming to rescue her? Impossible, Annie thought. I must be dreaming.

"We mean what we say, Preacher," another voice, one with an Eastern brogue, shouted. "Stop this wagon!" She'd heard the voice before, but where? Her mind was foggy with sleep. She'd heard the voice at her wedding—Badger Oberon, one of Mort Cranston's henchmen.

Suddenly Ned called, "Whoa," and she felt the wagon slow to a stop. Her breath caught in her throat when she heard her husband ask, "Just what do you gentlemen want with me and my missus?"

~10~

Into the Teeth
of the Storm

ANNIE SLOWLY BEGAN TO REALIZE THAT SHE was not just having a nightmare. Once she was wide awake, her brain struggled to process what was happening outside the wagon. She untangled herself from the layers of quilts that had become wrapped around her body and pawed around the floor beside the mattress for her carriage boots.

Her hands shook as she tightened the laces and tied the strings at the top. Her curiosity outweighed her fear, causing her to peer through a narrow slit between the canvas and the wagon wall in order to see what was happening. What she saw made her gasp. The three had their rifles aimed at Ned.

"Come now, Preacher Ward." When the leader of the group pushed back the brim of his black felt hat from his forehead, he gave Ned a crooked grin. "We know you and your buddy, Aaron Pownell, regularly aid and abet runaway slaves. And we finally caught up with you. A hangin' offense, if you ask me."

"Yeah," a third man spoke from the other side of the wagon. Annie suspected it was Jim Lair, the third man in the band of border ruffians that disrupted their wedding. She shuddered at the memory of the oafish man with the sandy brown hair, ragged beard, and cold brutish eyes. "It's a great day for a hangin'."

"My wife has been ill. She's asleep in the wagon." Ned's voice sounded tense, as if he were ready to leap onto the barrels of the men's rifles.

"Oh, Ned," Annie whispered, "don't lose your temper now. And please, dear God, send someone to help us." When she blinked open her eyes, she saw Badger Oberon's scarred face leering at her through the canvas opening at the rear of the wagon.

"His wife is in here, boss." Oberon whistled through a mouth of picket-fence teeth. "Purty thing. What you want me to do with her?"

"Leave her alone!" Cranston demanded. "We don't want a repeat of what happened in Baton Rouge, do we?"

Remembering that Ned kept his shotgun in the corner of the wagon inside the driver's bench, Annie grabbed the quilts and slid to that corner of the wagon as if she were scurrying out of his reach.

Outside, the bandit whined like a spoiled child. "That was a white woman, boss. No one would give a hoot about what happens to a—"

"I said no! Lair, go back there and keep Badger in line." Cranston snarled.

The man called Badger disappeared from her view, which gave Annie time to slide her hand along the wall of the wagon. "I know it's here somewhere," she muttered under her breath. "Oh, dear God, the gun has to be here somewhere."

Her hand brushed up against the smooth, metal barrel of Ned's shotgun. Quickly, she hauled the deadly weapon from under the covers. She'd never shot a gun before, nor held one for that matter. Gingerly, she rested the gun barrel on a round of her rocking chair, aimed it at the canvas flap, and waited. All she could hope for was to look mean enough for the ruffians to believe she'd actually pull the trigger.

Annie's breath caught in her throat upon hearing Cranston shout, "Preacher, get down off the wagon—slowly! Keep your hands where I can see them, and don't get any heroic ideas. Me and my men would shoot you in the blink of an eye, man of the cloth or not."

"Don't chicken out now," she thought as she peered through the gun sight. "Ned's life depends on it." When she saw the canvas flap move, Annie flexed her forefinger above the trigger. Badger's scarred face appeared under the flap. The man's insolent sneer turned to surprise when he found himself staring down a shotgun's barrel. In an instant, the man aimed his rifle at Annie.

"Ho, boss, we got a frisky one back here. She's got a gun," he called. "Easy now, lady. No one needs to get hurt." His voice was even and steady; his eyes hard as coal. "Hand the shotgun to me or your man gets a bullet hole where his heart is."

At that instant the face of the third man, Jim Lair, appeared from beneath the canvas, then disappeared as quickly as it had appeared. Annie heard him shout to Cranston, "Boss, the gal's sho'nuf got a shotgun aimed at ole' Badger."

"Mrs. Ward," Cranston called out in his cultured English dialect, "give the shotgun to Badger or I will shoot your husband dead. Do you understand? I will count to ten, then I'll plug your husband right between the eyes. One—two—"

Annie looked at the vile man called Badger. Already he was leering at the prospect of subduing her. His hand was extended, and he was flexing his fingers as if saying, "Gimme' gimme'."

"Three—four—five—"

Eyeing the gun in her hands, she took a deep breath. The weapon was their only hope.

"Six—seven—eight—"

The best she could do was to shoot Oberon, and then Ned would die. Reluctantly, she scooted toward Badger's outstretched hand.

"Nine—I'm not joking, Mrs. Ward. Give Badger the shotgun." The steely cold tone in Cranston's voice assured her he was serious.

"Annie! Give the man the gun!" Ned shouted. "Our protection doesn't come from guns and knives. You know that."

"All right! I'll give him the gun," she replied in a belligerent tone. "But God helps those who help themselves; isn't that what the Good Book says?"

The barrel of the shotgun had barely touched the man's fingertips when the weapon was snatched from her grasp and she was flung from the wagon onto the roadway. She landed flat on her stomach and chest. For an instant she couldn't breath. Then she felt a sharp pain in her abdomen. From somewhere in the distance, Annie heard her husband shout her name. Suddenly his arms were around her, despite Cranston's fury. They ducked as a bullet zinged over their heads and were only vaguely aware of Cranston and his horse standing over them while the other two ransacked their wagon, so great was their gratitude to be alive.

"Oh, darling," Ned whispered, rocking her tenderly in his arms, "what a brave and foolish woman I married. I love you so much, you crazy little pole cat."

"There's nothin' here boss," the man called Lair shouted, "not even a cache of money."

"I told you, sir." Ned glanced up at the border ruffian. "I am a simple circuit-riding preacher visiting my parishioners." He'd barely finished his protests when the butt of Cranston's rifle cracked against the side of Ned's head causing him to collapse on top of Annie.

Annie screamed, scrambling to protect Ned's unconscious body from any further blows. Blood spurted from the wound.

"Hey boss, there's someone comin'!" Lair shouted as he leaped from the wagon onto his horse. "Looks like it might be the sheriff and his posse!"

Cranston's horse was already galloping in the opposite direction of the approaching horsemen when Badger emerged from the wagon choking on a strip of dried venison. Lair wasn't far behind by the time the wiry outlaw mounted his horse and tore down the road after his leader.

Annie shook her husband and cried, "Ned! Ned! Wake up!" Blood oozed from the wound, staining the front of her dress and the back of her husband's jacket and trousers.

"Stop the bleeding," she told herself. "I must stop the blood." Trying to maintain self-control, she tore off the bottom ruffle of her petticoat and wrapped it around Ned's head several times. His blood saturated the white cotton fabric almost immediately.

"Oh, dear God," she held his head in her arms and rocked back and forth as she prayed. "Save Ned, your servant. Don't let him die. Please don't let him die!"

Minutes later Sheriff Maxwell and his posse rode up. "What happened?" The sheriff slid off his horse and rushed over to where Annie cradled her husband's inert body. He glanced about the area for signs of an accident. "Was it the Cranston gang?" He asked. "Which way did they go?"

The grieving woman nodded and pointed toward the east and the Kansas/Missouri border, then buried her head in her husband's neck. The sheriff uttered a mild expletive under his breath. "Maybe we can stop them before they cross into Missouri." He leaped on his horse and ordered two of his men to stay and help Annie with Ned while he and the rest of his posse rode after the three miscreants. The two posse members lifted Ned into the wagon and stayed with Annie until she was safely deposited in Jess Tyler's arms.

Annie didn't experience the first contraction until Jess and Billy had Ned bedded down and fresh bandages had been applied to his head. Then, as she began to relax, the first one came, followed by another, then another, until Annie was sure they would never stop.

How the sheriff's deputies knew to bring her and Ned to Jess Tyler, Annie didn't know. It didn't occur to her to ask until the next morning when Jess assured her that Ned was out of danger. Annie had awakened to find herself ensconced in the Tylers' guest room, while the Tylers had given up their own bed to make the preacher comfortable.

"Our closest neighbors to the south, the Richardsons, had an unwelcome visit from the Cranston gang. No damage, just a lot of shouting and threats should they be housing runaway slaves," Jess chuckled. "Somehow I can't see the Richardsons getting involved in the Negro cause for any reason. Billy and I hardly exist as far as they are concerned."

Annie stared at the open-beam ceiling above her head.

"Anyways," Jess continued, "the sheriff and his posse stopped at the Richardsons after running into you folk along the road. When Kermit Richardson told the sheriff which way the Cranston gang had headed, Maxwell smelled trouble."

"I'm certainly grateful the sheriff came along when he did. I think Cranston intended to kill us both. He was clearly frustrated when he didn't find any runaways or money in our wagon." Another spasm gripped Annie, doubling her over in the bed. When it subsided, she took a deep breath, then continued. "I think they were looking for someone in particular. The Railroad has many spurs along the Missouri/Kansas border. Aaron and Ned's is only one. But why am I telling you this? You know more about the operation than I do."

Jess smiled and plumped the pillow under Annie's head. "No more talk about runaways and ruffians for now. Both you and your baby need to rest for awhile."

"When can I see Ned? I want to see my husband."

Jess shook her head. "Don't worry about Ned. He has a hard head. Why, less than an hour ago he was saying the same thing about you. It took Billy's silver-tongued palaver to keep the man on his back."

"Then he's conscious?" Annie asked.

"Oh, yes, a kickin' up a storm. He'll be up and about long before you will, little mommy."

Annie rose on one elbow. "What do you mean?"

Jess's smile faded. "Your baby is struggling to live, Annie. You need to help him by staying in bed and sleeping as much as possible. The rest is up to God."

Annie fell back against the pillow, her eyes flooding with tears. God, she thought. A lot of help He'll be. It was Sheriff Maxwell and his men who saved Ned's life. And it will be Jess Tyler who saves my baby's life. "Where is God in all of this?"

"Right here with you, darling," Jess reminded. "God and I are partners when it comes to birthing. Don't you worry none. Neither of us are going to forsake you."

Annie had aches and bruises from her fall, but nothing, not even the cramps in her abdomen hurt more than the pain in her heart. All day and throughout the long night, they came like white caps on the stormy Atlantic, one after another, after another. Annie tried to sleep, but whenever she closed her eyes, she saw Badger Oberon's leering and pocked face looming over her, intent on doing her harm.

At some point during the night, she awakened to find Ned sitting in a rocker beside her bed holding her hand. His head was swaddled in white gauze; his jaw rough with a day's growth of beard.

"Ned? What are you doing here? Aren't you supposed to be resting?"

"Jess thought I should be with you for a while." He bent and kissed her fingertips. "I love you, Annie. I love you so much."

"I love you too, but . . ." She glanced toward the stoic-faced Jess. "What's happening? What's wrong?"

Ned brushed his hand across Annie's forehead. "Sh, sh, don't get upset, honey."

"Don't get upset?" She laughed hysterically.

"Sh, sh," Ned insisted. "It won't do any good to get riled."

"What do you—" Another contraction tightened the muscles in her abdomen, and she had the uncontrollable urge to push. "Jess, I think I'm going to lose the baby."

With smooth, unhurried motions, Jess lifted the blankets and felt Annie's abdomen.

"Please help me," Annie gasped. "I don't want to lose this baby."

"Brother Ned, go take a walk or something." Jess didn't wait for the worried young preacher to obey. One glare and she knew he would. "Remember Annie, it's not uncommon for a woman to lose her first child early on in her pregnancy. There'll be others. Nature's good at that." The midwife adjusted the quilts around her patient. "Annie, just relax as best you can and breath deeply. You will be fine."

"But it's too soon," Annie wailed. "My baby . . ."

*   *   *

The Sunday after Annie lost the baby, a procession of drawn faces filed through her bedroom following the morning service. While the women of Ned's congregation hurt for their new friend's loss, their condolences made Annie angry, angrier than she'd ever been in her life.

"You're young; you'll have another."

"Might have been something terribly wrong with the babe."

"God knows what's best."

"Bringing a child into this world of sin? If you ask me, that child is lucky."

"Without a little one to tie you down, you're freer to do the work of the Lord, Sister Ward."

Even Beulah Witherspoon, whose young son had recently died, could only mumble, "The Lord giveth and the Lord taketh; blessed be the name of the Lord."

Conscious of her role as the good pastor's wife, Annie smiled graciously and thanked the women for their concern, all the while biting her tongue and reminding herself to remain civil. She wanted to scream at them, "You don't understand. You can't know how I feel!"

After the last woman left her room, Annie turned her face to the wall. When Jess peeked in to check on her, she pretended to be asleep.

How can people be so cruel? she wondered as she picked at the lint on the cotton pillowcase under her head. *They simper and say they understand how I feel, but they don't understand; they can't. Their babies are fat and well and full of life. Mine's . . .* She couldn't finish her thought. In her heart, the grieving woman knew that no one meant to be unkind, but that knowledge didn't lessen her anger.

With her baby gone, Annie had only one thought in mind—going home. She was frantic to escape the unending train of sympathy and Jess Tyler's constant ministrations. Even Ned's efforts to comfort her grated on her nerves like fingernails scraping against a screen door.

When he tried to suggest they stay a few extra days to give her time to regain her strength, she sobbed into her pillow, "I want to be alone! Besides, you've accomplished what you came for! I know that you and Billy talked with the Judd family about your precious railroad! So your business here is done. And certainly mine is as well . . ."

She could see by the stunned expression on his face that her biting words had stung Ned's heart. He arose from the edge of the bed and threw his hands into the air. "Fine. We'll go home."

Annie had never before seen her husband so discouraged. Ned was always one to see the bright side of any situation. She was sure he could find something good in skunk spray. Yet the hard lump in the spot where her heart had once been refused to soften enough to share his pain.

***

The journey home was silent and cold. Annie reclined on the mattress in the wagon while Ned drove the team. As the wagon lumbered over the ruts and potholes, the grieving woman curled into a fetal ball beneath a stack of quilts. She tried to shut off her mind, but the thoughts refused to give her rest.

She was wracked with guilt and blame. If only the Cranston gang hadn't . . . If only the sheriff had . . . If only she hadn't picked up Ned's shotgun . . . If only Ned had been man enough to use the shotgun himself . . . If only she'd stayed at home . . . If only Ned had made her stay home . . . If only God had stopped the outlaw from throwing her to the ground . . . If only He had saved her baby . . .

It always came back to God letting her down. Anger seethed within her each time Ned opened his Bible to read. She nursed the bad feelings within her, never sharing them with her husband.

They reached home after dark. The house was cold and musty smelling. After helping Annie inside the cabin and over to the sofa, Ned lit an oil lantern and began unloading the wagon. Except for the immediate area around the lantern, heavy shadows, almost as dark as the ones in Annie's heart, filled the room.

On Ned's second trip, he carried in her rocker and placed it beside the shuttered window. "I'll open the shutters and start a fire in the fireplace after I bring in our mattress and make the bed," he said.

"No!" She shouted her refusal louder than she intended. Ned shot her a surprised glance. In a more controlled voice, she clarified her protest. "I mean about the window. I don't want the window open. It's too cold. There'll be a draft."

He cocked his head to one side. "Honey, are you sure? The window faces the east, and the wind comes from the west, remember? That was why we built the cabin as we did, so you could enjoy the window all year round."

"No! I said no. Isn't that enough?"

The energy behind Ned's eyes faded into resignation. "All right, dear. I'll go get the mattress."

As her husband disappeared from view, Annie buried her face in the nearest sofa pillow. She wanted to cry, but her tears refused to come. They'd stopped the day her husband prayed over their dead son's grave on a wind-swept hill at the Tyler Ranch.

It seemed foolish, digging a grave for a lifeless embryo hardly recognizable as human. Looking at it, it could have been a pig or a dog, certainly not the child she'd imagined would be hers.

Jess said it was probably a boy, since women seem to lose male babies more often than females. When Annie refused to give her son a name, Ned called him Thaddeus, meaning "praise to God."

"Praise to God?" She gave a derisive laugh. When she told Ned how utterly inappropriate she believed the name was under the circumstances, he disagreed.

"Scripture says, 'all things work together for good.' And like the prophet Habakkuk, I will praise my Father in all things. Someday we'll understand."

"Understand? The fickle whims of a faceless God?"

"Annie . . ." Ned reached out for her, but she snatched away her hand. ". . . you are so very wrong. God is a God of love, goodness, and faithfulness."

She'd turned away refusing to hear any more of his dribble, as she called it.

Annie had longed for the day she would return to her own one-roomed soddy. Now that she was here, the peace and the release she imagined she'd feel hadn't come. She stared at the open-beamed ceiling over her head, her mind devoid of thought.

When Ned returned with the mattress, Caleb was helping him carry the other end. Behind the two men, Serenity, with Sammy in her arms, rushed into the cabin. After setting her young son on the floor beside the sofa, Serenity drew Annie's limp body to her. "Annie, I just heard. I am so sorry. You poor, poor dear."

The grieving woman's heart didn't melt like it once would have at the sorrow in her friend's voice. "How are you feeling, darling? Are you going to be all right?"

Annie tightened her lips into a thin hard line. If she didn't, the young woman feared she'd shatter into a thousand pieces of crystal. She averted her gaze to a spot on the far wall beyond Serenity.

Like everyone else, Serenity wanted to help, though at the moment, Annie called it "taking over." "Honey, I have plenty of room at the inn," Serenity reminded. "You and Ned are welcome to stay with us until you get back your strength."

Caleb glanced cautiously at the two women as he passed through the cabin with an armload of logs for the fire. Annie didn't miss the men's exchange of worried glances as they lit the fire in the fireplace and started a fire in the iron cook stove as well.

"Stay for a cup of tea?" Ned filled the teakettle and set it on the burner to heat.

Annie was so sick of everyone's pity. She hated the way they treated her as if she were a fragile china doll ready to break, the way they tiptoed around her as if she were a case of black powder, ready to explode. "Thank you, Serenity, but no, I don't need anyone. I just need time alone, time to think things out."

"Are you sure?" Serenity asked.

Annie pushed her friend away and fell back against the sofa pillows. "Serenity, I know you mean well, but I just want to be alone!"

Serenity's brow wrinkled into a frown. "Do you think that's wise at a time like this?"

A rusty iron edge tinged Annie's speech. "It is what I want. Do you understand? Why can't everyone just leave me alone? I just want to be alone!"

Serenity drew back from the agitation in her friend's voice. Annie saw the look of surprise and hurt in Serenity's caring face, and for an instant, her lower lip quivered. But, instead of softening like she would have in the past, she hardened her jaw. "Serenity, in case you forgot, I am no longer your servant or your playmate. I can make my own choices, believe it or not. I am not an empty-headed twit."

"No, no, you're not." The woman rose to her feet, then picked up her son in her arms. "You're understandably tired. It's been a long day for you. We can talk about this tomorrow, after you've had a chance to rest."

"There is nothing to talk about!" Annie shouted so loud that Sammy burst into tears. "Oh, I'm sorry." Her agitation intensified with the volume of the child's wail. "Please, just leave!"

Serenity swallowed hard. The disappointment in her face was evident. Since their childhood days together, Annie had always done whatever Serenity wished. *I'm not a gullible child anymore,* Annie told herself as she turned her face to the wall.

***

Over the next few weeks, the pregnant Josephine visited Serenity and Caleb for Sunday dinner. Each week Serenity invited Ned and Annie to join them, but Annie declined.

Aaron and Lilia visited once, as did the Blackwings. Gray Sparrow brought with her an herbal concoction that would help Annie's body to heal. Annie graciously thanked her, then turned her face once more to the wall.

Members of Ned's local congregation stopped by. The women cooked, cleaned, and fussed over Annie until she thought she'd scream and run to the outhouse to hide.

The week before Christmas, the one-room soddy with shuttered windows and one lit lantern remained dark and cheerless. When Ned suggested he find a tree to decorate, "like the white folk do," Annie shrugged.

"Do what you like. What do I care?"

Upon Ned's return with the tree, Annie wasn't ready for the invasion of her friends. He'd barely stood the bare tree in the corner by the fireplace when Serenity came bearing cookie dough. Seconds later, or so it seemed to Annie, Josephine arrived in her sleigh bearing fancy Christmas decorations for the tree.

The two women quickly shooed Ned out of the cabin. "Go visit Caleb and Sammy in the blacksmith shop," Serenity suggested.

A few minutes later, Lilia burst into the small cabin carrying pine boughs along with red satin ribbon and wire. "We're gonna' make wreaths today," she announced as she plunked her bundles down beside Annie's rocker. "Hey, wasn't Dory bringing the pie fixings?"

"She'll be here in a few minutes," Josephine assured her friend. "Abe needed to stop at the post office on the way here.

Can't have Christmas without Dory's pecan pie. That woman makes the best pecan pie I've ever eaten, and that's something for a lady of the South to admit."

"And cookies too. We're making Christmas cookies like we used to. Remember?" Serenity glanced toward Annie whose eyes still looked vacant and uninterested. "I bought some candies and colored sugars from Jones's Mercantile. Caleb made me a few tin cookie cutters, too, just like Mama had." She held each one up for inspection. "A star, a bell, a sleigh, and a tree. Aren't they great?"

Lilia slipped into a red-and-white gingham apron she'd brought with her. "We should start with the cookies, I think."

Serenity laughed at Lilia's "take charge" nature. It was the first laughter there'd been in the silent room since their return from Kansas. "All right then, let's get cookin', er baking, I mean."

Christmas cookies—Annie's heart lurched within her. A wave of tender memories washed over her, memories of wearing aprons too big, of standing side by side with Serenity on kitchen stools, inspecting the cast iron cookie cutters, and tasting the colorful candy dots and sugar sprinkles. Once again she saw the steam-covered windows, felt warmth billowing from the oven, and heard her beloved Miz Charity and Dory harmonizing on "Silent Night" while the women rolled out the cookie dough.

Annie fought back a sudden rush of tears. *Those days are long gone. You are no longer a kid, Annie Ward. The real world is a cold, hard place, no room for pretty fantasies from long ago.*

"What's with these closed shutters? We need some light in here." The outspoken Lilia rushed to the window and flung open the shutters before Annie could protest.

"No!" Annie cried, but it was too late. The brilliant sunlight, sparkling down on a thick layer of snow, burst into the room with a force that couldn't be contained.

Annie fell back against her pillow in defeat. She failed to see the look of displeasure that passed between Serenity and her stepmother.

"Come on, young lady." The diminutive Josephine bustled over to the bed and hauled back Annie's covers. She tossed a Mother Hubbard apron at the startled young woman. "Here, up and at 'em, lady fair. Out of that pretty nightie of yours and into a housedress. And wear the apron. You don't want to get cookie dough or pine pitch on your clothes."

Josephine swung Annie's feet over the side of the bed and inserted them into her slippers. "Now, do you need help getting dressed?"

"N-no," Annie sputtered in surprise as the intruder in her somber little cocoon refused to take no for an answer.

"Here, brush your hair back," Josephine ordered, grabbing Annie's hairbrush from the bedside stand. Annie silently obeyed. With Annie's hair brushed and secured in a chignon at the back of her head, Josephine helped Annie slip into a gray linsey-woolsey dress, one with a stiff white Puritan collar.

After slipping the apron over Annie's head and tying the strings into a bow, the woman led the reluctant Annie to the table and set her down at one end. "Here. You be the cookie cutter. Serenity, you roll, I'll transfer the cookies onto the cookie pans, and Lilia will supervise the baking; how's that? By the way, where are your cookie pans?"

Annie feebly pointed toward the pantry.

"Good. Did anyone bring popcorn so we can string it with my cranberries? These berries came all the way from Cape Cod,

Massachusetts. They dried out a little, but that makes them even better for stringing." Josephine popped one in her mouth and made a face. "Ooh, that one was sour."

Annie shook her head in frustration at the tiny little blond lady bouncing about the one-room soddy. Josephine always took control of every situation. So did Lilia. The two women battling it out in the same small space would prove to be entertaining. Annie smiled in spite of her discomfort. Skirts of calico and gingham swooshed about the room while Annie watched in amazement.

After the last of the Christmas cookie stars was cut and placed on cookie sheets for baking, Serenity cleared the tabletop to make room for the pine boughs. "This was your suggestion, Lilia. I'll watch the cookies while you show us how to do this. What are we making, anyway?"

"Back home, each Christmas Mama and the household staff gather around the kitchen table to make evergreen wreaths, one for each window in the house." The woman placed a spool of wire and three pairs of heavy wire cutters in the center of the table. "After they make the wreath, they add all kinds of stuff for color. Sometimes berries, sometimes toys, sometimes pretty tree ornaments, and always a big red bow. The evergreens make the rooms of the house smell woodsy. Here, Annie," she said as she thrust the spool of wire at the surprised woman, "you start."

~ 11 ~

Holiday Cheer

"WHEN DID YOU SAY DORY WAS COMING?" Annie asked as she wrestled to untangle two recalcitrant pine boughs. "I can't do this. I'm all thumbs," she exclaimed, throwing the bows onto the table. She hated how her fury was never far from the surface. Her friends ignored her outburst as they had all the others since they arrived earlier that day.

"So, how many are you having for Christmas dinner?" Lilia asked Josephine.

The woman laughed. "At the last count, Dory said twenty-two. I guess my Sam is right. I enjoy complicating my life."

Serenity cast her stepmother a broad grin. "We'd be disappointed if you didn't. Your holiday dinners are becoming famous in these parts. By the way, will Judge York and his daughter be in town?"

Josephine nodded. "Margaret sent a note saying she wouldn't miss my dinner for the world."

A self-satisfied grin crossed Serenity's face. "And, of course, you're inviting daddy's law partner, Felix Bonner?"

"Of course." Josephine cocked her head to one side and asked, "You aren't thinking what I think you're thinking, are you?"

"Oh, come now . . ." Serenity wound a strand of wire around a cluster of pine boughs. "Don't tell me you haven't thought what you think I'm thinking as well."

"What? What?" Lilia leaned forward, her eyes sparkling with curiosity.

"Serenity Cunard, you're bad!" Josephine gave a huge sigh. "Margaret York and Felix Bonner? It never crossed my mind."

"Oh, yes, I'm sure," Serenity chuckled.

"It's going to take a very strong and patient man to corral in the indomitable Miss York," Lilia admitted.

"She is very quick," Serenity reminded.

"And a mouth unbecoming of a lady of class." Lilia clicked her tongue. "The woman's wit decimates most men faster than a woodpecker attacking a tree stump."

"Now, Lilia, be kind," Serenity reminded. "You're both my friends, remember? Besides, if any man can fire a great retort, it's Felix. He's no dummy, you know."

"The wagon." Annie leaped from her chair and ran to the front window. "Dory is here." She smiled in spite of herself. Why the woman hadn't come to visit sooner after the loss of Annie's baby, Annie didn't know, but whatever the reason, it no longer mattered.

Annie met the older woman at the front door. "Dory, I'm so glad you could come. Here, let me take your coat."

"Later, first you and I need to talk." Dory turned to the other women. "If you ladies will excuse us . . . Annie, put on your coat and bonnet. We're taking a walk to the top of the hill."

Bewildered, Annie hurried to obey her mentor and surrogate mother. They strode to the little cemetery on top of the hill in silence. Annie could tell Dory had lots to say, and she knew better than to hurry the woman.

When they reached the large boulder at the crest, Dory climbed on it and sat down facing the west. She patted the area on the rock beside her, asking Annie to join her. Annie did. After a few seconds, Dory began, "Annie, I'm sorry you lost your baby."

The muscles in Annie's jaw tightened. *Not Dory, no, not Dory,* she thought. *I can't take another cheery little talk with all the accompanying, "I understand." I just can't.*

Annie started to slide off the rock when Dory's hand grabbed her wrist. "Annie, my girl, you aren't the first woman to lose a baby, and you won't be the last."

How could Dory be so crass, so cold? Annie stared in disbelief at the woman she'd loved and admired since childhood.

"As painful as it is, it's not the end of the world."

Annie's lower jaw dropped open in disgust. She wanted to shout, scream, and cry out in anger, but she couldn't convert her rage into words.

Dory continued. "You have a husband who loves you deeply, friends who would do anything for you . . ." Then, gesturing toward the soddy, "and a home hundreds of women would envy. And here you are moping, whining, and cursing God. For shame!"

"Uh-uh-uh . . ."

"No one said life will be easy. You, of all people, should know that. Life is full of disappointments and hardships. It's time someone set you down and talked turkey to you. Annie Ward, you need to grow up!"

Enraged at the woman's startling rudeness, Annie slipped off the rock. "How dare you!" She stomped her foot. "How dare you speak to me this way. You have a son to love. Mine is dead!" Her wail echoed across the surrounding prairie. "Don't talk to me about how I should feel until you've walked in my shoes!"

Annie whipped down the pathway toward her home. She'd gone but a few feet when Dory called to her. "Annie, here." Annie turned to see the woman extending toward her a well-worn pair of lady's boots. "Here. Try mine on for size."

"What?"

"I said, 'Try mine . . .'"

"I know what you said, but what—"

Dory slid off the rock and walked to Annie, still extending the scuffed and worn brown ankle boots toward the younger woman. "Annie, darling, I do understand how you feel. I've been there. I lost five babies before my precious son was born, and after that I lost another boy two days after his birth. So, here, try wearing my boots."

Annie gasped and looked at the ebony-skinned woman through horror-struck eyes. "You lost five babies?" For the first time in days, tears glistened in her eyes.

A teary Dory gathered the grieving woman into her arms and held her tight. "Yes, and I love every one of those little bodies." Her words caught in her throat. "And while I don't understand the reasons right now, my God promises that I will one day."

Inside Annie, a dam of misery finally burst. She laid her head against the older woman's abundant bosom and sobbed uncontrollably. For several moments Dory comforted her.

When Annie's tears subsided, she admitted through a series of hiccups, "I was so angry with the women telling me they understood as they stood bouncing their healthy little babies in their arms."

"I know, I know. I was grateful to have Miz Charity there when I needed her. She lost two babies before she had Serenity."

"Really? I didn't know that."

"Not many people did."

"But she was always so happy." Annie couldn't understand. "How did she do it?"

"The same way I do today. First you weep, then you turn to God for strength and healing. He promises to heal all our diseases, including a grieving heart. And that takes time."

Annie stepped out of Dory's embrace. "Why didn't you come to see me sooner?"

Fresh tears streaked down Dory's tear-stained face. "I didn't visit you sooner because, even now, the memories of my losses hurt. But I knew I had to come, sooner or later, so when your friends planned their invasion today, I decided this was the day. Please forgive me for my weakness."

Annie bit her lower lip. "I'm just glad you're here."

Dory put her arm around Annie's slim waist, and together they started back down the hill. "Miz Charity would come to our cabin with a pot of herbal tea, a plate of shortbread cookies, and a heart full of love. I have the tea leaves and shortbread cookies in the wagon."

Annie swiped at her own tears and gave a chuckle. "This is the first time I've cried since . . ."

"I know. I know."

"But you had Abe." Annie couldn't put into words her feelings of contempt for her own husband. It had been Ned's job to protect her. Even as she thought it, she realized how unfair she was being.

"And you had Ned. That poor boy walks around like a whipped puppy. He's blaming himself, of all things." Dory removed a handkerchief from her coat pocket and blew her nose. "Abe did the same thing each time we buried a child. And

I confess that I blamed him too. Somehow, when I blamed him, I could stop blaming myself, but eventually I stopped punishing us both for something that was out of our control."

Annie's brow knitted with thought. This nugget of wisdom was hard for her to swallow. She'd thought of her giant, gentle husband as her protector, and in her mind, he'd failed her and their baby. Likewise, she knew she had failed to protect the tiny embryo as well, and God had also failed. She gave a huge sigh. Losing the baby had to be somebody's fault.

"Be kind to him, Annie. Remember that he lost a son as well. More than ever, you need to lean on each other."

Annie hadn't considered the fact that Ned had also lost a child. She'd been so caught up in her own grief, she hadn't seen his. "I don't know what to say. I can't forgive; I can't forget."

Dory took hold of Annie by her upper arms and gave her a gentle shake. "Losing babies is part of living and dying, like I said before. Pregnant women and their unborn children have weathered worse disasters than Cranston and his men. Why this child didn't, only God knows. It's as simple as that. To try to understand further is like delving into the mind of God."

"God . . ."

"Yes, God. His hand is weaving the threads of your life into an intricately patterned tapestry. He knows what's best for you and for the beautiful person He knows you can be."

Annie curled her lip in disgust. "And losing my child was for my good?"

"All things work together—"

"I know. I know. I've heard it before. Believe me, I've heard it before."

"Oh, honey, don't you see? Your life is like your embroidery. You need both light- and dark-colored threads to define the pattern you, the artist, are trying to create." She warmed to her subject. "So it is in life. God uses, not causes, the good times and the bad to define the pattern in our lives. That's how 'all things work together for good . . .' As He weaves His creative beauty in us, we become a work of art for all the universe to admire and appreciate."

Annie listened to Dory's metaphor, her mind eager to point out the errors in the woman's illustration. "But when I embroider, I can see the pattern developing."

Dory smiled. "As can God, your Father. You remember when you first were learning to embroider, the back of the fabric would be a tangle of threads?"

Annie smiled at the treasured memory.

"Think of it this way. Since God is doing the embroidering, He sees the top, the lovely scrollwork, and the delicately designed flowers. We look up from here below and all we can see is the back side, a tangle of threads, strings, and knots." A grin widened on Dory's face. "One day He promises to show us the finished product." Her voice grew tender. "And when He does, He'll smile and say, 'Well done, my child. You are so beautiful to Me.'"

The woman's analogy had hit its mark. Annie blinked back a fresh round of tears.

A note of assurance filled Dory's voice. "I know my wonderful heavenly Father, Annie. I know, without a doubt, that my little babies, all six of them are safe in his big old callused hands. And one day He's gonna' set me up in a golden mansion that will burst at the seams with chubby little babies to love."

What a naïve dream, Annie thought. "Oh, Dory, I wish I could believe."

"You can. God places in every person's heart a tiny droplet of faith. Yours too. You may think you've lost it right now, but you haven't. Look for it. I know you'll find it again."

***

Annie's winter of despair didn't end abruptly with Dory's wise counsel, but it did become easier as she pondered Dory's words in her heart. As she finished the needlepoint project she'd started for Josephine in time for the woman's New Year's party, Annie considered Dory's analogy.

The holidays came and went. Josephine's Christmas party was a huge success. Annie did her best to enjoy herself. She even fooled Ned, or so she thought.

After the New Year, the snows came, leaving the two families housebound. From her rocker in front of the window, she would watch the winter-white world with its subtle changes. It wasn't long before the roads to town became impassable.

While the two men spent their days working in the blacksmith shop, Serenity and Annie sought out each other's company. Serenity was delighted when Annie asked if they could study the Bible together, especially God's promises.

"I can't depend on promises I don't know," she explained to her friend.

They took turns meeting at each other's home. Serenity shared with Annie some of the texts that helped her deal with the death of her mother. Psalms 23 and 91 were her favorites. Annie memorized both to ward off the demons that haunted her nightmares. If Ned noticed the subtle changes occurring in Annie, he didn't say.

The icy barrier constructed between them the first days after losing Thaddeus remained solidly intact. Winter continued into the third week of March. Then one day Annie noticed the icicles on the eaves outside her window beginning to melt. Joy trickled down into her soul as well, stirring the ashes of a long-forgotten song to life.

"Joyful, joyful we adore thee, God of glory, Lord of love . . ." She couldn't remember the rest of the lyrics, so she just hummed the melody as she stitched the intricate nosegay of flowers on a piece of cotton fabric that would, when finished, become a pillow slip.

As she worked, Ned passed by the window, his shoulders stooped, his steps heavy, his face lined with grief and worry. He was carrying an armload of firewood. Her heart melted within her. It was time for the ice wall between them to melt as well.

The cabin door swung open, and the young husband stepped inside. "Thought the wood bin might be wanting," he explained as he dumped his load into the cast iron wood bin beside the kitchen stove. "The snow's melting on the roads. Caleb and I are making a trip to Independence tomorrow morning in the cutter, before the roads become impassible with snow runoff. Serenity and Sammy are going. Would you like to come along?"

Annie's eyes brightened. "I'd love to. Oh—" She sprang to her feet and tossed her sewing supplies onto the chair. "I need to make a shopping list. We're out of so many things." Visions of money popped into her head as she glanced down at the piece of embroidery she'd been working on. "If I finish this tonight, I could deliver it to Josephine tomorrow, and that would give us some extra cash."

Her enthusiasm must have surprised Ned, for at the corners of his mouth, a slight smile appeared, the first in a very long time.

Excited by the idea of going shopping, she had more important things to consider. What would bring her husband joy? A special dessert? Ned loved sweet potato pie. Her sugar supply was low. A hot bath with fragrant bath salts? A polish and shine on his Sunday-go-meeting boots? Annie scurried about the cabin all afternoon checking for other supplies that might need replenishing.

The following day's trip to town proved to be all she'd hoped. Her first stop was at Josephine's, where Serenity left her son with Grandma for a few hours.

Serenity and Annie giggled like schoolgirls as they trudged through melting snow from one shop to the next, trying on hats at the milliners and dabbing each other with samples of gardenia-rose and lemon-verbena toilet water at the chemist's shop. She bought bath salts for Ned, an herbal fragrance, manly in nature, she told herself.

When Serenity asked about the bath salts, Annie gave her a sheepish grin and arched a suggestive eyebrow. This gesture sent Serenity's eyebrows into her hairline.

"Maybe I should get some for Caleb," Serenity purred. "Wouldn't he be surprised?"

Josephine had paid Annie generously for the fancywork she'd commissioned, leaving the delighted young wife more than enough funds to do all the things she'd planned and to throw in a pink-ruffled flannel nightgown, a bevy of grosgrain ribbons, and a bottle of sweet-smelling lotion to use on her hands.

By the time the men picked up their wives at the Pownells' place, the sun was low in the western sky. Baby Sammy was asleep. Annie thought she might soon be too. However, that night, when her head hit her pillow and Ned was snoring beside her, she blinked awake. She was too excited to sleep.

In the darkness she could see the curves of her husband's body beside her. A wave of gratitude swept over her for the patient man lying by her side. She stared past her husband to the simmering red glow of dying embers in the fireplace. "Oh Lord," she prayed, "thank you for Ned and his easygoing nature. I haven't been able to live with me these last few months. How has he managed to do so?"

She studied the narrow beams of moonlight seeping between the slats of the window shutters. Restless, Annie crawled over her husband and slipped her bare feet into her Arctic boots. Then she slipped into her fleecy wool winter cape, lifted the hood over her hair, put on her woolen gloves, and fled out the front door—all without waking her husband.

As she gazed up at the sky, Annie reveled in a paradise of stars sharing the glory of the night with a full moon. Peace filled her as she climbed the hill to her "thinking" rock. Once comfortable atop the boulder, she took a long, deep breath. When she exhaled, she could see her breath.

"How beautiful," she whispered as she watched a shooting star flash across the sky. A warm furry body brushed against her leg and caused Annie to yelp.

Onyx gave a comforting "woof!"

"You big old bear . . ." She ran her fingers through the soft hairs along his spine. "You scared me."

"Woof," he barked again.

"All right, sh-sh-sh. You'll wake everyone." Except for the dog's panting and the steady beating of her own heart, the night was silent. Softly, unexpectedly, she began to sing a lullaby she remembered as a child. "Go tell Aunt Rhody, go tell Aunt Rhody . . ." *Where did that come from?* she wondered. "Go tell Aunt Rhody, the old gray goose is dead . . ."

Lightly thumping his tail against Annie's leg, Onyx watched the young woman intently as if the lullaby was a "doggie lullaby" sung mainly for his enjoyment. It wasn't until the second verse of the old ballad that a memory, frozen in time, surfaced in her head, the memory of a weathered oak rocker and a tiny porch outside an equally weather-beaten slave shack in Louisiana.

"My mother . . ." She inhaled sharply. For the first time in more than fifteen years, she remembered her mother's face. She'd been told by the plantation overseer that her mother had died in childbirth.

Instinctively Onyx pressed closer as Annie wrapped her arms about herself under the folds of the cape and gazed at the moon in an effort to recall more of her childhood memories, but none came. "Go tell Aunt Rhody . . ." she whispered in Onyx's ear. The big old dog, who'd been a part of her life since she first came to the Pownell estate as an eight-year-old child, gazed lovingly up at her. The woman chuckled to herself. "Imagine, me singing two songs in the same day? Whatever is happening to me?"

Annie and Onyx stayed on the rock until the moon had drifted toward the west and the cold from the rock seeped through her clothing and created a chill. Before leaving her perch, she prayed. "Now I can see that You were right beside me through my troubles, and I can see the times You rescued me from danger. Be patient with me, Father; I seem to learn very slowly." Then she reluctantly climbed off the rock and trudged back to the cabin with the dog by her side.

When she opened the cabin door, Onyx tried to push his way inside. "No. You know better," Annie whispered. "You stay outside."

The dog whimpered. "You've got a thick coat of fur to keep you warm." She closed the door. After one or two scratches on the heavy oak door, the dog gave up his campaign.

Annie removed her cape and boots, then heated a kettle of water to make herself a cup of chamomile tea. The hot drink would help her sleep. With teacup in hand, she padded to her rocker to continue watching the moon glide across the sky.

Outside the cabin, Onyx stretched out to sleep as close to the window as possible. Looking at the dog, Annie had to laugh. "Hmm," she whispered to herself, "it might be nice to have a dog of our own some day."

* * *

Annie hummed to herself as she fixed Ned's breakfast the next morning. By the time he returned from doing the morning chores, the aromas of hot blueberry pancakes and freshly brewed coffee filled the air. Corned beef hash sizzled in the cast iron frying pan on the stove.

"Umm, something sure smells delicious. Are you making blueberry pancakes, my favorite?" He set his wooden bucket of frothy white milk on the dry sink and removed his gloves.

"You guessed it, and with maple syrup too." She poured hot coffee into the two cups on the table. "Make yourself comfortable while I flip the next batch of pancakes."

He hung his coat on the peg behind the door, then took his place at the table. "Boy, a man could get used to this." When he saw the sudden sadness in her eyes, he said, "I mean, it smells really good."

Annie turned to dish up the corn beef hash so that he would not see her tears. In the last few weeks she'd barely fixed hot oatmeal for her husband's breakfast, and his other meals hadn't been much better. She knew Serenity often took a lunch to Caleb as he worked in the blacksmith shop. She always packed extra for Ned. And Annie had been happy to let her. But no more. Annie was determined to fulfill her wifely duties, all of them.

At the end of breakfast, Ned told her that he was riding into town to see Aaron Cunard. Annie bit her lower lip. Going to see Aaron always had something to do with the Underground Railroad and a fresh season of runaways.

"I know you don't like it, but—" he began.

"No, it's all right, darling. I won't fight you again on this, I promise." She closed her eyes momentarily, praying that she could keep her promise.

"Oh, uh, that's good." He seemed lost for words, as if he was afraid he might say the wrong thing. "I'll be home in time for supper, if that's all right. I'd invite you to come with me, but—"

"Don't be ridiculous," she sputtered as she gathered the dirty dishes from the table. "I was just in town yesterday. I have much too much to do here to traipse to Independence two days in a row."

Ned sighed with relief. She could tell he'd expected an argument from her, or at least, a pout. *Have I been that bad?* she wondered as she spooned the leftover hash into a smaller dish for later. That's when she remembered. "Ned?" she asked.

He was searching the Bible for an appropriate morning reading.

"Ned?" she called again. "What would you think about getting a puppy?"

He looked up in surprise. "You want a puppy?"

"Or a grown dog, it doesn't matter. He would be a great comfort to me when you're gone, and he'd be a good watchdog."

"Onyx does a good job of that," he reminded.

"Yes, and I love him dearly, but he's Serenity's, not mine."

Ned rolled his tongue around inside his mouth for a few seconds. "I'll see what I can do."

She threw her arms around his neck and kissed him hard on the lips. "Oh, thank you," she squealed.

"If I knew the promise of a puppy would bring about that kind of surprise, I'd agree to an entire litter."

She could feel the heat rising in her face. But he had spoken the truth. She couldn't fault him for that. "One puppy will be enough," she assured him as she returned to clearing the table.

~12~

Romantic
Reunion

ANNIE HUMMED A LITTLE TUNE AS SHE refilled her largest cast iron kettle with water and put it on the burner to heat. Everything was going according to plan. Earlier she'd scrubbed everything in the soddy from top to bottom, even polished the silver on the dented pewter creamer Ned had brought home one day. He'd found it alongside the road, probably abandoned by one of the families heading west.

Along with the three large kettles of water heating on the stove, a lentil stew simmered in a pot on a back burner. There was nothing Annie loved more than the aroma of hot stew simmering on a cold day.

Steam covered the windowpanes, adding a toasty sense of intimacy to the room. Every candle she owned was lit, along with all four of her oil lanterns. An hour earlier, Annie had dragged the big round oak washtub she used for washing clothes into the kitchen and began filling it with hot water. After taking a quick bath of her own and washing her hair, she began refilling the tub.

She thanked her absent husband for building their cabin around a natural well and for installing an indoor hand pump.

Not having to haul water from an outdoor well was a blessing any wise woman would appreciate.

The table was set for supper. The bread was baked and cooling on the cutting board. She'd even milked the cow to save Ned the trouble.

While fresh water heated on the stove, Annie dried her hair in front of the fireplace. Then she brushed out the snarls and gathered her tousled curls back into a pink satin ribbon she'd bought in town the previous day. She smiled at her reflection in the mirror. The perky little bow on the side of her head made her feel young and sassy.

Her hands were sweaty with eager anticipation as she slipped into her new pink nightie. She'd never before greeted her husband while wearing night apparel. Then methodically, she glanced about the cabin to make sure everything was perfect for his homecoming. To calm her nerves, she curled up on the sofa in front of the fireplace intending to read from her husband's Bible.

Long shadows of evening streaked across the prairie before Annie saw Ned's wagon approach the barn. She felt almost giddy as she watched him hurry two people out of the back of the wagon and into the barn. After a few minutes he reappeared. His steps were slow and deliberate.

Annie used the time to pour another kettle of hot water into the tub and to sprinkle a generous amount of bath salts into the steaming water. She paused long enough to take a whiff of the refreshing aroma of the herbal salts diluting in the bath water.

The cabin door burst open. Annie held her breath for an instant. What if Ned didn't want to reconcile? What if he wouldn't forgive her for all the stupid things she'd done? What if the loving relationship they'd known before she lost the baby could never again be?

Ned entered the cabin, shed his coat and cap, and hung them on the peg behind the door before he noticed Annie's surprise. Then he slowly turned and scanned the room, sighting everything from the turned-down bed and fluffed pillows to the candles on the mantle and on the sofa table, to the gleaming dinner table set for two and the stew simmering on the stove.

She smiled shyly as his gaze settled on her. "Annie," he whispered, a smile widening across his face. "You look beautiful. What's the occasion?"

Tipping her head to one side, she gave him a coy smile and ambled slowly toward him. "Welcome home, darling," she cooed. She slipped her arms about his waist, stood on her tiptoes, and kissed his surprised lips. "Did you have a good day?"

"I-I, uh, yes." He waited, acting unsure of himself, as his wife slowly unbuttoned his shirt and slid it off his broad muscular chest, then let it drop to the floor.

"I've drawn a hot bath for you before dinner." She gestured toward the wooden tub in the corner of the kitchen. "If you sit down, I'll remove your boots and then your trousers."

His eyes widened in surprise. He'd never before heard his comely wife use the word *trousers*. Her come-hither glances baffled the bewildered young husband. Reading his thoughts, Annie arched an eyebrow and called him to her with her finger.

Ned obediently sat in one of the table's straight-back chairs while Annie removed his boots and socks. "Oh, you have a hole in the heel of this sock. Tomorrow morning I'll wash them out and darn it for you." While she acted self-assured, inside she quivered like grape jelly.

"I-I-I can get the pants. I-I-I—"

"All right," Annie hopped to her feet and flitted across the room to the stove. "Your bath is ready for you, kind sir. Just climb in and I'll bring you a cup of hot tea to warm you inside as well."

Numbly, the man did as he was told. Annie smiled to herself as he eased his body into the hot, steamy bath water. *Ned really is a lion of a man,* she decided. And the fact that he loved her made him irresistible. If he still did love her, that is.

She poured a cup of hot chamomile and cinnamon tea into her best teacup, then carried it to him. He thanked her and relaxed against the wood side of the tub. His knees protruded out of the water, but that didn't seem to bother him. "This is wonderful."

"The tea or the bath," she asked, trying to keep her tone light despite the desire for her husband growing within her. She'd never felt comfortable before in their short married life together to initiate romance. Her hands trembled as she knelt on the floor behind Ned and handed him a bar of oleander-lilac soap.

He looked at her, then at the soap, gave it a sniff, shrugged, and began soaping up. When she offered to wash his back, he handed her the soap and sighed as she massaged his shoulders.

"Your muscles are tight," she whispered, kneading the knots in his neck and upper back. "Relax."

"I would if I had any idea what you will be up to next." She laughed and kissed a soapy spot on his neck.

He groaned with pleasure. "Oh, Annie, I love you so much."

"I love you too, Ned, and I'm sorry . . ." She threw her arms around her husband's neck. "Can you ever forgive me for losing our baby? If I hadn't been so stubborn, to insist on making the trip to Kansas with you . . . If I hadn't picked up the shotgun . . . If I hadn't . . ."

Water splashed from the tub as he turned to take her into his arms. "No, no, I'm sorry. I should have been a better husband. Why I didn't discuss the purchase of the wagon and my plans for the new underground route, I can't imagine. Worse yet, I've made the same mistake again by going ahead with my plans without consulting you. I'm so sorry."

"Sh-sh, it's all right. We both did stupid things, I guess." Tears streamed as she cupped his face in her hands, closed her eyes, and blindly sought his lips. She felt Ned's muscular arms take her by the waist and lift her, nightgown and all, onto his lap, in the tub of hot water.

"Ned," she squealed. "I'm all wet!"

"So?" he chuckled and captured her lips once more.

"You are insane."

"Insanely in love."

Annie giggled and promptly forgot about her wet clothes and the waiting supper. She remembered Dory's pre-nuptial advice about the joy of submitting to Ned. For the first time in her marriage, her thoughts were focused undividedly on her husband and the pleasure she could give him.

***

The glow of their lovemaking lingered as they dined on stew and freshly baked bread. They grinned across the table at each other like grade-school sweethearts. The sweet potato pie seemed sweeter and the whipping cream, creamier in a home freed of resentment and guilt.

While Annie cleared the table and washed the dinner dishes, Ned dragged the washtub out of the cabin and dumped the bath water onto ground already mushy with the spring melt.

Later, side by side on the sofa, they talked long into the night, confessing what needed to be confessed and admitting to hurts they'd both kept silent.

"Trusting always has been difficult for me," Annie admitted.

"What do you mean?"

"When I came to the Pownells', I looked at Miz Charity as my protector, I guess. When she died, I was scared. I had no one to protect me. Mr. Pownell was on the run from the law. He couldn't help me." Annie gave a deep sigh. "When Miz Josephine came along, I trusted her to take care of me until I was kidnapped in New Orleans. After that I began having the terrible nightmares. Then you came along."

Tenderly he gazed down in her eyes, holding her hands in his, and listening as she spoke her heart.

"I think it was your size and strength I fell in love with first. If anyone could protect me, you could. And then . . . Oh, Ned, I'm so sorry, but I've hated you for . . ." She collapsed against his chest. The beating of his heart comforted her. He hadn't moved away. He hadn't left her side.

"It's over, darling. We've confessed our sins to each other and to God. It's over. They're buried at the bottom of the sea. Let's leave them there."

She sniffed and straightened. "But I was so unfair."

"As was I, my love. My expectations for you as my wife were far and away beyond the realm of reality." He recaptured her hands. "I confess that I expected you to be the perfect hostess like Miz Josephine; the perfect partner like Miz Serenity; the playful playmate like I imagined Miz Lilia to be; the gentle, caring nurse like Miz Jess; and that was just the beginning. I had such high expectations for you, I didn't give you any room to be you."

"You think Miz Lilia is a perfect playmate?" The thought miffed her.

"I don't know. She was just an illustration."

"Um-hum, so you've been looking at other women?" A smile teased the edges of Annie's lips.

"No, no!" Ned was becoming agitated. "I-I-I just meant . . ."

"Sh-sh-sh . . ." She placed a kiss on his lips. "I was just teasing you. Ned Ward, I have never, for one minute, doubted your faithfulness. Even when I was most furious with you, I knew your affections belonged to no one but me."

A huge sigh escaped the man's lips. "I am so glad for that, Annie, because you're right. When I said my vows, I meant every word. My body is yours, and from now on, my mind is yours as well."

Annie shuddered with joy. "And I am yours. I want to submit to you as the bride does to Christ—completely."

"And I promise again to love you as I love my own body. But Annie, darling, I am only a man. I can't promise that I will be able to protect you from all evil. Only God can do that."

"I know. At least, I think I know. I'm still learning how to deal with that." She cuddled up next to him, her ear closest to his heart.

"That's something we all need to learn, I think." He cleared his throat. "I must admit, there've been times since the baby that I've accused God of not doing His job. So God is working with me as well. Speaking of which . . ."

"Yes?" She sat up and eyed him speculatively.

"You probably know about the runaways hiding in the barn."

"Yes?"

"Do you think I could take them the leftover stew and a few slices of bread?" He blinked his eyes expectantly.

"You need to ask? This is your home, remember?" She leaped to her feet. "Those poor people must be starving. Let me fix them some bread with honey butter on top while you grab a few bowls and the stew pot."

The family of a husband, wife, and five-year-old son thanked them over and over again for the hot food. "We 'un don' know when we dun ate so good last."

"I'm glad you enjoyed it. You will keep the rest of this loaf of bread, won't you? You might get hungry later in the night."

The young wife nodded, her eyes misty with gratitude. "Th-th-thank you."

"You're welcome. I'm sorry it took us so long to get something out to you," Annie confessed, glancing shyly at her husband. By the bemused grin on his face, she suspected that if he were a white man, his face would be bright red by now. "I, uh, we got detained."

"Oh, no, we be glad for whatever," the quiet man by the woman's side admitted, his face glowing with pride and determination. "We do anytin' to be free, ma'am. Our boy, he's gonna' growed up free."

***

Annie and Ned strolled back to their one-room soddy hand in hand. Once inside, she gazed about the simple, one-roomed home with a new sense of gratitude and pride. She felt wealthy beyond measure. Fear or not, she would encourage her husband to help these people and all the rest who would come through her barn in search of freedom.

As the couple cozied by the fire to watch the dancing flames burn to embers, Annie snuggled against his side. She found it so easy to feel secure when Ned was so close. *What will it take to find the same peace in Ned's God?* she asked herself.

When the first rays of light streamed through her window, Annie was surprised to find herself in their bed. She opened her eyes and stretched. The pillow beside her was empty. Ned's boots were gone, as was his jacket. If all had gone well, the runaways were safely in Kansas at either the Tylers' or the Judds' home.

Visions of the Cranston gang flashed before her eyes. "No! I won't think such thoughts." She threw back her covers and hopped out of bed. "It's going to be a beautiful day! And I have too much to do to lay abed and worry myself sick."

As she sipped a cup of cinnamon apple tea, she munched on a slice of honey-buttered bread and the promises of Psalm 91. A smile drifted across her face at the familiar words, "For he shall give his angels charge over thee, to keep thee in all thy ways. They shall bear thee up in their hands, lest thou dash thy foot against a stone. . . . He shall call upon me, and I will answer him: I will be with him in trouble; I will deliver him, and honour him. With long life will I satisfy him, and shew him my salvation."

Dropping to her knees beside the table, Annie prayed, "Thank you, Father, for your faithfulness. Forgive me for my unbelief. I want to trust you. Open my eyes so that I may see your salvation."

***

Throughout the day Annie recited the comforting words of the psalm. She straightened the house and did the morning dishes before settling down to her needlework. Eager to begin the work on Jess's angel quilt, Annie spread her pencils, erasers, and paper out on the table, brought an oil lantern close for better light, and began sketching. Cocoa-brown babies with big almond eyes and tight curly hair playing with their toes, and black-skinned babies with full, rose-bud lips and chubby cheeks flying through the air began to take shape on her sheets of newsprint paper. Her third pattern was an olive-brown cherub asleep on a cloud with its tiny wings folded.

Next, Annie sketched the babies onto each of the fabric squares and cut out the pieces to be appliquéd. On her shopping day in Independence, she'd purchased yardage of brown and black cotton and various colorful remnants. Spreading the fabric pieces out on her table had triggered her creative instincts.

As she organized, measured, and cut, Annie recalled Josephine's suggestion that she should start a business. While any pioneer woman worth her salt could quilt, not many had developed the skills required for doing intricate needlework.

Maybe it isn't such a far-fetched idea, she thought. *It would be one way I could travel with Ned and pay my way. I could visit the women in their homes and display my work. Plus, I could sew much of the fancywork on the trail.*

By the time Ned returned home that evening, Annie had worked out a plan. Her trust would bankroll her initial costs. She gave herself a self-satisfied smile. She'd become a woman of commerce, like Lydia of the New Testament and like the woman of Proverbs 31. This time, however, she would approach her husband differently with her revolutionary idea. A hot meal ending with his favorite molasses cookies, some time to relax in front of the fire, maybe a back rub, and then she'd spring it on him as a suggestion and not as an accomplished fact.

His response pleased her. "If that's what you'd enjoy doing," he said. "I liked having you with me, and I was afraid you wouldn't want to go again. That's why I've been putting off making my next trip with the wagon. I'd like to finish the project we started, to the Arkansas border."

"Great!" She leaped from the sofa. "When do we leave?"

He chuckled at her enthusiasm. "I was thinking of next Saturday. That way I could hold services at the Tylers on Sunday."

"Terrific. That will give me enough time to get much of Jess's quilt top completed. I feel badly that I haven't worked on it till now. I could have had it all done by now."

"I think she'll understand, sweetheart," Ned reminded. "By the way, Jess and Billy send their regards. Jess was hoping you'd come with me too. She gets lonesome, you know."

Annie spent the next morning appliquéing angel bodies onto the quilt squares. She was adding the finishing fancywork to one of the squares when Serenity appeared at her door. She was carrying a pie plate of oatmeal cookies.

"Here," she said as Annie invited her into the cabin. "I made two batches and thought you might enjoy one. And I came to invite you to dinner. The Blackwings are coming. Would you and Ned like to join us?"

Annie's smile broadened at the suggestion. "We'd love to, or at least, I would. I'll talk to Ned when he comes in to eat lunch. Which reminds me, how would you and Caleb like some molasses cookies in exchange for your oatmeal? I made them yesterday afternoon."

"M-m-m, sounds good." Serenity handed Annie the pie plate, then removed her coat. She ambled over to the rocker where the quilt pieces were scattered about. "So, what are you working on?"

"A quilt top for one of Ned's parishioners in Kansas." She looked around for Serenity's little boy. "Where's Sammy?"

"With his daddy. They're taking a carriage Caleb repaired to Mr. Albert. Ned's with them, I think." Serenity thumbed through the newsprint sketches. "How adorable. Did you draw these?"

Annie remembered that Ned had told her about the short trip they'd be taking this morning. "Yes. Would you like a cup of tea?"

"You are very good. Josephine's right. You do have a rare gift, Annie."

Annie poured the hot liquid into two mismatched cups and handed one to Serenity. "Thank you. It's fun to do. I could teach you."

Serenity threw up her hands in mocked horror. "Oh, no, you don't fool me. Have you forgotten all those hours Mama tried and failed to teach me? And the tangle of threads on the back of my sampler while yours looked almost as good on the back as it did on the front?" She shook her head. "I know my limitations."

Annie laughed. "Isn't it funny how you have become such a great cook, thanks to Dory, and I've become a seamstress thanks to your mama?"

Both women laughed, then sipped at their hot tea.

"Speaking of sewing, I've decided to set up a business, first as a seamstress, but my specialty will be my fancywork. And I will ply my trade to the farmers' wives while Ned does his preachin' and animal care. Springtime is birthin' time on the farm." A shadow of grief passed over Annie's face, which was instantly replaced with a brave smile.

Serenity patted her friend's hand tenderly but rushed on. "That's a great idea. Josephine will be delighted. She loves what you did for her."

A sense of pleasure flooded through Annie. "In *Goedy's Ladies Book* I see that cut work is high fashion this season. I thought I'd bring along a number of my magazines so my customers can see what's popular back East this year."

"Hey, I'll bet Josephine will give you her older copies if you ask," Serenity volunteered. "They'll be at dinner tonight."

"Thanks, I'll do that."

Serenity sipped at her tea. "When will you be leaving then?"

"At the end of the week."

"That soon?"

Annie smiled thinking how much she treasured Serenity. "'Fraid so."

"I'm going to miss you." Serenity's face saddened. "I've enjoyed our weekly Bible readings."

"I can never tell you how important those times have been to me." Annie touched Serenity's hand gently. "I'm not sure I would have made it through those bleak winter days without you."

Serenity blinked back her tears. "It's been mighty special to me as well, dear sister."

Serenity's words warmed Annie's heart. "We really are sisters, aren't we? Not by birth or even because we grew up side by side, but as daughters of the heavenly King. We've become more like family than family."

Serenity could only nod in response. The two women talked for a few more minutes before Serenity had to leave to begin fixing the evening meal.

"Can I bring something?" Annie called as her friend headed toward the inn.

"Bring your needlework. Josephine will love seeing your little angels, probably want a quilt of her own, in fact."

"See you tonight," Annie called.

Without having to worry about cooking for supper, Annie returned to her sewing, pausing only long enough to assemble a sandwich of honey butter and applesauce for Ned when he returned.

He agreed to dine with the Cunards, or at least, that's what she thought he said. Her mind was just racing with new ideas. He seemed genuinely pleased to listen to them.

* * *

That evening Annie's great new business venture was the topic of conversation. Sam Pownell gave her advice on setting up the business side of the plan while Serenity and Josephine bombarded her with creative ideas. The silent Gray Sparrow's eyes sparkled with excitement as she listened to them discuss the possibilities. Only Baby Sammy seemed uninterested as he played on the shiny oak floor with the building blocks his daddy had made for him at Christmas.

The men drifted to the fireplace to talk. Annie couldn't help but overhear their discussion of the latest happenings in Congress regarding the slavery issue and the influx of eastern troublemakers on both sides of the issue.

"Annie, Serenity said you could use my old issues of *Goedy's*. You're welcome to them. I have a terrible time with magazines piling up in my reading room." Josephine clicked her tongue. "I don't know where I'll keep them once the baby comes."

At the mention of the birth of the Pownell child, Annie experienced a bittersweet moment, sadness over her loss and joy for Josephine and Sam Pownell. She comforted herself with the thought that she was young and healthy and had time on her side. There would be other babies, maybe . . . In the back of her mind, she worried that maybe not . . .

"It can't be long now." Annie forced herself to respond with enthusiasm. "So, what are you hoping for?" It was the question everyone asked.

"Of course, Sam wants a boy to carry on the family name, but I don't care, as long as it's healthy."

Annie nodded. "If Jess Tyler is right, she'd say you're carrying a boy."

Gray Sparrow smiled, nodded, and patted Josephine's stomach.

"How can you tell?" Josephine asked.

The Indian woman extended her hands to the front of her abdomen, then gestured toward the men. Then she pointed to her sides and at Serenity.

"She's saying that women carrying boy babies carry them out front, while they carry girl babies back in the hips," Serenity volunteered. "My stomach was so extended with Sammy that I spilled food on everything I wore."

The women laughed. Anyone looking in the windows of the inn that night would have thought the scene unseemly as the four couples, as varied as the colors of a rainbow, mingled with comfort and good humor. Always cognizant of her color, Annie paused. Only in the West, she thought.

-13-

Hitting the
Road

"ONE SHORT STOP IN TOWN AND WE'LL BE ON our way." Ned urged the team forward toward Independence. "Billy Tyler asked me to pick up a harness he ordered for his team last fall."

With a nippy breeze blowing in her face, Annie straightened her back and inhaled the fresh aroma of springtime on the prairie. Being on the road wasn't the life she would have chosen, but now that it was hers, she vowed to enjoy every minute of it.

The annual Oregon migration and the Santa Fe mule train trade had begun. For weeks, as the snow began to thaw and the first sprigs of green appeared on the prairie, traders, trappers, muleskinners, and pioneers eager to begin their westward trek gathered in Independence Square.

As the Ward wagon lumbered through the center of town, Annie noted the raised window sashes and the anxious faces watching the drama unfold. She cringed as a mule skinner cracked his long leather whip over the backs of his unruly team. The rattle of trace chains and the echo of lowing oxen were punctuated by impatient cursing. Plush carriages jockeyed for position with farm wagons and Conestogas heading for Council Grove and all points west.

Annie's heart raced to the syncopated beat of excitement that permeated the air. Though she and Ned would only go as far west as the Tylers' ranch, she couldn't help but catch the spirit of these adventurous people.

Men and women perched on wagon benches, their faces either glowing in anticipation or resigned to their fate; children and dogs ran alongside the canvas-topped wagons, shrieking and laughing with pleasure. The overloaded wagons creaked from the weight; water sloshed from the water barrels strapped onto the sides of each wagon. Every pioneer knew that the wide, unfenced land ahead, yet unbroken by a plow, would be painfully dry.

Ned parked the wagon by a hitching post and hurried into the leather shop. Annie contentedly watched the wagons roll past—watched and wondered what might be ahead for each the families. How many would reach their promised land? How many would realize their goal? How many would turn back? How many husbands, wives, or children would be buried on the great American desert?

As Ned climb up into the wagon, Annie shook herself and smiled at her husband. "Ready to go?" she asked. Studying God's Word with Serenity, she'd learned not to dwell on the bad but to anticipate the good. To leave civilization behind for the empty nothingness of the prairie, one had to trust that the good far outweighed the bad.

It took more than an hour for Ned to maneuver the wagon through the sea of vehicles clogging the streets of Independence. Finally they reached the western side of town and the turnoff toward the Tylers' place. This time they wouldn't need the services of the raft owner. Instead, they fell into line with the wagon trains snaking toward the horizon.

The wagons continued westward, four abreast. This formation allowed for better protection should trouble arise. Renegade bands of Indians had been harassing the outlying settlers throughout the winter. Except for their stolen pies, Annie and Ned hadn't had any such trouble. Neither had Serenity and Caleb. Annie imagined it was due to their friendship with the Blackwings, since the Blackwings were well-respected in the community.

As Ned and Annie's wagon veered north from the stream of wagons heading toward Council Bluff, Annie settled down beside her husband, eagerly anticipating seeing Jess Tyler again. So much had happened since they had last seen each other.

Annie took out her embroidery hoop and sewing basket, intent on working on Jess's quilt top, but the wagon bouncing over ruts, fords, buffalo wallows, and prairie dog colonies made it impossible. About all she and Ned could do as they rode was talk or sing. Ned chose to sing.

"In the mornin' when I rise; give me Jesus . . ." His rich, baritone voice filled the air. Her husband's songs of faith renewed her own spirit of trust. She knew she could face tomorrow's challenges as long as Ned was by her side. She tried not to think about how she'd cope if he were not with her.

Starting softly at first, she began to harmonize with him. Ned glanced down at her and gave her a grin of encouragement. Before long, she joined him full voice. Whether the prairie dogs or the coyotes took exception to their music, Annie didn't care. She relished being in close harmony with her man.

By pushing the horses, they arrived at the Tylers before nightfall. What a night the two couples had, catching up on everything that had happened since the fall.

"Did you hear that the border raiders broke into a Free-Soilers' meeting in Lawrence last winter and started a riot?" Billy Tyler stayed abreast of the happenings up and down the Kansas/Missouri border. "It seems there was a spy among them. When he was found out, the man vowed to return with twenty thousand Missourians and wipe the emigrants off the face of the Kansas Territory."

"Did he? Return, that is?" Annie asked.

Billy gave a derisive snort. "Yeah, with twenty or so men. The sheriff and his posse quickly convinced all but three that they really wanted to be elsewhere."

"In Missouri, once the snows came, the border ruffians disappeared until spring thaw," Ned said as he grinned mischievously. "As a result, we safely transported a good fifteen or twenty runaways."

"Yep," Billy sagely nodded his head. "As long as the Missouri militia continues to meet at Fort Scott, we encounter little resistance up this way."

"But for how long?" Ned asked, tapping his fingers on the table before him. "What with President Pierce threatening to give U.S. marshals the authority to enforce the Fugitive Slave Act anywhere in the United States, no one will be safe this side of the Canadian border."

Consternation filled Jess's face. "I hate having to break the law."

When the men protested, she raised her hands. "I know, I know. There is a greater law, God's law, but I still wonder if there isn't a better way."

Billy pounded his fist on the table. "Jess! How can you say that? You've looked into the eyes of pitifully abused children. You've talked with families fleeing everything they've ever known just so they can stay together. You've treated backs bruised by the overseer's whip. Surely you can't believe God wants these people to remain in bondage."

The woman shook her head sadly. "No, of course not. It's just that . . ."

"Well, seems to me," Ned interjected, "we, being free Negroes, are hardly the ones to question the actions of the oppressed whose only sin is the desire to live free. Surely our memories aren't that short."

"I know you're right. I just wish we didn't have to go against the laws of our nation."

"Jess, look at history. It took a revolution to free us from England." Ned warmed to his subject. "If George Washington had politely asked for the colonies' freedom, do you think the English Parliament or King what's-his-name would have granted it with a smile and a, 'Have a nice life?'"

"Of course not, but . . ."

Ned interrupted the woman again. "It takes men and women of courage to stand against tyranny. Then, once they've proven the nobility of their cause through bloodshed and the laying down of their lives, lawmakers begin to rethink their positions."

"I'm sorry, Pastor," she argued, "but I'm afraid that when Congress voted for popular sovereignty, thus repealing the Missouri Compromise, they fired the first shot that will eventually divide the country."

Annie had been listening intently to the discussion. "But won't that destroy America?"

Jess shrugged. "It easily could." She turned her attention toward Annie. "You'll see the difference tomorrow. The men keep their pistols loaded and their rifles at arms' length. At a moment's notice a meeting of God could break up into a massacre."

"Jess," her husband scolded, "no such thing has happened yet and probably never will."

"But it could with everyone ready to kill at the click of a safety cock." The woman tightened her lips.

The two men and Jess talked into the wee hours of the morning. Annie, deciding nothing earth-shattering would be settled in the Tyler kitchen, snuck off to bed some time around midnight.

The next morning people from all over the region gathered in the Tylers' barn for worship services. Annie's heart was touched when Jess and the women laid their hands on Annie's shoulders and prayed for her to conceive once more.

A giant potluck followed with an abundance of fried chicken, potato salad, fried okra, stewed greens, cabbage salad, pickled beets, and yellow cake with strawberry-preserve frosting for dessert.

After dinner, while the men met in the barn to discuss the latest political happenings in Washington, D.C. and the children romped in the hayloft, a sewing bee sprang up among the ladies. Several of the women had brought along their sewing projects and were eager to show them to Annie, the resident expert. As the preacher's wife gazed about the circle of friendly faces, her heart overflowed with gratitude toward her sisters in Christ.

Ned and Annie got an early start Monday morning, despite staying up late a second night with the Tylers. A drizzling rain chased Annie inside the wagon for the day-long ride. To keep from getting drenched, Ned huddled under a heavy oil-cloth rain slick as he urged the team of horses over the muddy road.

At midday, they stopped long enough to eat a piece of fried chicken and a powder biscuit Jess had packed for them, then continued until nightfall.

That night Annie fell asleep listening to the rain pelt the canvas. The next day the rains hadn't let up. They pulled into the Judds' ranch by mid-afternoon. Ned hopped down from the wagon, ran through the rain to the Judds' front porch, and knocked on the door.

A short, round dumpling of a woman opened the door and stepped out onto the porch. She gestured for Ned to come inside and waved for Annie to do the same. Ned ran back to the wagon to help Annie around the sticky mud puddles.

Annie's stomach lurched at the thought of meeting the Quaker family for the first time. Ned had met them while she was recuperating at the Tylers'. Would they like her or would they look down their noses at the colored couple, even though Ned was a preacher?

Hattie Judd proved to be a jovial woman who seemed to be looking for an excuse to laugh. Her abundant girth jiggled with joy as she spoke about the most mundane of things. Nary a wrinkle creased the woman's yellow calico dress and starched blue gingham apron. Annie was drawn to Hattie's rosy cheeks and snappy blue eyes, evidence of a quick mind. The woman left no doubt in Annie's mind that her and Ned's visit was most welcome.

Her tall, gaunt husband, Herman, was as opposite to his wife as possible. His stern face appeared cast in granite. His gray-green eyes dissected everything and everybody he saw. The way he ruminated the inside of his mouth with his tongue as he listened, fascinated Annie. His canvas trousers hung from his body by a pair of green-and-yellow-striped suspenders. The patched and faded blue shirt he wore indicated many hard scrubbings on the washboard.

Hattie ushered them into the neat little farm kitchen. Yellow gingham tie-back curtains covered both of the small, four-paned windows. A matching oilcloth covered the rough-hewn table.

"Take off thy wet clothes before thee catches the grippe," she ordered. "Make thyself comfortable while I make thee a cup of hot tea."

"Make mine coffee," her husband growled as he dropped into the end chair at their table.

"Of course, honey." Hattie shrugged her shoulders and scurried into the pantry for the necessary cups and saucers. "I made a batch of molasses cookies yesterday." She appeared around the pantry door, her hands and arms full.

"Here, let me help you." Annie leaped to her feet.

"No bother, no bother. I am so glad to finally meet thee, Miz Ward. When your husband visited last fall, he told me thou art quite a seamstress. I'd love to see some of thy work." The woman giggled. "Me, when I sew, my fingers come away worse for wear."

The farmer's wife suddenly noticed the scars on Annie's hands. "Oh, I'm sorry. I hope thee didn't do that learning to sew!"

Annie laughed. "Hardly. I burned my hands during a house fire. Actually, my love for embroidering brought life back into my fingers. It was difficult at first, but I was determined."

"That's remarkable." She glanced over at the two men seated at the table. Annie suspected that Ned was filling the farmer in on the latest news regarding the conflict.

"It's so nice to have someone to talk with besides Herman He's one of those silent Quakers, in and out of church on

Sunday mornings." She laughed at her reference to her husband's taciturn habits. "He's really as meek as a spring lamb," she confided. Looking at the man, Annie questioned Hattie's assessment.

"We've been married thirty-five years come September. Raised six kids on the ranch, four girls and two boys—one's a professor at a college in St. Louis, and the other boy runs a mercantile up Kansas City way." She poured the hot tea in the cups as she spoke.

"My girls are each married with kids of their own, seventeen, in fact. With the boys' five, that comes to twenty-two grandchildren in all. Talk about a lively place at Christmas!" She paused to glance about the small kitchen. "This year they didn't come to the farm. Herman Jr.'s wife insisted we visit them in St. Louis."

Annie listened as the woman spouted out personal family information faster than a hoard of mosquitoes draining blood from a man's arm. She wondered if Hattie ever paused to catch her breath.

"Now, St. Louis, isn't that the place?" The woman laughed. "Last time I was there, I about started a stampede on Main Street. I didn't mean to, of course. I didn't know the mare would be skittish when I accidentally stepped in front of her. Reared, she did, right in front of city hall. I screamed, which caused the horse tethered beside her to do the same. A third horse, a gelding, kicked his hind feet into the air, upsetting a crate of apples his owner was getting ready to load in his saddlebags. Why thee would think I'd started a five-alarm fire or something."

In a conspiratorial tone, she added, "It was funny watching men and their parcels, women and their parasols, and smaller species of animals scurry out of the way of the horses and their hooves. Herman was upset with me for days!"

The woman clicked her tongue and sighed. "So was my daughter-in-law, Herman Jr.'s wife. She's one of these high-falutin' city gals who's afraid of her shadow. I do love her, or at least I try."

By the time the two couples retired for the night, Annie's head buzzed and her ears hurt from the woman's chatter. If Annie had been previously worried about having to keep up her side of the conversation with the farmer's wife, she realized now that the fear was unfounded. Yet Annie had to admit she'd enjoyed spending the evening with the conversation-starved woman.

The isolated life on the prairie is most difficult for women, Annie decided. To take a young bride from her family and friends in the East, away from the tea parties, afternoon soirees, the family gatherings, and the heady round of social events, then drop her in the middle of the great American wasteland without another human being for forty miles or more in any direction was difficult—no matter how much she loved her man.

Tilling the sod and tending cattle from dawn till dusk might be a man's dream, but a woman's dreams were more often wrapped up in the man himself. Again Annie was grateful to have Serenity and Caleb nearby.

The next day Ned and Annie were off with the first light. It took four long days of hard riding to reach Fort Scott. The first night they stopped near a one-room sod house owned by a Scottish family, the McGregors. Beside the tiny cabin stood a massive barn. The McGregors had five tow-headed blond children, two black-and-white-speckled sheep dogs, a Jersey cow named Belle, and two plow horses.

Mr. McGregor had a thick Scottish brogue. Annie had trouble understanding him when he gave them permission to spend the night on his property. The man eyed the couple with suspicion. Ned's wide grin went a long way to rest the man's fears. Being an itinerate preacher helped as well.

Mrs. McGregor seemed as shy as her children, and equally as curious. Annie imagined that they'd never before seen black people, or at least been close enough to speak to them. While the youngest, a three-year-old boy, hid behind his mother's skirts, the oldest, a boy around eight, asked if he could touch Ned's hand.

Ned smiled and extended his hand. The boy timidly ran his forefinger lightly across the back of Ned's hand, then examined his finger. The child's brow knitted in confusion. He rubbed the back of Ned's hand a little harder, and again examined his own finger. Then the child rubbed his own two fingers together and then checked for markings.

While the parents acted embarrassed with their son's curiosity, both Ned and Annie laughed aloud when the child turned to his brothers and sisters and announced, "It doesn't come off."

"Nope!" Ned assured the children. "No matter how hard I scrub my skin with lye soap, the color just won't come off. Come," he beckoned to the other children, "see for yourself."

The three older children, a boy and two girls, inched closer and cautiously touched Ned's hand. One of the girls turned to her mother, "Look Mama, it really doesn't come off. See?"

The woman gave an uncomfortable smile, glancing quickly toward her husband, then back at Ned.

"It's all right, ma'am. Children are curious. And curiosity is good." Ned tousled the older boy's straw-blond hair. The boy's eyes widened, and his hand flew to the spot on his head where Ned had touched.

Ned laughed. "The color won't come off, I promise." The boy reddened and hung his head.

"So you say you're free Negroes? And you're travelin' through the area to see your parishioners?" Mr. McGregor rubbed his jaw slowly. "And you know something about animals?"

"Yes, sir." Ned held his head high.

"Hmm, a man of God. Not one of those Papists, are you?"

"No, sir. Baptist, in fact," Ned assured him.

"Well," the Scottish farmer thought for a moment, "I'm not sure about the dunkin' part, me being Anglican and all, but I've known others of your kind who were good people. And you say you know something about animals?"

"Yes, sir."

"Well, I have a mare who's been actin' mighty strange the last few days. I think she may have gotten into a nettle patch." The farmer turned to his wife. "Mavis, get this man's wife a cup of tea or something. Kids, you got chores to do."

Summarily dismissed, the children reluctantly scattered in different directions. Only the youngest clung to his mother's skirts as she led Annie into the tiny sod house. While the place was immaculately clean, it was dark and gloomy due to a lack of windows. Also, the walls were the color of the natural sod, a muddy brown. The only sources of light came from the fireplace and one lone oil lantern on the counter beside the dry sink.

A ladder made of logs led to the loft above the parents' rough-hewn log bed. The multicolored quilt atop the bed added much needed color to the room. Beyond the trestle table and benches, there were two rockers, one on each side of the fireplace, with a footstool and a rag rug between them. A Bible lay unopened on the hearth.

The only wall decoration, a sampler, attracted Annie's attention. "Mavis Griswold, age 10. B. July 15, 1829, Glasgow, Scotland," it read. Annie glanced toward her hostess. The woman was less than four years older than Annie, but she looked to be a good fifteen years her senior.

"I was just admiring your handiwork, Mrs. McGregor," Annie said. "I do fancy needlework as well."

"Call me Mavis. It's just cross-stitch, and not very neat, at that," the woman apologized.

"Oh, no, it's lovely. I think a sampler adds so much personality to a home. And please, call me Annie, Annie Ward."

The woman smiled. Her eyes softened. "I came from Scotland as a bride of thirteen, you know. There were ten young'uns in my family. We were dirt poor, nothin' to eat much of the time." For an instant the farmer's wife frowned as she if were recalling bittersweet memories of home.

"Robert paid my father five pounds for my hand in marriage, enough to keep my family in potatoes for quite a spell." Then, as if she read Annie's mind, Mavis added, "Robert's good to me and the young'uns. Always food on the table," she added proudly.

"You have a fine family, Mrs. McGregor. You must be proud of them."

The woman beamed with delight. "I am. You know my son, Herbert, the one who, uh, introduced himself to your husband? Well, Herbert could read and write before he turned five, he could. Of course, Robert doesn't think much of readin' and such."

She tipped her head shyly to one side. "He says, 'Readin' can't plow a field.'" She smiled sadly. "I guess he's right. My daddy was dirt poor, wasted all his money on books, so Robert says."

"Do you like to read?" Annie asked.

"Oh, yes. I have one book beside the Good Book, that is. I have read it so many times, the binding is loose." Excited to share her treasure with someone who was interested, Mavis McGregor rushed to the other side of the cabin and hauled out a book from under her side of the corn-cob mattress. "See? Jane Austin's *Sense and Sensibility.*"

"I've read that one too," Annie volunteered.

"You did? Oh, which of the three sisters did you favor most? Me, I liked Margaret best. Elinor was too clever for me."

Annie laughed. She'd never imagined herself discussing the three heroines of a Jane Austin novel with a Scottish farmer's wife on the Kansas prairie.

"Have you read Miss Austin's *Pride and Prejudice?*"

"No, no. I only got to read this one. My husband bought some junk at a farm auction, and the book came with it. I rescued it from the garbage. He was going to throw it away." The woman looked distraught at the very idea. "Did I tell you that Herbert has read the Bible through five times?"

"No, but that is remarkable, especially when you consider suffering through the Chronicles or Lamentations," Annie admitted. The two women laughed together as they sipped on their tea.

Mavis set her cup down on its saucer. "Herbert's teaching Sara, my younger daughter, to read. My older daughter and the other two boys are like their pa. They don't have a hankerin' for learnin', at least so far."

Annie could hear the longing in the woman's voice. A look of pride replaced the woman's moment of vulnerability.

"Of course, there's not a lot of time for book learnin' on a dirt farm like ours. Doesn't leave much energy for doin' one's letters or numbers at the end of the day."

The young preacher's wife had heard the tale before, working from sunup to sundown, growing old long before one's time, too many mouths to feed, too many children to clothe.

As Mavis collected the cups and carried them to the dry sink, Annie glanced about the place. *And what will they have to show for their hard work?* she wondered. A sod shanty and six feet of ground for burial? Was Mavis any better off in America than she would have been in Scotland? Did a woman like Mavis McGregor, bought and paid for by her husband, need emancipation as much as a rich woman's chambermaid or a cotton picker on a southern plantation?

That evening, as she slipped under the covers beside Ned, Annie wondered if Mavis Griswold McGregor loved her husband or if she endured the hard life on the prairie because she never had a chance for a better life.

Throughout the long ride the next day, Annie couldn't shake the memory of Mavis McGregor. As night fell Ned eased to a stop in a small Negro community outside of Aubry, Kansas. The wagon hadn't come to a stop when Ned's parishioners came running from every direction to welcome the pastor and to take a "gander" at his beautiful wife, so Beatrice Devers told Annie the next morning.

"Why every woman in this place wanted to meet the lady who stole our preacher's heart," the robust Miz Devers informed her. "It wasn't as if your husband didn't have a swarm of interested honeybees buzzing about the best looking, single man between Independence and Fort Smith! But don't let those gals bother you," she advised. "Remember, he chose you."

That's comforting, Annie thought as she eyed the bevy of doting females surrounding her husband. What tweaked her nose was that he didn't seem to mind! Deciding she had to do something, Annie sided up to Ned, slid her arm around his waist, and gave his admirers a sicky-sweet smile. "Honey, don't you think you should introduce me to all your friends?"

Annie fought back the giggles when Ned cleared his throat and swallowed hard. "This here's Marabelle Bender, and this is Elsie Woodward and Susan Langley . . ." He introduced each girl in the circle. Most of them were still in their teens. Only one or two would be any kind of threat as far as Annie was concerned.

The pastor's wife acknowledged each female with a big smile and a friendly greeting, accompanied by a compliment on the girl's clothes, hair, or features. She assured herself that she wasn't lying. Elsie Woodward did have beautiful almond eyes, and Marabelle Bender did look pretty in pink.

That night Annie teased her husband as they settled in Miz Devers' four-poster guestroom bed. Ned, like many men bent on a mission, found his wife's teasing disconcerting. His brow creased with worry. "Honey, if I'm doing anything improper to attract these women, please tell me. It's you I married. It's you I love."

Reaching out and caressing his neck and shoulder with her one hand, she assured him he'd done nothing wrong. "You can't help it if I snagged the best catch between Independence and Fort Smith, and that's a quote, I'll have you know."

"Hmmph! That's balderdash," he sputtered, turning his face away from her.

Gently caressing his shoulder and back, Annie whispered in his ear, "As long as you always remember you belong to me, I don't care how many bees buzz about my honey."

Ned turned toward his wife with concern riddled on his face. "Darling, when I vowed to love you 'till death us do part,' I meant it. There's no other woman for me."

"I'm glad." A smile spread slowly across Annie's face as she leaned forward and kissed his waiting lips.

~14~

Heading for Home

FOLLOWING TWO MORE DAYS OF TRAVEL, THEY pulled into Fort Scott, Kansas, near sunset. The fort had been built by the United States Army twelve years earlier to control what the United States government called, the "permanent Indian frontier." It was named after General Winfield Scott. However, after the founder, General Charles Bent, died while visiting Santa Fe, the United States Army failed to assign someone to take his place, and the fort deteriorated despite the small town growing up around it.

When he introduced himself to the commanding officer, Ned quickly discovered there was no place for Negroes to stay for the night, either in town or at the fort.

The officer on duty suggested that Ned make camp south of town by the cemetery. Ned asked if it would be safe there. The military man shrugged. "As far as I know," he said. "We ain't had any trouble from the border ruffians or the Indians since last fall."

It was at the cemetery that Willy came to live with them. Willy, a medium-sized dog with wiry gray hair, adopted Annie the moment she stepped down from the wagon. His bark startled her, but it was quickly evident that the bone-thin mutt wanted nothing but her love and the scraps left over from lunch.

"He's terribly skinny. Do you think he belongs to anyone? Can we keep him?" Annie asked as she scratched the animal behind his ears.

"We can ask around tomorrow." It was evident that Ned wanted the dog as badly as did Annie. During their evening meal, they tried a number of "doggie" sounding names on the creature, but none fit until Ned suggested "Willy," after a dog from his plantation days. "He was the bright spot in my days," Ned explained. "He would come looking for me at night when I was alone in my bunk. He seemed to know I was homesick for my family."

Before she fell asleep, Annie prayed, "Dear Lord, you say you want to give us the desires of our hearts. Here's your chance. Please let us keep Willy. Amen."

Annie's prayer was answered. The next morning Ned stopped at every farmhouse they passed and inquired about the owners of the dog. Everyone agreed that Willy was an abandoned stray waiting to be adopted by Annie and Ned.

Fort Scott was abuzz with news from the East. The latest issue of the *Leavenworth Herald* reported that three Massachusetts businessmen had formed what they called the New England Aid Company, whereby they would assist immigrants from Europe in relocating to Kansas. This thinly veiled attempt to populate the Kansas Territory with Free-Soilers promised to supply the equipment for saw mills, grist mills, and printing presses that the immigrants could rent for very little. They could also purchase cut-rate railroad and steamboat tickets.

With more than four hundred thousand immigrants from Europe landing on the eastern shores in 1853, it made good business sense to move these homeless people to a place where they were needed.

The reporter went on to write, "Mr. Eli Thayer, a wealthy businessman from Worchester County, along with Mr. A. A. Lawrence and J. M. F. Williams have arranged with a group of thirty German emigrants to be the first to avail themselves of their services. Mr. Thayer told reporters, 'The New England Aid Company is eager to protect naïve immigrants from being swindled by unscrupulous scalawags.'"

Annie lingered in the general store for several minutes behind a shelf loaded with bolts of fabric, listening to the clerk and three fellow pro-slavers rant against this latest threat upon their way of life.

"Kansas would and should be a slave state! Those rich men from the East and their money! They think they can overrun us with ignorant foreigners! We'll meet them with guns a blazing, that's what we'll do," one bushy-faced hothead declared.

Swallowing hard, Annie clutched her white leather reticule to her chest, wishing she could become invisible behind the bolts of gingham, calico, and plaid.

Another man, smoking on a pipe and wearing a wide-brimmed Stetson added, "Sure, let the citizens of a territory decide for themselves whether or not to become free states. Right. Those Free-Soilers might have gotten their way in New Mexico and Utah, but by cracky, they won't find it so easy here."

The clerk who'd read aloud the article wagged his head in disgust. "With the proposed transcontinental railroad comin' through Kansas Territory, it's imperative to the Southern cause to be able to ship their belongings across the country without the risk of their chattel escaping while the train crosses a free state."

"George," the first man asked of the clerk, "what's imperative?"

The clerk gave the man a look of disgust. "Something very important, Manny."

"Oh . . ." the first man rubbed his beard. "I get it. Yeah, imperative." He thought for a moment again. "And what's chattel?"

The clerk gave an exaggerated sigh. "Horses, cows, slaves, Manny. Slaves."

"Hmm, 'magin that, Rupert. It's imperative for me to buy some smokes before I leave town. Right?"

"Right, Manny." The clerk rolled his eyes toward the ceiling.

The man called Manny scrunched up his weathered face as if struggling with a new thought.

"The Blue Lodges are havin' a meetin' tonight, ain't we?" A tall, angular man with a graying mustache and a beard that covered most of his upper chest chewed on a licorice stick as he spoke.

"Hey, does my wife count as chattel?" Manny asked.

The clerk clicked his tongue in frustration. "I suppose the law might think so, Manny. But I've met your old lady and I know she keeps you harnessed tighter than you do her." Manny reddened as his buddies laughed at his expense.

"But what about the meetin' tonight?" the bearded man asked again. "We gotta' do something before we're completely overrun."

"Sh-sh-sh! We gotta' keep it secret," the clerk hissed, glancing about worriedly. "We don't want the law snooping around."

Suddenly he spotted Annie peering around the corner of the fabric shelves. "Whatcha doin', girl?" he shouted. "Spyin' on us?"

"No, sir. No, sir." Annie's heart leaped to her throat as the store clerk strode menacingly toward her.

"You one of them runaways? Ya' think you're purty smart, don't ya'?" His eyes grew threatening and his mouth hard as he rounded the pickle barrels and a counter of kitchen gadgets. "On second thought, you ain't a runaway. You're one of those thieving outlaws who harbor our slaves, ain't ya'?"

A thick support beam and the fabric display stood between the clerk and Annie. Annie stared back at the man. A note of defiance entered her mind. She doubted the man had ever had enough money to own a slave in his entire life. Chances were, he didn't even own the store but worked for someone else.

Leaning against the heavy oak support was a homemade straight broom. The clerk grabbed the broom and swung it at the startled woman. "Girl, you git out of my store, ya' hear?"

All thought of purchasing fabric and needed spools of threads disappeared. She had no doubt that he meant business. *Run,* her brain shouted as the broom breezed past the side of her head. Annie hiked her skirts and fled the store as fast as she could go. *Find Ned,* she thought. *I have to find Ned and the wagon.*

She raced down the wooden sidewalk toward the livery stable where Ned said he was going to check one of the horses' hooves. Annie rounded the end of the block without slowing down and plowed into the hard chest of a man completely clothed in deerskin from his moccasins to his bent-rimmed hat. Thick deerskin fringe dangled from his sleeves and down the sides of his trousers. He grunted from the impact.

Startled, she lost her balance, but he caught her before she fell on the wooden sidewalk. "Howdy there, Senorita. In a hurry, are you?"

Terror filled her heart when she looked up into his weathered, brown face. "Sorry," she gasped, wrenching her arms free from his grasp. "Sorry."

"Are you all right?" he asked. His words sounded strange to Annie's ears.

"Yes. Yes, sir, I'm fine. I'm so sorry. I was in a hurry and didn't see you coming."

The stranger tipped his hat toward her. "That's all right. I was moving at a mighty clip myself." He touched the edge of his hat. "Now, if you will excuse me? I still am in a rush."

"Uh, yes, yes. Excuse me too," she muttered as she whipped about, only to find the latch on her reticule caught in the fringe of one of his sleeves. "Oh, uh . . ." Annie tugged at the purse, but it remained hopelessly tangled.

The man laughed and proceeded to free her purse from his garment. When he broke free, he chuckled again and touched his hand to the brim of his hat. "Senorita, till we meet again?"

"Yes, thank you." Annie whirled about and hurried down the muddy alley toward the livery stable. When she saw Ned she just fell into his arms. Willy came bounding around the corner of one of the horse stalls, barking his greeting.

Ned ignored the puppy and grasped his wife by the arms. "What's wrong?"

At first she couldn't speak, she was so out of breath. Annie's heart seemed to be pounding its way through her chest. The dog sensed her fear and whimpered by her feet. "It's all right, Willy. I'm fine." She bent down and patted the eager puppy's head. He licked her hand and tried to lick her face. Annie laughed in spite of herself.

When she arose, she could see the concern in her husband's eyes. "I overheard a group of men talking about what they called a Blue Lodges meeting tonight. Isn't that one of those secret societies the pro-slavers have organized, the ones who advocate using violence against the Free-Soilers?"

"Yes. Did they try to hurt you?" Her husband asked, checking her over as he spoke.

"Only the clerk—when he swung his broom at my head, but I moved too fast for him." Tears blazoned in her eyes. "If I hadn't run into that foreigner, I think they would have chased me. I could see the very presence of evil in their eyes."

"What foreigner?"

"I-I-I don't know his name. He spoke funny, that's all I know, and he dressed Indianlike, in deerskin."

Ned thought for an instant. "Hmm, sounds like the explorer and mountain man who just left the stables. If it's the same one, his name is Jorge Lopez, and he spent the winter at his home in Southern Mexico and is now on his way north to Colorado. I helped him treat a sore under his horse's saddle. A real gentleman, he is."

"I felt so foolish when my reticule caught on the fringe of his right sleeve. First the poor man had to catch me when I started to fall, then he had to disentangle us. How embarrassing."

A chuckle erupted from deep in Ned's broad chest. "It's all right, Annie honey. The important thing is that you're safe." He drew her into his arms despite the presence of a gawking livery boy. "We'll be leaving here in no time."

"Good." Annie glanced about her nervously. "It can't be soon enough for me. I wish I were home."

Taking her face in his hands, Ned studied his wife's tear-stained face. "Annie, honey, we have a few more places to visit before we return home. You realize that, don't you?"

She nodded and sniffed back her tears. "I'm sorry. I didn't mean to fall apart like that. I know better. I know God will be with me and, and . . ."

"Honey, honey, honey." He drew her close and rocked her in his arms. "It's all right to be frightened every now and then. I get frightened sometimes when I read what Stringfellow and his ilk say to the news reporters." He patiently massaged her back and shoulders. "Fear can be a good thing as long as we remember that perfect love, the love that God gives, casts out our fears, and that He will give us the power to walk among poisonous snakes. And by the sound of it, the men you met in the general store sound like they qualify."

Annie chuckled as she imagined the clerk and the other men in the store as defanged rattlesnakes—a lot of noise but no bite.

"And remember, darling, for every hate-filled outlaw who is using the slave issue as an excuse to become violent, there is a good man, a kind gentleman, like the one you met on the street corner. Remember too, there are equally evil men who are using the Popular Sovereignty Act as a means to line their pockets with other men's gold."

Annie knew her husband was right. It was easy to class every Southern sympathizer as evil and all anti-slavery supporters as holy. Only God knew the condition of a man or woman's heart. If God hadn't softened the heart of the plantation owner who bought Ned, Annie would never have met and married the man holding her in his arms.

When Ned was certain she had calmed down, he harnessed the horses to the wagon. "I repacked the axle with grease," he said as he helped Annie onto the wagon bench, then led the team out of the barn and into the courtyard.

"Here, Willy," he called as he hopped on board. The dog bounded out of the barn and hopped onto the wagon and into Annie's waiting arms with one leap. And that's where he stayed mile after mile and day after day as their wagon rolled south to Baxter Springs and the Oklahoma border.

The news that a Negro preacher was coming through the area traveled ahead to each tiny settlement along the Kansas/Missouri border wherever free coloreds lived. Annie marveled at the number of people that traveled several miles to hear Ned preach. There were baptisms and marriages to perform, prayers to pray, and funerals to conduct.

The couple traveled on tips from one sympathizer to the next, trying to find people who were willing to be stations along another underground route. A Methodist and a Baptist mission, a Presbyterian and a Quaker community, rugged dirt farmers who scratched out meager existences from the soil and wealthy landowners whose hearts beat for the cause of freedom willingly agreed to risk their lives and livelihood to be a part of the vast interconnecting route that would spirit runaway slaves to the safety of Canada.

Annie and Ned didn't need to remind these people of the risks they were taking. Many had seen the violence the ruffians were capable of and they'd heard their fiery rhetoric. Several refused to put their families in danger. They argued, "It's not our fight."

Annie understood. She would prefer to stay home toasting her toes in front of a cheery fire, too, but she'd seen too much to turn back now. She found that to maintain her courage and dedication she needed to study God's Word regularly. While Willy helped Ned reload the wagon each morning, she would find a quiet spot and put to memory the promises she needed to see her through the difficulties of the day.

Annie found traveling from one place to the next to be a pleasure. She enjoyed seeing groves of trees, white with apple blossoms, as well as blossoming plum trees and wild grapes growing on the high rolling prairie. As they crossed westbound trails, they'd see broken-down wagons, abandoned to the elements. Occasionally she would spot an isolated Shawnee settlement in the distance. One of her favorite memories would be hearing the songbirds at sunset.

Annie also enjoyed meeting the wives of farmers and ranchers along the way. The women would pore over her *Goedy's* magazines, oohing and aahing over the styles of clothing women were wearing back East. The most common remark was, "How do those women get a lick of work done wearing those great, big hoops? Why, one good wind and they'd find themselves sailing into the Atlantic Ocean."

Several of the wealthier wives commissioned her to add delicate fancywork to their favorite garments and bedroom linens while she was with them.

The Wards steered clear of the larger white settlements for fear of encountering border ruffians and other vigilantes. When a shortage of supplies forced them to stop in a potentially unfriendly town, they bought what they needed and got out before the sun set. At night Ned took care to camp within the borders of a Negro settlement or on a friendly white rancher's property.

The most dangerous part of their journey came when they turned their wagon north and crossed into Missouri. For the underground route to be successful, they needed to find willing conductors and stations in the slave state of Missouri as well.

They spent their first night in Missouri at a small Negro settlement south of Carthage where they heard wild tales of secret societies raiding the homes of Negro farmers as well as bands of ruffians terrorizing foreign immigrants who were establishing claims across the state line into Kansas territory. One local white farmer had been hung because he dared to speak out against the atrocities.

As Annie climbed into bed beside Ned, she whispered, "It will be good to finally get home, won't it?"

He slid his arm about her waist and drew her close. "It won't be long now, precious one."

They spent a week in Jasper where two exciting events occurred. First, Annie told Ned she was again pregnant. Second, when Annie went to the local mercantile to replenish her thread supply, she met Margaret York. Her father, Judge York, was in town hearing the cases of miscreants arrested throughout the winter. They were staying in Auntie Sue's boarding house at the edge of town.

It felt so good to see a familiar face once again. From her reaction, Miss York felt the same way. They talked for some time before Annie mentioned her reason for being in the store.

"Oh, yes, your sewing. This is absolutely wonderful," the judge's daughter began. "My father and I are going to Washington, D.C., later this year, and I am in desperate need of several traveling gowns. The ones I wear here in Missouri are, well, you know, hardly suitable for Eastern society. Would you consider making them for me?"

Annie choked back her happiness. What a privilege it would be to make garments to be worn in the capitol of the United

States! She studied Miss York's diminutive figure, her peachy pink complexion, and fiery red, curly hair. "I'd love to. Do you have any styles or fabrics in mind?"

"Actually, I do." Margaret York was as excited as Annie. "Walk back to the boarding house with me. The latest *Goedy's* has sketches of some exquisite gowns for summertime travel."

The two women started down Main Street toward the boarding house. Talking and laughing together like old friends, neither heard a middle-aged woman with unkempt hair and clothing shout at them from an upstairs window until she called a second time.

"Aren't you getting a little chummy with your slave girl? You one of those darkie lovers from back East?"

Miss York stopped abruptly and looked up at the mottled-faced woman. "Were you speaking to me?" she asked.

"Yeah, honey, I was. Are you one of those . . ." She started to repeat her question again.

The judge's daughter's eyes flashed with anger, and her lip curled into a snarl. "Actually, yes. Annie is my very dearest friend, as if it's any of your business."

"A real lady wouldn't be caught dead on the street with one of those colored folk," the woman shouted.

"Sh," Annie hissed. "Don't pay any attention to her. Come on, let's get out of here." By this time a small crowd had assembled to watch the interplay.

The scrappy Margaret York would not be deterred. Her ire was up, as her father often said, and no one could stop her. "And I wouldn't be caught dead on the street with the likes of you!" She shouted for everyone to hear. With that Margaret whirled about, slipped her arm in Annie's, and sashayed proudly down the street.

At the same instant, the woman in the window dumped the contents of her chamber pot out the window, intending to hit the two women.

Fortunately her aim was as keen as her intellect, and she missed. The contents splashed behind them on the wooden sidewalk. The crowd laughed. Annie almost choked when Miss York turned and gave them a genteel curtsy and was cheered and applauded by the crowd. Embarrassed, Annie glanced toward the window again. It was closed, and the draperies were drawn.

"I am so sorry that happened," Annie began as she walked faster to get away from the area. "It was because of me that she . . ."

"No! I am the one embarrassed by the woman's stupidity," Margaret insisted. "You did nothing wrong, Annie. Nothing at all. One of the reasons for my father's trip East is to appear before the members of Congress to warn them of the dangers resulting from the passage of the Popular Sovereignty Act."

Margaret took Annie's arm and hurried down the street toward the boarding house. "The majority of the cases my father sees have to do with hoodlums on one side or the other taking the laws into their own hands. He's hoping he can talk some sense into Washington's pea-brained politicians."

Annie chuckled at the woman's outspokenness and her snappish nature. The more she saw of her, the more she admired the indomitable Margaret York. Yes, Serenity was right. It would take a man like Felix Bonner to tame her. Then again, knowing Mr. Bonner, it would take a woman like Margaret York to tame him as well.

Before Annie and Ned left town the next morning, Miss York commissioned Annie to make three gowns, a lightweight linen suit, a cotton lawn print, and a cotton brocade for evening wear. The judge's daughter would order the fabric by telegram from St. Louis, and it would be waiting for Annie when she returned to Independence.

"If you have any extra time at all," the woman added, "I would dearly love an embroidered cotton batiste camisole like you made for Mrs. Pownell."

Annie promised to try. Since the gowns would also involve some embroidery work, it would take working day and night to finish everything before August 1, the Yorks' departure date.

"Oh, did I tell you?" The judge's daughter's eyes brightened. "Mrs. Pownell had her baby—a boy, seven pounds, eight ounces, with a shock of black hair like you've never before seen. They named him Wesley James, after absolutely no one, so the proud mama says."

Joy filled Annie's heart as she hurried back to the livery stables where she and Ned had agreed to meet two hours earlier. "Well, little one," she whispered to her unborn child as she rushed into the stable yard, "it looks like you'll have a playmate."

～15～

Home Sweet Home

SERENITY SHRIEKED WITH LAUGHTER WHEN Annie told her about her encounter with Margaret York and the chamber pot lady. She laughed so hard that she not only got the hiccups but also awakened Sammy, her napping son.

"How did you manage to keep from laughing?" she asked Annie as she helped her son put on his socks and shoes. "I've never heard anything so funny."

Annie gave a shudder. "Laugh! I was too terrified to think of laughing, especially when the crowd began to gather. I wasn't sure they wouldn't lynch the both of us right there in broad daylight."

Serenity began snickering again. "I'm not sure who had the most audacity, Margaret or the woman in the window. She's going to turn those D.C. snobs upside down and inside out. The government will never be the same again."

This time Annie chuckled at the idea of Margaret York shocking the wives of Washington's politicians with her forthright candor. "Miss York could stand a touch of refining."

Laughter burst from Serenity once again. "Refining Margaret would be as likely as training a hungry polecat. But you know, Margaret York might be what those stuffy matrons need most, a breath of fresh air!"

"It's not that she's unrefined, exactly. She's outspoken. Her mouth gets her into trouble." Annie grinned and shook her head. "She'll probably start her very own war between the states before she returns home."

"She is a spunky one," Serenity admitted. "This is really a lovely cotton, so light and soft."

The fabric for the first of Margaret's three gowns, a pink flowered cotton batiste with a light-green background, was spread out on Annie's dinner table waiting for the first cut from her scissors. The soft tones in the feather-light fabric would compliment the woman's titian red curls and peach blossom complexion.

As Serenity watched her friend deftly cut out the pieces for the gown, she marveled at Annie's dexterity and skill. "How do you do that, and without a pattern, no less?"

"It takes practice." Annie remained focused on her work.

Little Sammy gently touched the cloth. "Pretty," he said.

"Careful, Sammy," Serenity cautioned. "We don't want to get the pretty fabric dirty."

"He's all right." Annie ran a corner of the cloth between her fingers and smiled at the child. "Yes, it is pretty, isn't it?"

Serenity ran her fingers through her son's tousled hair to give the thatch of wiry blond hair some order. "Doesn't it scare the liver out of you that you'll make a mistake and ruin the fabric?"

"Sometimes, especially when I'm working with imported silks or satin brocades that can't easily be replaced. Then I move very slowly, carefully thinking through each move before I make it," Annie admitted.

Serenity took her son's hand in hers and walked to the door. "Go see Daddy. He's in the shop." When she opened the cabin door, Sammy ran outside into the June sunshine. "You are remarkable, Annie Ward."

Annie laughed at her friend's assessment of her. "Serenity, you are such a good friend."

Serenity closed the door and strode to the stove. "Can I fix you a cup of tea?" Annie barely looked up from her project. The two women felt completely at ease in each other's kitchens—not at all surprising for two friends who had taken to calling each other "sister" since Annie had returned home.

"When do you think your baby is due?" Serenity asked as she put the teakettle on the burner to boil.

"Let's see. I think I got pregnant soon after we began our journey to Kansas. I haven't had any morning sickness for about a week, so I'd say I'm three months along now."

"That would mean you're carrying a Christmas baby." Serenity's eyes shone with anticipation. "Won't that be fun?"

"Yeah," Annie groaned. "With my luck we'll be snowbound, and Ned will have to deliver it."

"Nonsense." Serenity gestured with her hands. "If worse comes to worse, I'll be here for you—although I do get queasy at the sight of blood."

Annie grimaced. "Thanks. You sure do know how to inspire confidence."

"Absolutely!" Serenity chuckled aloud, hurrying to rescue the singing teapot. "One sugar or two?"

"None. I've been eating too much lately. It seems like I'm always hungry," Annie admitted. She held up for inspection two of the four pieces that would give the dress's gathered skirt its volume. "I have no idea how I will get all three dresses done in the next two months."

"I'll help," Serenity volunteered.

Annie looked at her friend incredulously.

"Hey!" She looked insulted. "I can sew a straight seam, and that would free you to do the fancywork."

A frown crossed Annie's face as she thought about the prospect. "Would you want to do that?"

"Of course." Serenity lifted her nose defiantly in the air. "I wouldn't have volunteered if I didn't."

"Great! Then let's get busy." For the first time since Annie took on the task she felt confident of completing it on time.

For the next two months the women worked side by side, cutting, sewing, and embroidering the promised garments. Annie's kitchen became part tailor shop and part canning factory as the task of preserving food for winter continued regardless of anything else.

At the same time, guests came and went at Serenity Inn, keeping Serenity running between the two homes. Fortunately, as the summer progressed and the garden produce came in, the number of guests staying at the inn dwindled.

When it looked like they could never finish the dresses by August, Serenity put out a call for help. Esther Rich volunteered to help with the work at the inn, freeing Serenity to spend more time sewing. Serenity's sister-in-law, Lilia, also offered to help.

When Lilia arrived ready to work, she came equipped with a gunny sack of vegetables in one arm, her sewing basket in the other, and her daughter Anne at her side. Little Anne played outside the soddy with Sammy, Onyx, and Willy while pots of vegetables stewed on the stove and the ladies sewed.

One morning, as Annie helped Serenity harvest a crop of string beans from their kitchen garden, Serenity asked Annie how she was feeling. "You look peaked, like you're not getting enough sleep. Surely you're not staying up late sewing. We're on schedule with the dresses."

"You're right. I'm not getting enough sleep lately," Annie demurred.

"It would be all right with Lilia and me if you took a short afternoon nap, if that would help," Serenity assured her. "We could go back to the inn and gossip over a pot of snap peas."

"No, no. That isn't the problem. If I could sleep at night . . ."

Annie felt her friend studying the dark circles under her eyes and the sallow hue beneath her usually warm, honey-brown complexion.

"What do you mean? Is the baby keeping you awake?"

"If only . . ." Annie's momentary smile faded. "I hate to admit this, but my nightmares have returned."

"Nightmares?"

"Yeah, the ones that followed my kidnapping are jumbled with the house fire. And now, the men from the general store are a part of them too." She knew her frustration was evident in her voice, but she didn't care. She needed help. "I've prayed about it—every morning and every night before getting into bed—but nothing has helped."

Serenity pursed her lips. "Have you prayed with Ned?"

"No, I haven't told him. He knows I'm restless, but I've blamed it on the pregnancy. I don't want him to worry," Annie admitted. "On the good side, Willy, Onyx, and I have taken a lot of walks to the cemetery in the middle of the night. When I force myself to go back to sleep, I awake with a frightful headache and an overpowering sadness."

Serenity thought for a moment before answering. "I don't have a secret telegraph line to heaven, but I do know that Scripture promises 'where two or three are gathered' in Jesus' name, He'll be there. We are two, and if we add Ned and I add Caleb, we'll virtually have an army praying for you."

"I don't know . . ."

"Nonsense. You can't control the subject of your dreams, but God can. And one of the benefits of being a member of God's family is a ready army of help at your fingertips. We need one another." Serenity waited for Annie to respond.

Admitting she'd fallen back into having terrible nightmares after all the spiritual victories she'd had made Annie uncomfortable. When fighting her fears, she'd claimed the Bible promises, and she'd found the promised strength. She believed the words of Nehemiah 8:10, "The joy of the LORD is my strength."

Seldom did she allow herself to mull the bad things from her past, and she'd replaced the negative with songs of praise. *Why now,* she wondered, *when, for my baby's sake, I want to keep my mind set on heavenly things, have the nightmares reappeared?*

"Tell you what. Let's plan a war strategy to battle the demons of your sleep." Serenity's eyes blazed with excitement. "First, you've got to tell Ned what's happening. He deserves to know. Next, at bedtime each night Caleb and I will pray for you to have a good night's sleep. You and Ned pray for the same thing."

Annie listened patiently, despite a definitely skeptical spirit inside her scoffing at the idea. "Is that it?"

"Oh no." Serenity was just beginning, Annie could tell. "Throughout the day you need to recite to yourself Psalm 23. Then at bedtime, go to sleep quoting praise texts like

Psalms 111, 117, and 118, just for a start. We'll help you memorize while we work."

Annie groaned. "Oh, no, Lilia and Esther have to know about this too? I feel so foolish."

"Nonsense! We all love you. Who better to fight for you?"

Annie laughed in spite of herself at the belligerent glint in Serenity's eyes.

"The father of lies has put out the challenge, and through the power of the cross of Jesus, we'll beat his little demons to a pulp!"

"You really take this seriously, don't you?" Annie couldn't keep from chuckling.

Serenity straightened her back and leveled her gaze at her friend. "More seriously than I do the threat of border ruffians and militant pro-slavers! These are the real battles of life. The others, while they may annoy us for a time, will eventually evaporate."

"I wish I could believe that."

Esther Rich's carriage eased to a stop outside the cabin. Annie glanced at Serenity, then at the woman making her way to the front door.

"It's time we charge the devil's fortress for that baby's sake!" Serenity's last remark touched a responsive chord in Annie. She took Annie's hands in hers. "Will you do it? Will you give my plan a try?"

Annie sighed, knowing that when Serenity got a bee in her bonnet, nothing and no one could stand against her. "All right. I'll give it a try."

"Good. Yes!" Serenity did a little jig and rushed to open the door for Esther.

That evening Annie kept her promise. She and Ned talked long into the night. She wasn't surprised to discover that he'd known about her sleeplessness but had followed her lead by saying nothing. After praying together, she melted into his arms. "I don't know why I hesitate to share things like this with you," she confessed. "Perhaps it's because I want you to be proud of me, to think well of me. I am a preacher's wife, after all."

Instead of laughing as she'd expected, he grew grave. "Honey, you've been so honest with me; I need to be as open with you. I have the same problem, keeping things from you. For me it's a pride thing. I'm the husband, the head of the house, and I don't need to answer to you."

Annie bristled until she saw tears glistening in his eyes. She waited patiently as he ruminated his tongue against the inside of his cheek for several seconds. "And, like you, I hate to have you see my flaws. I do so want you to be proud of me."

"Proud of you?" Cupping his face in her hands, she gently kissed his lips. "I couldn't be more proud of you. I'm the weak one, the one always falling down and needing help to get up."

"Oh, Annie, my love, if you knew the demons I battle and how often I fall down, would you still love me?" He buried his face in her chest and sobbed.

She held him for several minutes. She'd never seen Ned more broken up. Instead of feeling nervous or fearful over his display of weakness, Annie felt closer to him than ever. Maybe Serenity had something in her theory about gaining strength by sharing our burdens with one another.

As Annie rubbed her husband's back, she admitted that she couldn't imagine him falling against any foe, human or otherwise. He turned his face to one side and remained cradled in his wife's arms.

"There are nights when a fugitive and I are crouching behind a scraggly bush hiding from Cranston who is less than a couple of yards away, and I am praying with every ounce of strength in me for the God of David to hide me in His presence. At that time I am numb with fear. I couldn't run if I had to."

Annie couldn't believe her husband's confession. *Ned, frightened?* The idea was as foreign to her as dining with the king of Siam.

"And there are times when I encounter Cranston alone. I look at the fancy British ascot about his scrawny neck and think, 'One snap and I could free the world of a despicable glob of English swamp scum.' Murder . . ." He fell silent. "How can a man of God harbor murder in his heart? Yet, at times I do."

Agitated with his disclosure, Annie wanted to defend her husband against himself. "Cranston is the lowest of the low. He deserves anything he gets."

"Yes, but not at my hand. 'Vengeance is mine, saith the LORD. I will repay.'" Ned straightened and pounded his fist against the palm of his other hand. "I preach it, but I'm not so sure I'd practice it if the right time came."

Annie cuddled up to her husband's chest. "I think you're too hard on yourself. You are a brave, courageous man of God, and you're human."

"No, that's my sinful nature, not a state of humanity." Ned clenched his teeth together. "I must be honest before God can remove my sinful desires."

Annie thought about Ned's words long after they tumbled into bed. Ned was snoring before she remembered to quote a psalm of praise to help her fall asleep. "O praise the LORD, all ye nations: praise him, all ye people. For his merciful kindness is great . . ."

The hot July sun was heating the soddy before Annie completed the verse, ". . . toward us: and the truth of the LORD endureth forever. Praise ye the LORD." A smile spread across her face. She'd had no bad dreams, no nightmares of leering men and raging fires.

As usual, Ned was already doing morning chores when she popped out of bed eager to face the new day. Through tears she breathed a prayer of gratitude. "Lord, it worked. You kept Your word. I love You, dear friend."

Annie patted her slightly protruding stomach. "It's going to be a scorcher today, little one. Of course, you'll be comfortable in your cozy little bubble. Of course, it could be worse for me. I could be in my eighth month."

Many women had told Annie how fortunate she was not to be in her last trimester during the heat of the summer. "I've never been so uncomfortable in my life," Mrs. Tucker, one of Ned's local parishioners, told her during a church family barn raising. "I couldn't breathe half the time because my baby was pressed so high against my lungs."

Annie idly rubbed her stomach as she spoke. "You, little one, have been a delight. Even my morning sickness was worth it."

"One night down, a lifetime to follow." As she washed and dressed for the day, Annie caught a glimpse of herself in the mirror. Her eyes sparkled and her complexion glowed with happiness. "In the mornin' when I rise, in the mornin' when I rise. In the mornin' when I rise, give me Jesus . . ." The old favorite bubbled out of her unbidden.

***

The corn was high in the Cunard-Ward garden by the time Margaret York showed up for her fitting. Serenity, Lilia, and Esther were on hand to see Annie accept the accolades.

Margaret York marveled at how precisely the garments fit her tiny figure. "You, Mrs. Ward, are not only an artist at this incredible needlework, but you've made the gown fit so perfectly." The judge's daughter fingered the delicate cut-work embroidery along the jacket hem of the traveling suit. "Are you sure I can't take you to Washington with me?"

Annie gulped. "I don't think so."

The woman continued to rave over the workmanship.

"I had help," Annie reminded. "These ladies made it possible for me to put in extra time on the fancywork."

"Well, I can't thank you all enough. You went above and beyond anything I expected. The fashion hounds of D.C. will drool in their teacups when they see these dresses."

Annie doubted the woman's hyperbole, but she gratefully accepted the payment. When the judge's daughter insisted upon paying extra to cover the other women's time and efforts, all of the women protested.

"Nonsense! In St. Louis I'd pay double what you charged, Mrs. Ward, for designer, one-of-a-kind creations. At least let me salve my conscience by paying your staff."

"My staff?" She looked bewildered toward Serenity and Lilia. Serenity gave her a wink. The two other women chuckled at Annie's discomfort.

"You really should consider opening your own shop, Mrs. Ward." Margaret was not to be deterred. "I have friends in St. Louis who would die for dresses like these."

***

With the sewing project completed and Margaret York on her way to Washington, three of the four women poured their combined energies into preserving food for winter. Esther Rich had to drop out of the group when Doc Carpenter had a small stroke and begged for her to help him. Everyone in the area knew about and trusted Esther's unusual healing touch. Since Annie had benefited from more than one of Esther's pain-relieving back massages, she couldn't begrudge the doctor Esther's help. The other women agreed.

"Her knowledge of herbs and poultices is remarkable," Serenity admitted. "And since she spent time with Gray Sparrow, her gift seems to have multiplied."

"I know. Last spring, when Baby Anne fell into a hive of bees, I thought she'd die from the stings." Lilia bit her lower lip. "Esther was visiting us at the time. She immediately plastered mud on each sting. Anne calmed down within minutes, and before the night ended, she was sleeping peacefully. Esther stayed by her side the entire night."

There was no doubt that the quiet, unassuming Esther Rich had an extraordinary gift.

"I wish we could find her a husband," Lilia admitted as she quartered a tomato for stewing.

"Now, Lilia . . ." Serenity eyed her friend. "I know it's hard for you to imagine that a woman can be happy without the benefit of a husband."

The twice-married Lilia glanced up in surprise. "Well, she can't, can she?"

Annie threw back her head and laughed. Strolling to the window, she gazed out at little Sammy rolling on the grass with Onyx while Baby Anne watched and Willy barked from the sidelines. Behind her, Serenity and Lilia continued their sputter. How she treasured their days together during the summer of '54.

The last Tuesday evening of August, Annie puttered about her kitchen fixing a light supper for Ned. She was tired. She and Serenity had spent the whole day gleaning the last of the season vegetables from the garden, culling the bad and storing the good in the storm cellar. The back of her neck and shoulders ached. "I wish Esther were here tonight," she mumbled, stretching and twisting to remove a kink from her middle back. The thought of a short nap before Ned returned home was enticing.

The night before, Ned had transported cargo to the Tylers' place. She knew he would sleep a few hours before coming home, giving her enough time to catch a few winks herself.

Annie had barely stretched out on the bed when the cabin door flew open and Ned stepped inside. The man's ebony skin glistened from sweat. He looked upset. "Ned! It's you. You're early. What's wrong?" She hopped out of bed and hurried to his arms.

He brushed his lips against her cheek, then strode to the sink and put his head under the hand pump. Cool fresh water gushed out onto his head. She heard him sigh with pleasure. When he stopped pumping and straightened, she handed him a clean towel.

"M-m-m, that feels good." He dried his short black hair to a damp shine as he spoke. "Annie, do you feel up to a trip to the Tylers'? Jess needs you."

"What? What's wrong?"

Ned blew a stream of air from his lungs. "Jess thought she was pregnant, but she was wrong. When the doctor told her she was going through her change, Jess went into deep depression."

He shook his head; his eyes were filled with sorrow. "She and Billy wanted a baby so badly. Anyway, she's so discouraged that Billy is afraid to leave her alone. He thinks you might be able to help her. Nothing I said made a difference."

"Of course I'll go to her." She looked expectantly into her husband's face.

"Are you sure you're feeling up to the ride? I don't want to put our child at risk."

"I can do it. I'm as healthy as a horse." She gave him a sly grin. "And we know how expert you are at treating ailing horses."

"This isn't funny, Annie. We'd have to leave tonight."

"Tonight?"

He nodded. "And I would have to leave you with Jess for a few days. The traffic has been heavy on the Railroad, what with all the talk of it threatening to close because of the Fugitive Slave Act."

She closed her eyes for a moment, then slowly nodded her head. "I can be ready in an hour."

"Fine." He kissed her on the forehead. "I'll see to the horses and the wagon. Will it upset you if we're carrying cargo? Aaron will drop off a male runaway immediately after dark." Ned studied his wife's face.

She didn't know what to say. It was one thing to risk her baby to help a friend like Jess, but for strangers?

"Thou wilt keep him in perfect peace whose mind is stayed on Thee, Lord," she whispered, worrying her left pinkie with her thumb.

"I could tell Aaron to deliver them himself, but he's been on the road for twenty-four hours."

It would be ridiculous to have Aaron make the same trip to the Tylers' because of her own fears, Annie decided. "I'll be fine. Let Aaron go home to Lilia."

As she packed the necessary clothing and food for their journey, Annie recalled bits and pieces of a verse that talked about laying down one's life for a friend, which she decided, she had no intention of doing. Laying down one's own life for a friend was one thing, but the life of one's unborn child was quite another. She would do everything possible to guard her precious one's life. And woe be unto the man or woman who threatened that life. She placed her husband's Bible on top of her clothing and clasped shut her leather-bound travel case.

Annie had filled a basket with food and a leather canteen with water when the wagon pulled up in front of the cabin door and Ned hopped down. He loaded the mattress onto the wagon against her protests. "I'll be all right," she protested. "It isn't that long a trip."

"Just in case," he argued. "Besides, should we be stopped near the border, we want the wagon to look as natural as possible. And that includes a bed and a stack of quilts. I filled the water barrels and threw in a sack of feed for the horse, so I guess we're ready to go."

Annie took a deep breath when Ned helped her into the wagon. What was she doing? Either she was the stupidest woman on the face of the earth, or God was giving her courage like she'd never before known.

"Can we pray for Jess before we leave?" she asked as Ned climbed onto the seat beside her.

Ned gave her a questioning glance. "And for us as well."

"And for us as well . . ."

~16~

Dancing
Through the
Flames

THE WAGON ROLLED TO A STOP IN FRONT OF the Tyler place as the first streaks of dawn lit the eastern sky. They'd traveled all night, stopping once to eat. The boy, hidden in the well of the wagon, appeared to be fourteen or fifteen years old. Ned had determined that the child had been shanghaied from his West African village and had escaped from a Tennessee plantation within weeks of his purchase. While the boy spoke little English, Annie suspected he understood more than he pretended.

As Ned helped Annie from the wagon, the Tylers' front door swung open and Billy stepped out on the porch and waved. "Annie! Ned!" he called, taking the porch steps two at a time. "It's so good to see you. Thank you, Annie, for agreeing to come."

After giving her a hearty hug, he held her at arm's length. "Look at you! Aren't you the most beautiful mother-to-be?"

"I've never felt better!"

The man shook his head and grinned. "I believe it. You positively glow."

Annie glanced over his shoulder, expecting to see Jess appearing in the doorway at any moment. "Where's Jess?"

"Upstairs, in bed. Annie, she seems to have lost her spunk. I don't know how else to describe it." He gestured toward the second-floor window, the one with the curtains drawn.

Annie thought she saw the edge of the curtain move, but she wasn't certain. "Does she know I'm here?"

"I don't know." Billy shrugged, his face drawn with grief. "So we can't have any kids of our own. It isn't that I love her any less. And as to having my own children, God knows, I'd give a home to any child God might send our way—black, white, red, or yellow."

A sad but gentle smile tilted the corners of Annie's lips. "Billy, I know you are sincere, but as a woman, I can tell you, Jess doesn't see things in the same way, at least right now. Maybe, in time . . ."

Billy gave Annie a helpless shrug, then turned to help Ned bring in Annie's luggage. "I'm sorry, Pastor Ned, to make you do my run, but I don't dare leave Jess right now."

Ned shook his friend's hand, then gave him a hug. "It's all right. Who knows what the future holds for any of us? You may bail me out someday." Pointing toward the wagon, Ned continued, "Speaking of which, why don't you see to our cargo, give him some food and water, along with a little exercise and a visit to the john, while I settle Annie into the guest room. That is where you'll want her to stay, isn't it?"

"Yeah, I suppose so." His shoulders slumped and his head hung low. The usually exuberant Billy Tyler resembled a mistreated mongrel as he slowly walked to the back of the wagon.

Ned and Annie exchanged pitiable glances, then started for the house. She paused at the foot of the staircase and called out to her friend. "Jess, it's Annie. I'm coming up."

Silence greeted her. Determined, Annie lifted her skirts and ascended to the second floor. She hesitated at the master bedroom door and knocked, uncertain whether Jess had heard her greeting. Again, silence followed.

"All right, woman," she muttered under her breath. "I'm coming in!" Annie flung open the door to find Jess burrowed under several quilts with her head covered. A wave of heat accosted her. She suspected that the room temperature exceeded 100 degrees.

"Jessica Tyler! What are you doing?"

The mound beneath the quilts didn't move.

Annie rushed to the window, pushed back the embroidered, white panel curtain, and flung open the window. The morning sunlight streaked into the stuffy bedroom. A refreshing breeze ruffled the curtains. Gratefully, Annie inhaled the fresh morning air. Glancing toward the west, she spotted dark thunderclouds forming on the horizon. *Good for the land and not so good for the wheat crop,* she thought.

Without a word, Annie crossed the room to the bed and threw back the quilts to find her flannel-clad friend curled into as tight a ball as a woman of her stature could curl, her eyes closed tight and her face buried between her chest and her knees.

"What is the big idea?" Annie asked. "What are you doing in bed on this beautiful morning? You have a house full of hungry guests waiting to be fed!"

The woman opened one startled eye. Annie's greeting was not what she'd expected. Annie could sense Jess watching as she flung open the doors of the hand-made oak chifforobe and removed a yellow gingham housedress from its hanger.

"This should do." She turned to hold the garment up for Jess's inspection and caught the woman's eyes snap shut. "Jess

Tyler!" Annie chuckled aloud and clicked her tongue. "Come on now. Up and at 'em!"

Slowly the woman lifted her head and eyed her friend. "I see you're pregnant. Around Christmas?"

Annie grinned and nodded before tossing the gown onto the bed. "Now, let's see, you'll need a camisole and a slip." She turned back toward the chifforobe and glanced over her shoulder. "Any one in particular you prefer?"

Jess grunted and hugged her knees to her chest.

"I'll take that as a no. Hmmm . . ." She examined the woman's three choices and chose the crinoline with a ruffled flounce around the hem. "Where will I find your camisoles? I don't think we need to bother with hose on such a hot day." She lifted her own blue cotton calico skirt and crinoline, revealing her bare legs and lightweight kidskin slippers. She laughed at the look of surprise on Jess's face. "Who's gonna' know with all these skirts?"

Jess's face widened into a smile as she held out her arms toward her friend. "Annie Ward, it's so good to see you again."

Annie rushed to her. They held each other until tears began to flow. "I'm so sorry, Jess, about everything."

"Oh, Annie . . ." was all Jess could utter before her emotions burst free. Her upper body heaved with grief as she sobbed onto Annie's shoulder. They clung to each other until Jess's tears were spent.

"Come on, honey. We can talk after the men leave." Annie urged Jess from her bed and into her clothing.

"For the last year I've been having female problems," Jess explained. "When I missed two months, I was certain I was pregnant. Besides, I felt a heaviness in my uterus. Then one morning as I was preparing breakfast, I . . ." She grimaced at the memory, then said, "I called Doc Reyes. After examining me, he gave me the news—no more babies."

"I'm so sorry."

"I thought I'd die. No, I wished I'd die. He ordered bed rest until the flowing stopped, and somehow it became easier and easier to stay in bed." Jess stared into a tortoise shell hand mirror while Annie combed the snarls from her hair. "I wonder how many women I've ordered to their feet after suffering a devastating experience? And me, I didn't have the strength to take my own advice."

"Don't be hard on yourself, honey," Annie cautioned. "It took a woman like you, who'd walked the same pathway, to force me to reason. You know, I think we must experience suffering before we can truly understand another's pain."

Jess glanced at her friend through the looking glass. A crooked smile tweaked her lips. "When did you become so wise?"

Annie gave a modest shrug. "Dory did it for me. I'm glad I can be here to help you a little, especially after all you've done for Ned and me."

Jess turned when a voice from the base of the stairs called. It was Ned. "Annie, I'm getting ready to leave."

"Oh, excuse me for a minute." Annie dropped the comb on the bed and rushed from the room and down the stairs to Ned.

"How's she doing?" he asked as he took his wife in his arms.

"A little better, but I suspect it's not over yet. I'm glad I'll be here for a few days to help her." Annie adjusted the collar on Ned's brown-and-green plaid shirt, then placed a kiss on his lips. "You be careful, ya' hear?"

"You, too, sweetheart," he said, returning her kiss.

As he turned and ran down the porch steps toward the wagon where Billy stood holding the reigns, she called, "I'll be praying for you."

"You too," he answered, leaping onto the wagon bench. Taking the reigns from Billy, he flicked them over the horses' backs and the horses lunged forward, eager to run.

"Take care of her," he called to Billy as he waved good-bye.

"I will, friend."

Annie didn't like the looks of the cloudbank in the western sky. Fortunately, Ned would be heading due north and probably outrun it. If a storm did hit, he'd be forced to spend the night at the next station, and she wouldn't see him till the morrow.

Slowly she turned to go back to the house and found Jess watching her from the doorway. "Hey!" Annie jumped. "You surprised me."

Though tiny and weak, Jess's responsive laughter encouraged Annie. She suspected that the smile had a similar effect on Billy who was nearby. Billy mumbled something about needing to muck out the horse stalls and headed for the barn while the two women entered the house together.

As Jess heated water for tea, Annie assured her that Ned had been in too much of a hurry to deliver his charge to linger over a big breakfast. "He has a tin full of soda crackers, a loaf of cinnamon bread, and a basket of apples. He'll be fine."

"But if I hadn't been such a weakling, Ned wouldn't have had to take Billy's place. I feel badly about that," Jess admitted.

Annie smiled to herself. She knew Jess had taken a second step toward her recovery by caring about the needs of another. "Don't you worry. He'll be fine. My husband is a resourceful man." She shuddered as she eyed the clouds from the kitchen window over Jess's dry sink. "This one looks pretty big."

Jess set out her best teacups and saucers on the table, along with two white cotton napkins appliquéd with calico teapots. "Yes, but it could be one of those dry storms, a lot of thunder and lightning with little moisture."

"We could use the rain," Annie added, her mind focused on Ned and his charge. "Take good care of him, dear Father," she silently prayed.

The women had enjoyed their peppermint tea and sugar cookies until Billy suddenly burst through the kitchen door. The screen door slammed against the kitchen wall with a loud bang.

"What the . . ." Jess exclaimed, leaping to her feet.

Energy drained from Annie's knees as she saw Billy with a gun barrel aimed at his temple. Behind him she saw the familiar evil faces of Cranston, Oberon, and Lair.

"Sit down, woman, or I plug your man," Cranston ordered, shoving Billy into the kitchen. "You sit down too, boy."

Oberon and Lair swaggered into the room behind their leader, waving their weapons in the air. "Well, well, well, what do we have here?" the grungy-looking Oberon snarled. "Imagine, Cranston. We arrived in time for high tea. Isn't that what you limeys call it?" He snatched a sugar cookie from the plate and shoved it into his mouth. The third man did the same, taking a handful and stuffing them into his vest pocket.

When Jess started to protest, Cranston shoved her back into her chair. "Sit down, girl, if you know what's good for you and your man."

Leveling his steely gaze at Annie, Matt Cranston asked, "Where's your man? Where's the preacher?"

"He's long gone," Billy snapped. "Too bad you missed him."

"He can't be too far ahead of us, boss," Lair interjected.

Cranston continued focusing his attention on Annie. "We know about his comings and goings, Mrs. Ward. We've been watching him for months."

"If you know so much," Billy began, "you'd have caught up with him before now."

"Shut up!" Lair swatted Billy on the side of the head with his pistol. Billy fell unconscious to the floor. Jess gasped and dropped to her knees beside him. "Someone get some water."

Annie started to her feet.

"Oh, no you don't, little mama." Cranston grabbed her by the neck and set her back down in the chair. "We want answers from you." He turned to his men. "Lair, you and Badger wake him up while I palaver with the preacher's little woman." He pulled an empty chair next to Annie and sat down, his handgun all the time aimed at her chest.

"First of all, we know that it was your husband who scouted out the new routes for the underground railway. While old Billy here might know the next station, the preacher knows every conductor, every station along every route that crosses Missouri, from the Mississippi River to the Canadian border." Cranston moistened his lips in eager anticipation. "So we decided to forget the minnows for now and go for the big fish."

"My husband?" She gave him a beguiling smile. "Really, Mr. Cranston, Ned's an itinerate preacher visiting members of his flock."

The ruffian snorted. "And I'm the king of Spain, aren't I, boys?"

The two men laughed. Suddenly Cranston grabbed her bun at the nape of her neck and yanked her head backwards, exposing her neck to the cold, metal barrel of his gun. "We can do this the hard way or the easy way, girl. It's up to you."

Jess gasped and started to her feet only to have Lair push her back to her knees. Tears sprang into Annie's eyes despite her determination to show no fear. "I can't help you."

"Or you won't," he added, snapping her head forward and releasing her disheveled hair.

"What should we do, boss," Oberon snarled, "kill 'em?"

By the glint in the man's eye, Annie could see the idea excited him.

"And have the sheriff and his men after us for murdering innocent people?" With emphasis on the word *innocent,* Cranston shot a condescending look at his dimwitted partner. "No, we gotta' go for Ward, but how do we lure him . . ." The man gazed thoughtfully at Annie. "Lure . . ."

A cold chill passed through Annie as she realized what Cranston was up to.

"By the heart, of course." With his free hand, Cranston curled one of Annie's ebony tendrils dangling from the side of her forehead about his leather-gloved pinky finger. Annie cringed at his touch. "What man wouldn't risk life and limb to rescue the woman he loves, who also happens to be pregnant with his first child?"

"Whatcha' thinkin', boss?" Oberon squinted at Annie, his lips curling into a sneer. Annie glared at the man. How she'd love to wipe that sneer off his face. *If Ned were here,* she thought. *No, if Ned were here, they'd probably torture him and hang him from the oak tree growing beside the barn.*

Cranston grinned at Annie as if he'd read her mind. She tightened her lips and looked down at the table. "Sooner or later, Ward has to come back for his missus."

"We can wait at the hideout," Lair suggested.

The leader of the gang acknowledged the man's suggestion with a wide grin. "For once you said something smart." He rose to his feet, dragging Annie by one arm. "We'll take little mommy with us for security. And you," he pointed the gun at Jess, "when that man of yours wakes up, tell him to find Ward. If he's not here in twenty-four hours, minus the sheriff's posse or any other posse he might assemble, well, I'm sure he can figure out the rest." Cranston ran the end of his gun barrel gently along Annie's jawline.

"And if Billy doesn't waken?" Fire spat from Jess's eyes as she crouched on the floor beside her unconscious husband. Annie feared what the woman might try to do.

"I think you know the answer to that question, girl." Cranston shrugged, then motioned for the men to follow him from the house. Annie stumbled along beside the Englishman as best she could. When she lost her footing on the bottom step of the back porch and fell, he roughly yanked her to her feet. "Don't do that again, Mrs. Ward," he snarled. "For the sake of your baby, you'd better cooperate. My patience is slim with obstinate women."

For her unborn child's sake, Annie kept up with the man's long strides as best she could.

"Oh, dear God, help me," she whispered. A familiar wave of fear began growing within her chest. She broke out in sweat; her sight blurred, as her body and mind slipped into the familiar pattern of hysteria. Dots danced before her eyes as Cranston dragged her over dirt clods and through a patch of thistles.

I'm going to faint, she thought. *He'll kill me, but I know I'm about to faint.* Alongside her paralyzing fear, a new voice appeared. It didn't speak, exactly, but it came through most clearly. "Fight your fear, Annie. Fight your fear!"

With all the strength she could muster, she clamped down on her tongue. "Ouch," she grimaced, tasting blood.

Three horses, two brown mares and a gray gelding, were tethered behind the barn. "Hey, what's she gonna' ride?" Lair asked.

Cranston gestured toward the gray gelding. "With you, you scrawny worm of a sow's ear."

"But boss . . ."

"Here!" Cranston shoved Annie toward the sour-faced Lair. "Don't give me any mouth or I'll . . ."

Lair cringed as if Cranston might take a swing at him. "I hope you know how to ride."

Annie shook her head. "No, I don't."

Lair threw up his hands in exasperation. "Of course, you don't! Did you hear her, Cranston? She don't know how to ride."

Cranston arched a smug eyebrow, shrugged, and swung his lithe body onto the larger of the two brown mares.

After much jostling, Lair managed to get Annie into the saddle then swung his body behind her onto the horse's rump. Annie shuddered as the wiry little man wrapped his arms about her and told her to hang on to the saddle horn. She caught one last look at the threatening sky before they galloped toward the Missouri border.

They rode eastward for approximately thirty minutes, though to Annie, who was praying for her baby's safety, the journey seemed interminable. "The joy of the Lord is my strength," she whispered, her voice breaking as she jounced along on the animal's back. "Lo, I am with you always . . . I will never leave you, nor forsake you . . . Thou wilt keep him in perfect peace, whose mind is staid . . ."

The promises she and Serenity had memorized together flashed through her mind. Determined to outwit the demons of fear in her mind, she recited them aloud, knowing her saddle partner could hear what she said with the wind whistling in their ears.

They came to a stop beside what looked to be an abandoned soddy. The weeds and prairie grass had grown up around it, partially hiding an iron plow and a broken-down carriage. Only the open well appeared in working order.

Annie didn't protest when Lair ordered her to dismount. She gratefully slid off the horse's back into Lair's surprisingly gentle arms. For an instant she saw a look of compassion in the middle-aged man's eyes. Then it disappeared into a snarl. "Git into the cabin."

Annie glanced about at the wide-open prairie. From horizon to horizon, except for the tiny sod house, there was nothing, not a tree, not a building, not a bluff—nothing but waving grass dried by the summer sun. A shiver passed through her when she saw a streak of lightning flash between the clouds and heard thunder roll across the open plains, followed by another and another.

"Hurry up," Lair jabbed her in the middle of her back with the barrel of his hand gun.

While Annie would have loved to shove the pistol down the little man's scrawny throat, she hobbled stiff-legged to the sod house. Lair swung open the heavy oak door and nudged Annie forward.

When her soft-soled slipper hit the bare earth floor inside the dusty smelling room, two mice scurried through the open door. From the flour in the open, half-filled gunnysack behind the door, she realized her arrival had interrupted the couple's luncheon.

The dusty air inside the cabin made her sneeze. She blinked several times to allow her eyes to adjust to the cabin's dark interior.

She strode to the middle of the room where a kitchen table, its white paint peeling and scarred from hard use, balanced on three legs. The fourth lay on the floor beneath it. A candle, burnt to the nibbins in its wooden holder, sat in the center of the dust-covered table. A second gunnysack leaned against one of the legs of the only chair in the room, a ladder-back also in poor condition.

To her left, her gaze rested on the empty, black yawn of a massive stone fireplace. A bucket of water, brackish with time, sat at one end of the stone hearth, while a stack of twigs sat on the floor at the other end. A pile of rubble had been dumped in the northeast corner of the shack. The windows on each side of the fireplace were so covered with grime and dirt that they let in very little light.

Spider webs swept across the fireplace's opening and the back wall, draping gracefully from the open beams and thatch of the roof to the sidewalls. A handmade hearth broom, its twigs tightly lashed together with rawhide, leaned against one corner.

Annie shuddered at the sight of the grimy straw pallet on the floor to her right. She could only imagine the vermin inhabiting it. At the foot of the pallet was a stack of heavy saddle blankets. The red and yellow crazy quilt folded on the top of the stack looked as incongruent to its surroundings as a delicate flower blossoming in a pit of shale.

Realizing the men hadn't followed her into the building, Annie whirled about, slammed shut the door, and immediately swung the heavy wooden bar down across the door into the metal guards. "There!" she exclaimed, brushing her hands together triumphantly. When one of the men banged his fist against the three-inch-thick oak door, demanding she open it immediately, she smiled to herself. "Not on your life."

Her victory turned to vexation when she went to the window and heard Matt Cranston laughing. "So she locked us out; she also locked herself in. Sooner or later, she'll get hungry or thirsty and have to open the door."

He was right. She knew he was right but vowed that she would need to be mighty thirsty and on the verge of starvation before she lifted that bar. In the meantime, as she gazed about the room once more, she wondered, *Now, what shall I do?*

A twinge of pain in her lower back reminded her of her uncomfortable horseback ride. She dusted the cane seat of the straight-backed chair and sat down. "Ouch!" She leaped to her feet. From the shock of sudden discomfort, she decided she wouldn't be sitting any time soon. That left the straw-filled pallet.

Heaving a sigh of resignation, she gingerly spread one of the saddle blankets on the pallet. The dust rising from the pallet as the blanket hit brought on a series of sneezes. Once she recovered, she covered the blanket with the quilt, then made herself comfortable for however long she would need to stay in her little prison. To her surprise, she fell asleep.

Annie didn't know how long she slept, but she awakened to the men pounding on the door and shouting something about a prairie fire. She ran to the door and swung the heavy bolt of wood out of its iron brackets, then opened the door to a gale-force wind that whipped the heavy door out of her hands, slamming it against the side of the house.

The sight that met her eyes alarmed her more than Cranston and his gang ever could. Heavy black clouds shrouded the sun. Smoke and blazing tongues of fire filled the western horizon. Nothing struck more terror in the hearts of farmers and ranchers alike than a prairie fire. Moving at up to sixty miles an hour, a prairie fire could consume every living thing before it slowed at the first river. And this one was definitely coming their way.

Cranston, who'd never seen what a raging prairie fire could do or how fast it could sweep across open grasslands, stared, fascinated by the unfolding drama. It was a mesmerizing sight to behold. Billowing towers of smoke and dancing flames, jagged bolts of lightning, scorching winds, and rolling thunder could daunt the stoutest heart. At the sight of a prairie fire, entire battalions of soldiers would break ranks and flee, each man for himself.

The three horses snorted and pranced in terror, struggling to break free of their tethers. "Whoa there, whoa there," Lair and Oberon shouted as they fought to hold the panicky animals still enough to mount them.

"We gotta' get out of here boss," Oberon shouted against the roar of the wind. "Those babies can move faster than scat across the prairie."

"You may be right . . ." The man pursed his lips and remained transfixed by the sight before him.

Oberon managed to climb onto his mount. "I know I'm right, and I'm getting out of here. No amount of reward on the preacher's head is worth losing my life over."

"Badger, you come back here!" Cranston shouted a string of

obscenities while waving his fist in the air. "When I catch up with you, I'll . . ."

The fleeing man didn't look back but rode south/southeast as fast as his mount could take him.

"Maybe Oberon's right," Cranston shouted over the roar of the wind. "The fire does seem to be getting closer." He strode across the clearing and mounted his frightened horse.

"But boss, what about the woman?" Lair glanced back at Annie, then at his horse.

Cranston's eyes appeared empty of emotion. "Leave her. The extra weight will slow you down."

The shock in Lair's eyes mirrored Annie's. "I can't do that, boss. She's pregnant."

"So? Do you want to burn for her sake?" The outlaw slapped his reigns against his horse's flanks and galloped in the direction Oberon had taken.

For an instant Lair fought with his conscience, but one last glance at the western horizon made up his mind. He cast a "please understand" look at Annie, leaped on his horse, and galloped after his friends.

The stunned woman didn't realize that she'd been holding her breath. It wasn't until the rider became a black speck on the horizon that Annie considered the seriousness of her situation. With the horrid realization came a strange ennui. Her knees became like jelly. She wobbled to the well and slumped against the pump handle.

Annie looked from horizon to horizon for a way of escape. She considered trying to outrun the fire. But where could she run, and how fast could she run before the flames overtook her?

As the black clouds drew closer and the flames shot higher into the air, the memory of the excruciating pain she'd endured following the New York house fire returned. She glanced at the ugly scars on her hands, then squeezed her eyes shut, leaning her head against the pump.

Annie knew she was going to die alone on the empty prairie, a pile of ashes blown away by the breeze. The babe inside her womb would never see its father or feel her kiss on its cheek. The thoughts enervated her spirit and her body.

"I can't go through that again, Lord. I just can't. Please don't ask me to. I'd rather die than suffer like that again." The dark foreboding weighed her down for several minutes.

When she raised her head and looked toward the approaching flames, it was evident that the fire would not be deterred. Annie staggered inside the sod house and barred the door. If she had to die in this fire, she would do so with dignity, not that anyone but God and she would ever know. As she saw it, her only choice was to lay down and die. She massaged the tiny bulge in her stomach. "I'm sorry little one. There's not much else I can do."

One of her favorite Bible stories, the one about the three Hebrew boys in the king's furnace, popped into her mind. She'd always pictured the three boys and Jesus, not posed like statues, but dancing together in the flames. She smiled at the familiar image and lifted her eyes to the thatch above her head. "All right, Father, I guess it's going to be you and me, dancing in the flames."

Where the idea came from would always remain a mystery, but in a flash, Annie knew she had to try something. Grabbing the filled water bucket on the hearth, she doused the quilt and pallet. Then she rushed to the well, refilled the bucket, and returned to soak the other blankets, making four or five trips. On her last return trip Annie barred the door, then wrapped herself in the smelly and soggy wool blankets and laid down to await her fate.

"He that dwelleth in the secret place of the most High shall abide under the shadow of the Almighty . . ." she began as the cold, mushy fabric slapped against her face, molding itself to her features. The three drenched blankets on top of her pressed down with the weight of ten.

The winds outside the house grew to a deafening roar as they whipped about the corners of the sod house. The heat inside became so intense that it felt as though a lid from the stove had come down on her, smothering the breath out of her. Her breath came in short desperate bursts.

Is this what it feels like to die? she asked herself. The urge to break free of her heavy woolen prison, to flee the burning building, was a deliriously appealing thought. *Die! Get it over with.* "No, No! I won't give up. For my baby's sake, I won't give up!" She fought to reclaim control of her mind.

"'I will say of the LORD, He is my refuge and my fortress: my God, in him will I trust. Surely he shall deliver thee from the snare . . .'" Tears burned in Annie's eyes, but she continued reciting Psalm 91, "'of the fowler, and from the noisome pestilence.'"

Outside, the roar of the fire grew as it attacked the mixture of grass and dirt on the walls of the small building. Pressure built up inside the cabin and inside her head until she was certain her head would burst. She covered her ears with her hands and closed her eyes and mumbled, "'He shall cover thee with his feathers, and under his wings . . .'"

She screamed when she heard what sounded like a shotgun shooting in rapid succession. Peering out from under her blanket, she saw that the panes of glass in the windows had shattered. The rafters above her head were in flames. Burning thatch dropped to the floor. One clump landed on her blanket. She flung it to the other side of the small room and pressed her body tightly against the sod wall behind her. "'Thou shalt not be afraid for the terror by night; nor for the arrow that flieth by day . . .'" She paused, unable to remember the next verse as the fire above her head became deafening.

"I will rejoice in the Lord!" she shouted. "'Although the fig tree doesn't blossom, neither shall the . . . the . . .'" she stuttered, trying to block out the intense heat surrounding her. She then continued, "'. . . fruit—neither shall the fruit be on the vines . . . the flock shall be cut off from the fold and there shall be no herd in the stalls; though the child in my womb must perish . . .' That's not in there, Lord, I know, but . . ." Her eyes burned and her throat ached. She knew she had only moments before breathing her last breath. "'Yet I will rejoice in the Lord; I will joy in the God of my salvation!'"

Annie gasped for oxygen but inhaled the acrid odors of burning thatch and scorched wool. The air was so hot that it scorched her throat and seared her lungs. Her hands clutched the wool blanket on top of her. With one last breath, she willed her fingers to let go. Slowly her fingers uncurled, releasing the blanket clutched in her hand as well as the one smothering her mind.

As quickly as the roar of the fire built to a crescendo, it faded and stopped. All was suddenly silent around her, except for the crackling of burning embers and the hiss of moisture escaping from wood. The hazy silence lured her into a state of calm. Her eyelids fluttered closed. Through swollen and parched lips, she spoke aloud the words of Psalm 23, "'. . . though I walk through the valley of the shadow of death, I will fear no evil: for thou art with me . . .'"

As the promise soothed her fevered mind, a rivulet of peace settled into her soul. A smile spread across her lips. For Annie no longer imagined herself dancing through the flames with her Lord, but rather, imagined herself cuddling in her heavenly Father's arms. If this was heaven, she was delighted to be there.

From a distance, she heard someone calling, "Annie, Annie." Her first thought was, *Go away. Leave me alone.* But the voice became insistent. She twisted her shoulders and grunted beneath the heavy weight holding her down.

Suddenly the weight was lifted from her body. It was if she were floating. A refreshing breeze blew across her face. Someone was touching her face and kissing her lips. As nice as that sensation was, the sweet silence and the comforting peace she'd been enjoying faded.

Reluctantly Annie opened her eyes and looked straight into Ned's frightened eyes. "You're alive," he whispered. "Oh, thank God, you're alive!"

Total darkness enveloped the room beyond the circle of light from his oil lantern. The air was acrid with smoking thatch and burning timbers. Annie started to rise, but Ned gently pushed her back against the damp blankets. "Stay where you are," he ordered. "Billy is bringing the wagon around to the door. We're taking you home."

"I'm alive?" she asked.

"Yes, praise God, you're alive." He showered her face and forehead with kisses.

"And our baby?"

He paused a moment. "Have you felt any pain?"

"No, except for lungs hurting before I fainted—I fainted?"

Ned chuckled, knowing how much she abhorred the idea of "having a case of the vapors" like a fragile society matron. "You were unconscious when I found you. I'd say you passed out from a lack of air."

"Good! What about the baby?"

"I don't know, but I'd say that if you didn't have any contractions, the baby is safe and secure for another four months. But we'll have Jess check you out before we make the long drive home."

"By the way, how did you find me?"

"The sheriff led us to you. He and his posse have gone after Cranston and his gang."

Annie smiled sadly. "I don't think they'll find them. You know, Jim Lair wasn't all bad."

"What? That little weasel of a man?"

She inhaled deeply of the fresh air flooding in through the open door. "How did you get in here?" she asked. "I barred that door before the fires came."

Ned shrugged. "I lifted the latch and it swung open. I didn't see you at first under the pile of blankets. If you hadn't moved, I would have searched elsewhere for you."

"I heard you call my na—" Annie's eyes widened in surprise at a sharp jab she felt in her abdomen. "Ned!"

"Are you all right?"

"Absolutely!" Her hand flew to her stomach. She began to laugh. "I felt our baby kick. Oooh! There it is again." She grabbed her husband's hand and placed it on her stomach. "Wait! Wait! Maybe he'll do it again."

Transfixed by the miracle of new life, they waited several seconds before they were rewarded with a sound thump. Ned gasped and looked at his wife. She grinned back at him through a film of tears.

"Our baby wanted to reassure us that he's alive and kicking."

"He could be a she," Ned reminded. "A she with her mama's spunk."

Annie looked at him in surprise. She'd always thought of others as having courage—Serenity, Miz Josephine, Miss Margaret York, even Lilia Pownell—but not herself.

"You are the bravest woman I have ever known, Annie Ward. Whether this baby is male or female, its mother is the most amazing and beautiful female God ever created, up to and including Eve."

"Oh, Ned, I know that's not true, but I love the fact you said it. And I love you so very much," she whispered, overcome with emotion.

"Oh, honey, if I could only put into words how precious you are to me. I thank God for you every morning and every night." At the sound of an approaching wagon, Ned straightened. "Billy's here. Let's go."

"Home . . ." Annie chuckled softly. "That sounds so good."

Jess hit the soddy with the force of a hurricane. With an oil lantern in one hand and a black leather satchel in the other, she whipped through the open door. "Annie! Annie! Are you all right?" Before Annie could answer, Jess dropped to her knees beside her. "I am so glad to see you. I brought burn medicine that should help—"

"I didn't get burned. Not even my eyebrows are singed. Everything around me burned. Even the rafters." Stars twinkled beyond the charred beams over their heads. "The table, the chair, the wooden bucket, everything but me and the horse blankets. Isn't God good?"

"Oooh, he sure is." With two fingers Jess lifted a corner of one of the horsey-smelling blankets and wrinkled her nose. "You found her here, buried beneath these?"

Ned laughed. "That's right. If I'd not seen the mound of blankets move when I called her name, I would never have found her."

Annie's eyes sparkled. "And do you know what? I barred the door before I crawled under the blankets. Yet when Ned arrived, he just unlatched it and walked inside. Talk about miracles!"

The preacher looked lovingly at his wife. "It's been a day of miracles. What do you say to returning to Jess's for the night?"

"I could use a hot bath, er, maybe, under the circumstances, it should be a cool bath," Annie grimaced.

"I'll bet you're hungry as well," Jess added.

Annie rubbed her stomach. "You can't imagine how . . ."

The other woman rose to her feet and picked up her lantern and satchel. "Then what are we waiting for? Let's go home. While you're soaking in bubbles, I'll boil up some eggs for egg salad sandwiches. How does that sound?"

"Hey, you convinced me." Ned scooped his wife into his arms and headed for the wagon where Billy waited.

***

Two days after the fire, Serenity and Caleb were waiting when Ned and Annie returned home. As the covered wagon eased to a stop in front of their place, Serenity came running from the inn. "Annie! Annie! Are you all right? We heard all about the fire." The woman nearly tore her friend off the wagon she was so excited to see her again.

"Let me look at you." She held Annie at arms length for an instant then crushed her to her chest. "What a nightmare for you. And the baby's all right?"

Annie nodded and started to tell her friend about feeling the baby move but didn't have the opportunity.

"Did you hear? The Cranston gangs' horses wandered into Independence yesterday, their backs and saddles scorched and their manes and tails singed, minus their riders. A charred boot was caught in the stirrup of one of the horses. God only knows what happened to the men out on that God-forsaken prairie."

Annie cast a quick glance toward her husband. "Hardly God-forsaken, I assure you."

-17-
Epilogue

ON CHRISTMAS EVE, AN HOUR BEFORE midnight, a lusty-voiced baby with pudgy cocoa-brown cheeks and a shock of ebony curls arrived at the Ward home. Ned and Annie named their daughter Faith Johanna Ward, meaning trust— God's precious gift.